THE
HUNTED

Alex Shearer lives with his family in Somerset. He has
written more than a dozen books for both adults and
children, as well as many successful television series,
films, and stage and radio plays. The BBC series of
his book *Bootleg* won a BAFTA award for Best
Children's Drama, *The Speed of the Dark* was short-
listed for the Guardian Children's Fiction Award and
Sea Legs won the Stockport Schools' Book Award.
Alex has had over thirty different jobs.

Books by Alex Shearer available from Macmillan

THE HUNTED

Alex Shearer

MACMILLAN CHILDREN'S BOOKS

First published 2005 by Macmillan Children's Books
a division of Macmillan Publishers Limited
20 New Wharf Road, London N1 9RR
Basingstoke and Oxford
www.panmacmillan.com

Associated companies throughout the world

ISBN 0 330 43190 0

1 3 5 7 9 8 6 4 2

A CIP catalogue record for this book is available from
the British Library.

Phototypeset by Intype Libra Ltd
Printed and bound in Great Britain by Mackays of Chatham plc, Kent

1

The Real Thing

'I tell you, kid,' Deet said, 'one day you'll grow up and then you won't be worth anything. Youth's the only stuff that matters these days. And you know why? – Because it's in short supply. People aren't being born like they used to be, and the ones that are here aren't dying. They're hanging on by their fingernails, their toenails and anything else they can cling on with. Youth, it's the only thing. I know plenty of people look young, but that's just fake, like a suntan from a bottle. It's the real thing that I'm talking about, kid, and you've got it. Or at least you have for a while . . . only it won't last, not even for you, and that's the thing to remember, and to make the most of it while it's here. One day, you'll even end up as old as me. So let's go make some money, while we can. Let's make that old hay while the sun is shining. And stack it up in the barn.'

Tarrin didn't really want to make any money. Not today. What he wanted was to meet another child, one to talk to, one to play with, but he hadn't seen anyone his age for weeks now. Most children belonged to rich people – the way most things belonged to rich people, which was why, no doubt, they were called rich. They owned everything. Or said they did. Maybe they had stolen it all once, and then had bought suits and got respectable. Tarrin himself had belonged to a rich person once, but Deet had won him in a card game. That was the story anyway. His owner had got drunk and had bet him on the turn of a card – and the card had turned up wrong.

But how had he belonged to the rich person? The rich person couldn't have been his father, for no father would bet his own child on the turn of a card. It was so long ago now anyway, longer back than he could remember. It had been Deet for years now, Deet and a whole succession of different ladies whom he was expected to call Mother for a while. But they soon tired of Deet, or he tired of them, and they packed their bags and then a few weeks later there was somebody else to call Mother.

One of them had tried to take Tarrin with her when she left. He had been ready to go with her as well. But Deet had suspected something. He had a nose for trouble. He hadn't let Tarrin out of his sight that day until she was long gone.

Tarrin always wondered about her afterwards, if she had really wanted him, or if like Deet she only wanted him in order to make money and then one day, when he got too tall, she would abandon him, and he would be just like anyone else in the world, worth only what a day's work could bring him. (Or a day's stealing, in some cases.) He wondered how many years he had left before even Deet didn't want him.

'Hey, cheer up! What're you worried about, kid?'

Deet said, both interrupting and seeming to read Tarrin's thoughts.

'It's a long time till you grow up. And, even then, there's always the PP. But you've got to have it while you're young. It's no good after. Then it's too late. What do you think, kid? What do you say? How about going for the PP? I'll stake you to it. We'll be made forever then. You and me. You can pay me back from your earnings, a little at a time. Sure, it'll take a while, as it's a big investment. It's more money than I've got, to tell the truth, but what the hell – live long and prosper – someone'll lend it to us if they know you're having the PP. It's security. They'll know you'll be able to pay them back. Sure, you'll miss out on a few things – the things that grown-ups do. But what the heck, I can do all those things for you, on your behalf. Why not stick to what you're good at? You're good at being a kid, you've got that kid thing off to a T. And I'm good at exploiting the situation and representing you. Don't I get you regular work, kid? Of course I do. Do I overwork you? Course I don't. Others would in my position, but not me. I'm not like that. Remember the old goose and the old golden egg? Well, that's how I see it. Why strangle the hand that feeds you, if you get my drift. Wouldn't you like to be a kid forever? Think of that. A kid forever. How about it? What do you say? A kid forever in a world of old folk. You'd be the toast of the town, like a movie star. What do you say?'

Tarrin said nothing. They walked on in silence, each absorbed in his thoughts. Deet thinking that if Tarrin had the PP, he'd be set for life, never have to worry again, ever, all the way to the end. Tarrin

3

thinking that Deet was overlooking one very essential fact – the PP was totally illegal now, and if anyone involved in perpetrating it was caught, it meant life. Life in prison. And these days, life was a long, long time. Life just went on and on now. On and on and on.

Yet the PP was tempting. Yes, in some ways it was. To be young forever, that was what it meant. That was why the operation was called the PP. It stood for Peter Pan, the boy who never grew up. To be a boy forever, there was something in that, and yet . . .

Another man, with a child beside him, was coming towards them. Tarrin's heart leaped. The boy was the same as him – his age, his height. It was weeks now since he'd played with anyone, even talked with, even seen, anyone like himself.

'Deet . . .'

'I see him, I see him. OK, you can have fifteen minutes together if his old man don't mind.'

But as they approached, Tarrin saw that there was something wrong with the boy – that he wasn't really a boy at all. Maybe many, maybe most older people would not have noticed. But Tarrin did. And Deet too.

'That's no father,' Deet said. 'He's minding him, same as I'm minding you.'

The man was tall and fair. The boy was dark, with black, curled hair. There was no way they were father and son.

'Hi, guys, how's it going?' Deet called as they drew level. 'Looks like we're in the same line of trade.'

The blond man's eyes looked Tarrin up and down.

'Yup.' He nodded. 'Looks like we are.'

4

They stopped to talk.

'Work good?' Deet asked.

'Turning it away,' the blond man said.

'Own him?' Deet asked, nodding towards the child.

The blond man shook his head.

'Partners,' he said.

Deet's eyes narrowed.

'How old is he?'

'Older'n me,' the blond man said. And he looked about forty.

Deet nodded slowly.

'Nice job,' he said. 'Cost you?'

'You'd better believe it,' the blond man said. He turned to the child. 'Right, Charlie?'

'Right.' The boy nodded. But he was looking at Tarrin. And Tarrin was trying not to look at his eyes.

They were frightening. They were small and black, but they weren't the eyes of a child at all, they were the eyes of some unknown creature.

The boy spoke. 'Hi.'

'Hi,' Tarrin answered.

Deet nodded at the two boys. 'Getting acquainted,' he said. 'Does he meet many his own age?'

'He meets plenty his own *age*,' the other man laughed. 'He just don't meet many his own *size*, if you get my meaning.'

Tarrin was studying the boy's face.

'How old are you?' Tarrin asked.

The boy paused a while before answering, then, 'Old enough,' he said.

'Don't be shy, Charlie,' the blond man said. 'Tell him how old you are.'

5

Charlie didn't answer.

'He's forty-eight,' the man said.

The boy looked offended. 'No need to tell him that,' he said. 'He won't play with me now.'

And it was true, Tarrin wouldn't. He was recoiling, moving gradually away, from the boy who was forty-eight years old.

'Well, we'd better be going,' the blond man said. 'He's booked for an hour in a little while and we need to get some lunch.'

'OK. See you around maybe,' Deet said.

'Maybe.' The blond man nodded, but he didn't sound as if it was very likely. 'We're moving on tomorrow – try another town. Eh, Charlie?'

'Yes, sure,' Charlie answered. 'Another town and then another one and another after that. Another day with this one or that one, another hour making up for the kid they never had. Yeah, it's great, it's just great, a great way to earn a living.'

His eyes turned to Tarrin.

'Never have the PP, kid,' he said. 'Never. Grow up, grow old and die one day. But never have the PP. I'm telling you.'

'Hey, that's enough of that, Charlie,' the blond man said. 'Partners or not, older than me or not, you ain't so big I can't take you over my knee and give you a good hiding.'

Charlie looked up and turned his gaze on the man. 'You can try it,' he said. 'And you may do it. But you'll only do it once.'

The blond man went on trying to look in charge, but he didn't really seem it any more.

'Good luck then,' Deet said. He wanted to be away

now. He didn't like this way of talking about the PP, not in front of Tarrin. 'We'd better not keep you.'

The two men and the two boys went their separate ways. The black-haired boy turned back once and shouted to Tarrin. 'You remember what I said,' he told him. 'You remember!'

'That's enough of that now, Charlie,' the blond man said, and he got hold of the boy's ear and twisted it. The boy responded by stamping his heel down on the man's foot. He let out an enormous yell.

'And next time I'll stick my penknife in you,' the boy said.

Tarrin and Deet walked on. It was a road Tarrin knew well; if anything he was overfamiliar with it and had long since ceased to notice its attractions. But there was one frontage that always held his gaze. It was the entrance to a small theatre club, and on a board outside were some photographs of a girl who looked about eleven or so, up on the stage of a tiny theatre, wearing red tap-dancing shoes.

'Miss Virginia Two Shoes,' the board proclaimed. 'Fifty-five years young and still dancing.'

Deet paused to admire the display.

'Now there's a pro,' he said. 'There's a real professional. This is what I'm talking about kid, you see? Fifty-five years young and still dancing. Now that could be you.'

Tarrin shuddered. He could think of nothing worse than to be fifty-five years old, but looking eleven, and still dancing.

'She's all upfront about it too, see, kid. Everyone knows she's had the PP, but so what? She's not hiding anything. And still they come to see her. She's a real trooper.'

Tarrin glanced at the other side of the board. There were more photographs of Miss Virginia Two Shoes. She was up on stage again, wearing a ginger wig and singing – at a guess – 'Tomorrow' from *Annie*, the old musical about the little orphaned girl. The caption under the photograph read, 'Miss Virginia Two Shoes – Everybody's Favourite Girl. Come see her dancing – the daughter you never had.'

Deet nodded. 'That could be you, kid,' he said again. 'That could be you. The son they never had. Upfront and out with it and not hiding anything and still making a living. Everyone knows she's fifty-five. In fact they change the numbers every year. First time I came through this town, that board said, "Miss Virginia Two Shoes – forty-three years young and still dancing." She was still dancing back then and she's still dancing now. And if you want my opinion, she'll be dancing till the day she drops, and even if she gets to be two hundred and ten, she'll still be everybody's favourite girl. And that's the way to be.'

He stared at the board and seemed in a reverie, maybe dreaming of all the money Miss Virginia Two Shoes might make from being everybody's favourite girl, between now and the hour of her ending. Maybe he was thinking of how he could help her spend it.

'Only she never got to grow up,' Tarrin pointed out.

'What? What'd you say, kid?' Deet asked, coming back to reality.

'I said, she never got to grow up and she never will now,' Tarrin said.

8

Deet looked at him, a curious expression of pity and maybe even compassion on his face.

'Grow up?' He grimaced. 'You think it's such a big deal – such a good deal – to grow up? The world's full of grown-up people, kid. They live a long, long time, until maybe they get so tired of it they wish they'd never been born. They don't look a day over forty or act old, and they're always sporting the latest styles, but they're ancient inside. Some of them have even already crumbled away to dust, deep inside where it matters. Those Anti-Ageing pills, they stop you rotting from the outside in, see kid, but they can't fix the inside out, not if you've got the old bored-with-living-but-scared-to-die blues. There's no pill for that.

'But you have the PP implant, you never feel that way. Not so they say. Anti-Ageing stops grown-ups getting older, but the PP saves you the trouble of ever growing up at all. You just stay young and hopeful and happy, and you go on singing and dancing – just like Miss Virginia Two Shoes here, everybody's favourite girl. I mean, look at that little angel face, kid, and those cute curls. You're a kid yourself, so how would you know, but for me, she's the cutest thing, just the sort of daughter I'd have dreamed of myself. She'd have been there when I came home from a hard day's work, and just the sight of her angel face and her head of curls would have made it all worthwhile.'

It was on the tip of Tarrin's tongue to ask Deet when exactly he had ever done a hard day's work, but he wisely kept the question to himself. As far as Tarrin could see, Deet did no work other than to live off him. Deet, no doubt, would have seen it differently. He would have talked about himself in terms of agent, manager, minder. He would have mentioned responsibilities and things like that. And maybe that was true, it was work to an extent, but it wasn't hard, and it didn't fill the day. It took up a couple of hours of his time at most, and the remainder of the day was his to do with as he pleased, and he normally passed it in spending Tarrin's money. His 'company' money, as Deet called it. The money Tarrin was paid just for keeping people company.

Deet went on admiring the photos of Miss Virginia Two Shoes. He seemed to have genuine feeling for her, as if she really was the daughter he had never had.

'She's a doll, all right,' he said. 'A living doll.' He turned to Tarrin. 'And that's another thing you don't understand, kid,' he went on, 'and if you go the PP road, you'll never have to. If you stay a child, you'll never want a child. But you grow up, kid, and watch the years go by and know you'll never have any son or daughter or family of your own . . . well . . . it's a bitter pill, kid, a bitter pill. And a hard one to swallow. Or why else would Miss Virginia Two Shoes still be packing them in those seats and selling out every performance?'

A queue was beginning to form outside the door for the first show of the day. There were couples, groups of friends, some men and some women on their own. Some were wearing Miss Virginia Two Shoes badges and were plainly regular fans.

'I hope she sings "The Good Ship Lollipop" today,'

a woman said to her husband. 'She hasn't sung that for a long time and it's one of my favourites.'

The door opened and the queue shuffled forwards. The audience paid their money and went on into the dim interior of the small theatre. They didn't know that Miss Virginia Two Shoes was already in her dressing room, putting her tights on and her buckled shoes. Every now and again she took a sip from a glass of whisky.

'Let's move it,' Deet said to Tarrin, looking at his watch. 'We'll get a bite, then I'll take you to the customer's. It's a straight one-hour – no frills, just basic be-a-boy stuff. I'll wait outside till you're done and then there's a twenty-minute break till the next one. We'll need to get a cab to that, as it's a few miles further on. Then there's a couple more to do, which should take us into early evening, and then we'll call it a day. Come on, kid, what are you looking at? Let's move it.'

The people in the street. That was who Tarrin had been looking at. The people in the street and, more particularly, the people in the queue, all lining up to pay their money for the privilege of seeing Miss Virginia Two Shoes dance in her silver-buckled pumps, with her little girl's body in her little girl's clothes – even though she was fifty-five and then some. The people were all different, and yet in some ways they all looked the same.

They all got stopped at the same traffic lights, Tarrin thought. And none of them could go any further.

That was it exactly. Time had stopped passing for them. There was no knowing how old any of them were. They may have been forty. In fact, the majority of them looked about forty. But these days, an octogenarian looked forty, a centenarian looked forty. You could go right on to about a hundred and fifty before you started to look much older. There were people who had reached their second century and who had passed on, still looking forty.

'It's a wonderful thing, medical science,' Deet said, as if reading Tarrin's thoughts. This ability of his constantly impressed and startled the boy, because he didn't believe for a moment that Deet was a greatly intelligent man, but he had bottomless reserves of shrewdness and cunning. He was astute, in a streetwise kind of way; he knew how to spot an advantage and how to read people's deepest desires.

'Come on, let's get a bite. Burger do you?'

'OK,' Tarrin agreed.

'Let's make it a fast one then,' Deet said, leading the way on down the street to a burger joint. 'Let's take a look at the menu and see what's on special today.'

They went on towards the burger bar. As they entered, Tarrin looked back over his shoulder, up the street towards the club which was the home of Miss Virginia Two Shoes, everybody's favourite girl. He briefly wondered what it must be like to be fifty-five years old yet still a child, never to have aged, never to have grown. What was it like for a girl never to become a woman? For a boy never to become a man?

'Come on, kid – time's moving!' Deet beckoned him in and Tarrin followed him up to the counter, where they ordered burgers, Cokes and fries.

'And make it snappy,' Deet told the server. 'We

haven't got all day.' Then, 'Fast food, huh?' he muttered to Tarrin. 'Even fast food don't seem quick enough any more.'

Yes, time was moving, that was true, time was always moving. But for the other people in the queue, with their forty-year-old faces, time stood still, or seemed to. There were days as long as eternity, afternoons which seemed impossible to fill, evenings that stretched forever towards an unending night. Life was long, life was long. And what did you do when you had done all there was to do? When you had experienced all there was to experience? When you had been everywhere there was to go? When you had read all there was to read? When you had heard all the music and knew all the stories, when you knew every cadence in every symphony, every hook in every song, every twist in every plot, every brush stroke in every work of art? What did you do then? What did you do?

You took a walk along the street and you bought yourself a ticket for Miss Virginia Two Shoes – fifty-five years old and still dancing, everybody's favourite girl and the source of eternal delight. And you sat and dreamed of the daughter you had never had and the son you had always wanted, and the children and the grandchildren you had never known and would never know.

You thought of the family you had always desired, and the sound of children's voices as they played out in the yard. You dreamed of the washing on the line and the plates in the sink, the untidiness in the rooms and the sounds of squabbling. You dreamed of birthdays, of the puff of breath blowing out candles, of

Christmases, of weddings and christenings, of a hundred different occasions. You dreamed of the pictures they painted, the bikes they learned to ride. You dreamed and you dreamed, you forgot and you remembered, as you sat in the darkness while Miss Virginia Two Shoes (who was surely your most favourite girl) sang her song and danced her dance. Then at the end when the applause came, sometimes, before you put your hands together, you reached to your eyes with the flat of your hand and you wiped away a tear.

2

A Child for the Afternoon

As they left the burger bar – Deet picking his teeth with a wooden toothpick – a man passing by looked down at Tarrin and smiled.

'My, that's a fine child you have there, a fine child,' the man said to Deet – his voice full of innocent appreciation.

'You want to rent him?' Deet asked. 'How long do you want him for? Minimum time is an hour. You can have him for less but you still have to pay for an hour. It's up to you.'

The man looked shocked – insulted even.

'Rent him? What do you mean, rent him? What sort of a person do you think I am?'

'Nah, nah, nah,' Deet said, 'nothing like that. Strictly legit. You can take him for a walk, take him for a burger – though he's only just had one so he may not be that hungry. Or you can take him to feed the ducks, take him to the park, play on the swings, skim stones across the pond – you can show him how, like a real dad, you know what I'm saying? And if you want to buy him a present at the end as a sign of appreciation – that's up to you. He gets to keep everything.'

No I don't, Tarrin thought. Not if it's valuable.

You either sell it or keep it for yourself. When anyone took him anywhere, Deet would stalk them, keeping an eye on whatever might happen. If he ever saw any presents being given, he always asked for them when time was up.

'You can't have him right now, mind,' Deet said. 'We've got an appointment. But I can book you in for later in the day, or maybe tomorrow would be better. I'm not too sure about next week, we might be moving on.'

Moving on? It was the first Tarrin knew about it. But that was Deet, always thinking of moving on. Not necessarily doing it, but thinking.

The man shook his head and walked on. He didn't want a child, not today. Or maybe he did, but he couldn't afford one, or maybe he could afford one, but it would just be too painful for him, it would make him think of the son he had always wanted, of the family he had never had.

So few people could have families now. Sterility was the price of longevity, it seemed. With advanced age and increased lifespan had come new viruses, which had all but destroyed the ability to reproduce. Only the rare and fortunate few had proved immune. Even those who declined to take the Anti-Ageing pills, for moral or ethical reasons, were equally susceptible. Yet if it hadn't been for this sterility, the world would have become so densely overpopulated – with a high birth rate and low death rate – that people would have been crammed into it like canned sardines.

Only a minority were still able to conceive children, and those who did have them wouldn't let them out of their sight – the way you wouldn't let your gold watch or your most precious possessions out of your sight, or someone would take them from you. It wasn't the bogeyman children had to worry about, it was Kiddernappers and, unlike the bogeymen and the monsters in the wardrobes, they were real enough.

'Come on, kid,' Deet said. 'Let's get you to Mrs Davey's – just up here and around the corner, if I reckon it right.'

They walked down a long street of terraced houses which widened at the end to two rows of detached and more expensive ones with large gardens. Deet checked his watch, led the way up the path to one of the houses and knocked on the door.

'Never trust doorbells,' he told Tarrin. 'Sometimes you hear them, sometimes you don't. And if you don't hear them, are they ringing inside or aren't they? But knocking – you know where you are. It's got a positive feel about it.'

A woman came to the door and looked out at them through a small glass panel. At the sight of Deet, she looked worried, but when she looked down and saw Tarrin standing next to him, her face relaxed into a smile and she reached to open the door.

'Good day to you, ma'am,' Deet said, so stiff and formal all of a sudden that Tarrin was afraid that he was going to break into a bow. 'I believe,' he continued, 'that you ordered a child for the afternoon, and I have the pleasure of bringing him right here to your door. This is he,' he said, nodding at Tarrin, as though Mrs Davey might otherwise have trouble working out which of them was the child and which

17

wasn't. He nudged Tarrin with his elbow and muttered, 'Say hello to the lady and mind your manners.'

Mrs Davey overheard him and smiled. 'No need to tell him to mind his manners,' she said. 'He seems like a nice, polite and well-behaved boy to me.'

Deet latched on to her words immediately, anxious to agree with them and to embellish them.

'Indeed he is, ma'am, indeed he is. A nicer boy would be hard to find. In fact, come to that, any boy would be hard to find these days . . .'

It was intended to be a small joke, but the childless Mrs Davey plainly did not find it amusing. Deet rapidly tried to salvage the situation.

'Yes, any boy would be hard to find, and any girl too. And a sad and distressing state of affairs it is, ma'am, for a woman like yourself, if I may say, who would maybe love to have a family, and who – if I may make so bold, ma'am – would make a fine, fine mother. A fine one, if appearances can be trusted, and, in this instance, I believe they can.'

Mrs Davey seemed well aware of the insincerity of his words, but was touched by them just the same. Tarrin saw her eyes grow cloudy.

'I would,' she nodded. 'And that is the truth Mr . . .'

'Deet,' Deet said. 'No first name, no after. Just straight Deet is how I take it.'

'Yes, Mr Deet,' she continued, 'I would love a family. As you can see, I haven't even begun to take the Anti-Ageing . . .'

'I can see you're still a young woman, ma'am,' Deet agreed. It was on the tip of his tongue to add,

'And a very attractive one,' but he rightly thought that this would be pushing familiarity too far.

'We would both love children,' Mrs Davey said. 'Both my husband and myself. But like so many other couples – so, so many other couples – alas, it has not proved possible.'

'Alas,' Deet sighed. 'Alas, alas. The way of the world. The way things go . . . things going wrong, and no one knowing how to fix them. Alas, alas.'

As he spoke he sneaked a look at his watch.

'Well,' he said, 'better get down to business. An hour, I think we fixed on. Payment in advance, I believe, was arranged. Cheque will do, but cash is preferable. Time starts from when you close the door, and it ends when I return and knock on it again.'

'You can use the bell,' Mrs Davey said, pointing to it. 'We have one.'

'I prefer knocking,' Deet said. 'It's more definite, more positive, it can't be argued with and that way there's no misunderstandings.'

He put his arm round Tarrin's shoulders in a fatherly way. The sheer, rank insincerity of it always gave Tarrin the creeps.

'Now you behave yourself, my boy, and you be nice to Mrs Davey and mind your manners. In you go now and have a nice afternoon.'

'Thank you,' Mrs Davey said. 'Are you coming in now . . .?'

Tarrin realized that Deet hadn't told her his name.

'It's Tarrin,' he said.

'That's a nice name,' Mrs Davey said. 'Unusual, but nice.'

'I gave it to him myself,' Deet told her.

Liar, Tarrin thought, but he didn't say anything.

'Will you come in now, Tarrin?' Mrs Davey smiled. 'And we can spend our hour together. See you in a while, Mr Deet.'

'No mister. Just Deet. Straight Deet,' Deet said. 'No forenames nor encumbrances.'

Maybe he had been hoping that Mrs Davey might invite him to wait inside and to spend the hour in front of the television, watching the horse racing and even drinking a can of Mr Davey's beer. But if such were his hopes, they were dashed. She was already closing the door.

'A moment, ma'am!' Deet all but screeched. 'A moment!'

She reopened the door and looked blankly at him.

'We forgot the . . . eh . . . the . . . recompense,' Deet said, almost sheepishly, like he didn't care to talk about it and that money changing hands was a grubby thing he would have preferred to have had no part of, but was forced into by a cruel and hostile world.

'Forgive me,' Mrs Davey said. 'I have it ready. It's all here.'

She handed him an envelope. Tarrin was afraid for a moment that Deet was going to open it up and count it there and then, right in front of the lady. But he somehow managed to contain himself until she had closed the door. He was sure the money would be all there, and he was right. He was a good judge of character and of honesty, even if he lacked those two qualities himself.

*

The door closed behind them. The house was cool. It was clean and tidy, a refuge from the bustle and heat of the afternoon.

'Well . . .'

Mrs Davey seemed as shy and as awkward as a young girl in a strange place. As the house was hers, and Tarrin was the stranger, he should have been the shy and awkward one, but he had done this too many times before to let his apprehension or his nervousness show. He maybe felt the way a seasoned performer does before he goes on stage to give a show. There was an edge of nervousness, but confidence too, and the nervousness would help him to give a good performance, to give value for money, the way Deet liked it. Because that way you got the word of mouth recommendations and more work elsewhere.

Strangely, there was not all that much return work, however. Tarrin would probably not see Mrs Davey again after this afternoon. Deet discouraged it. He felt that after two or three visits people were starting to get too attached, or there was a danger they would, and that could lead to problems. After a visit or two, most people never got in contact again anyway. It was obvious why – it was just too painful. The customers had wanted to know what it would be like to have a child, if only for an hour or two of the morning, if only for an afternoon. At first they enjoyed it and marvelled at it and they could hardly wait for the second appointment to come round. But around the second visit or the third, they grew melancholy after the boy had gone. They realized that they were only prolonging an inner agony, and that all their money was buying them was salt for their wounds, when they had sought to purchase balm.

'So what would you like to do, Tarrin?'

They often asked him that. It was their hour, and their money and their choice. Only when it came down to it, they often found they didn't really have much idea. For so long they had wondered what it would be like to have a child, and now he was here they didn't know what to do with him.

'What would you like to do? Anything?'

Tarrin could have made it easier for her, but he didn't, at least not immediately. He just made it a little more complicated.

'What would *you* like to do, ma'am. Whatever *you'd* like to do, I'd be pleased to do that. That would be just fine.'

She looked a little bit confused, then she started thinking, then she smiled.

'Please don't call me ma'am . . . call me . . .' Her voice drifted to silence, as if she were embarrassed, even a little ashamed to say.

Tarrin decided that he liked her. She had a nice face, she was clean and pretty, her house was calm and ordered and, more importantly, she was probably the age she seemed.

What she had said to Deet had probably been true. She hadn't started taking the Anti-Ageing yet. But no doubt some day she would. They all did. Every one of them. Nobody wanted to grow old, Tarrin reflected, or that was what they told themselves. Maybe the reality was that they *did* want to grow old. What they didn't want to do was to *look* old. What they wanted was to live forever and seem young forever. Maybe a small part of everyone was just like Miss Virginia Two Shoes, fifty-five, or sixty, or seventy, or ninety years young, and still dancing . . . dancing . . . dancing . . .

'Can I call you "Mum", ma'am?'

Mrs Davey smiled, a real genuine smile that crinkled her eyes. 'That would be lovely, Tarrin. That would be nice.'

They still stood in the quiet hallway. There was an old-fashioned grandfather clock in a corner, it ticked and tocked slowly, almost as though it were the wood of the case creaking and not the pendulum inside.

Tarrin wondered what Deet would be doing, where he would have gone. He wouldn't have gone far, that was for sure. 'Only hanging round protecting my investment,' he told the boy once when Tarrin had questioned him as to why he had seen him loitering outside the house he had been in for the last hour. Deet trusted him more now, but still not that much, and never entirely. He wouldn't have gone more than a few minutes away. He'd be right outside, leaning on a lamp post, reading the newspaper he kept folded in his pocket for half the day, squinting across at Mrs Davey's windows every now and again. Or he'd be sitting on a bench in a nearby park, doing the same. Or he might be in a coffee bar, trying to get friendly with the waitress. Or he'd be inside a local betting shop, losing money on the latest sure-fire winner he had chosen from the racing pages of his newspaper. But, wherever he was, he'd be back in sixty minutes. He'd be back in fifty-nine.

'Would you like anything to eat, Tarrin?'

'I'm OK, thanks . . . Mum.'

Mrs Davey looked a little disappointed. Maybe he shouldn't have had lunch. Maybe he should have anticipated the offer of food. It happened frequently enough. If she offered him a drink he would accept it. Not that he was thirsty. He was only doing his job.

'A drink, then?'

'That would be lovely.'

'Then let's go into the kitchen.'

She led the way. The kitchen was immaculate; it was light and airy and spacious.

'You have a lovely home,' Tarrin said.

'Thank you.'

'No, I mean it. I'm not just saying it because I have to.'

'You say a lot of things because you have to?'

'Deet tells me to say things to please people.'

'To keep the client sweet?'

'I guess.'

Honesty always disarmed them. Some might have thought that it was mere professionalism, a ploy in its own right, almost a slightly dishonest one, that deliberate frankness was a form of deceit. And maybe sometimes it was, but not today.

Mrs Davey smiled. She seemed to understand and not to resent him for his plain speaking. He didn't know quite why he was being so confidential today. Maybe he was tired, maybe he was sad, maybe it was the atmosphere of her safe, quiet home, which made him long for such a place – such a mother – for himself.

'We have milk, squash, orange juice, cola or . . .'

She looked shy again.

Or what? Tarrin wondered and waited to see what

24

it would be. She reached into the fridge and took out a glass jug, covered with a cloth.

Here it came. Like always.

'There's some home-made lemonade . . .?'

Tarrin would have chosen it even if he didn't have to. So it was neither effort nor sacrifice to smile and look pleased, almost excited, and say, 'The lemonade, please . . . Mum.'

For a moment she turned away and her hand reached to her face and her eyes. Then she pulled a piece of tissue from the kitchen roll and blew her nose and threw the paper into the bin and then she washed her hands. By the time she turned round to face him again, she was back in control, and her cheeks were dry, and he would never have known – if he hadn't had the experience of being in this same situation so many times before – that for a second there, she had been crying.

'Lemonade it is then. I'll have some too.'

She poured it into tall, plastic glasses, decorated with cartoon figures. Tarrin watched her. The tumblers were childish. They were new. She had bought them in anticipation of his visit. She had bought them for him. And maybe, when he had gone, she would take the one he had drunk from, and would put it away somewhere safe, and some time in the future, when she was alone in the house, she would take it out and hold it in her hands and press its rim against her face.

'Then maybe we can go out into the garden.'

'That would be great.'

'There's lots of space – and trees – and a swing – and a bicycle – and a skateboard – and a basketball hoop on the garage wall. I know what you boys are like.'

'*I know what you boys are like.*'

If only you did, ma'am, Tarrin thought. If only you did. If only it were all that straightforward and simple, and it could all be cured by a basketball hoop and a skateboard and a swing. If only. Only. Only.

But he didn't say, or even let his expression convey, any of that. No, ma'am. No sir. He just smiled his professional smile and nodded and said, 'That's right, Mum. That's right.'

Then he sipped at his home-made lemonade and said how good it was – and it was good too, he wasn't shamming – and then he followed her out to the garden, and as they went out he glanced up at the kitchen clock, and he saw that she, for her part, had glanced at her wristwatch. For a whole ten minutes had already gone. Ten minutes of her precious, expensive hour. Ten minutes of their time together. Ten minutes of their afternoon.

The garden was like the kitchen, like her, like the house. It was ordered and calm and cared for. There were an old oak and some sycamores growing, and the oak's trunk divided into branches quite low down near to the earth, so it was perfect for climbing. There were some rustic garden benches and there was a table with an umbrella in the middle to shade out the sun, and the umbrella was weighted down, being set into a heavy oval of concrete so that no sudden breeze could blow it away like a kite. There was a swing seat too, facing the sun. That was where she headed for and she invited him to join her.

'Shall we sit on the swing? We can sit for a while,

and then you can play . . . and maybe I can watch. Will you mind if I watch you play?'

'No . . . not at all . . . Mum.'

So they sat on the swing seat and sipped their lemonade. She set the swing in motion with the tips of her feet against the ground, and every now and then she would kick against the ground again, to make it swing some more.

Tarrin felt the sun on his face and the cool lemonade going down inside him. He looked at her and he wished that she really was his mother and that this really was his home, and he smiled. Or tried to.

'You look sad,' she said.

'No, ma'am,' he said. 'Not me.'

'Don't you ever get the grumps, kid. Don't you ever get moody with the customers. They're not paying good money for your long face. So you keep smiling, even if it hurts.'

'No . . . Mum. I'm fine.'

'Sure?'

'I'm fine.'

The swing seat went back and forth. He longed to reach out and take her hand. Maybe she longed as much to reach out and take his. He longed to snuggle up next to her, feel himself held in her arms, to smell the scent of her, to know he was loved, safe, secure, that he had a mother. He suddenly felt about three years old, lost in a shop, abandoned in a crowd, and aching for the arms of someone who loved him.

The seat swung. It creaked a little. Not much, just a little. The seat swung on.

'No contact. You appreciate that, don't you? Nobody's implying nothing and nothing's to be

inferred. But misunderstandings can happen, so it's best to define the boundaries and to have the definitions well in advance and that way we're all agreed. So no contact.'

Deet was quite protective of him in some ways. Tarrin was his investment and it was in Deet's own interests to look after him. He wouldn't let him go to a house he didn't like the look of, or with people he felt wrong about. Deet was a good judge of bad character, that had to be said. He knew a crook when he saw one, but maybe he'd developed that particular talent while shaving and looking at his own face in the mirror.

'Lemonade OK?'

'Lovely.'

'There's more if you'd like some.'

'Maybe in a while. Thank you.'

He didn't want to seem greedy. It didn't do.

'Got to project the right image, kid, got to live up to their dreams. The perfect boy, that's what they want and that's what you've got to be. So be on that old best behaviour – all the time. Don't let the mask slip, kid, you hear me? Heck, I know that kids are a pain in the butt half the time, but the customers don't know that. Not having any, they like to think it would all be perfect and hunky-dory all the time. So don't you go knocking those rose-coloured glasses off their noses.'

'Would you like to play now?'

'Can I climb the tree?'

'Yes, of course.'

Climb the tree, follow the branch that extended over the garden fence, drop down into the back lane, run for it. He could be out and away in thirty seconds. Run and keep running and he'd be gone before she could stop him. By the time Deet returned with his rap on the door and disinclination to use the doorbell, he could be two or three miles away. Mrs Davey would open the door to him and Deet would know immediately, from the look of fear in her eyes and the tears on her face and the way she stuttered, 'I-I'm ever so s-sorry, Mr Deet, ever so s-sorry . . .' Calling him *Mr* Deet too, though he'd told her it was just Deet, plain straight and simple and that was how he liked it. Deet would know that he had made a run for it, gone on the lam.

'*That little son of a . . .*'

And then he'd let out a whole stream of the kind of bad language you shouldn't use in front of a lady. Though Mrs Davey would more than likely have heard it somewhere before. Just as Tarrin had heard all that kind of thing before. Many times in fact. From Deet. When he'd been full up with beer again.

If Tarrin ran, then Deet would come after him. Not that he'd necessarily find him. But the chances were that somebody would. Where could he go? Where could he hide? How could he hide? How could any child hide in a world where a child was possibly the most conspicuous thing in it? When a child attracted attention everywhere it went?

The reality was that maybe Tarrin needed Deet as much as Deet needed him. Tarrin was Deet's living. Deet was Tarrin's protection – against something worse. He was probably one of the lesser of many potential evils. Like Kiddernappers, for one. There were rich people who'd pay good money for a child in prime condition and there were plenty of people ready to snatch a kid off the street to cater to the demand.

He could head for the police station. Only what would they do? Deet had papers, proper ownership papers, which proved that Tarrin was his. Though the boy knew that he wasn't. But how could he show otherwise? How could he demonstrate where he really belonged when he had no actual knowledge of it himself? Just faint memories now of a far-distant childhood, a babyhood, an infancy, memories of sunlight, a barking dog, a long, grassy lane overhung with trees, a woman's scent, a man's voice, the lowing of cattle, a harvest of hay, the feel of grain in his hand, trickling through his fat baby fingers like sand at the sea.

That was all he had – his passport, his identification, his personal ID – memories which could have belonged to anywhere, to anyone, to no one in particular.

So how could he ask them to send him home when he didn't know where home was? How could he demand that they return him to his father and mother when he didn't even know their names? And how did he know for sure that there even was such a home, such a family? Maybe he had invented the whole thing. Maybe longing had turned wishes into beliefs and hopes into certainties.

And Deet had the papers. Yes, Deet had the official guardianship papers, and there was nothing the police could do about that except send Tarrin back into his guardianship and protection.

Yet he couldn't stop himself from believing that

there was somewhere he belonged, that there were people he belonged to and who belonged to him, that he had been taken once, torn forcefully away from the family and the place he now scarcely remembered.

So why should he be afraid of Kiddernappers? Hadn't the worst that could happen to him happened already? Hadn't he been abducted once? What would be so bad about a second time? And in a few years he wouldn't be at risk anyway. Nobody would want to grab him off the street any more. He would be too tall, too old. Everyone wanted a child for the afternoon, but a tall, gangly teenager with the beginnings of acne on his face, no, they didn't want that, not at all.

Which was why Deet wanted him to have the PP, of course, so Tarrin could stay a child forever and go on making money for Deet forever, so that he could go on wasting it forever.

'Are you OK, Tarrin?'

He looked down at Mrs Davey from behind the leaves. 'I'm OK.'

'Not too high, mind. I wouldn't want you to fall and hurt yourself.'

'I'm OK . . . Mum. No need to fuss.'

'Sorry. Sorry, Tarrin. I don't mean to fuss, but a mother worries, a mother cares. I'm only thinking of you.'

'I know, Mum. I know.'

'There's a good boy.'

He climbed up higher. It felt good and a little dizzy too. He hadn't climbed a tree in ages. Mrs Davey remained in the swing seat, holding her own, half-full glass of home made-lemonade and his empty one. She watched him climb. He climbed confidently, with occasional hesitation, a typical boy, a real boy. She didn't like to think of anyone in terms of stereotypes, but he was everything she had anticipated, everything she had hoped: he was a real, real boy.

Maybe one day soon, if she could afford it, she could have a real girl for the afternoon. Would she want to climb trees too? Yes, maybe.

She'd save up and do that one day – hire a girl for an hour or two. There had to be somebody who had one. And it wasn't illegal. Maybe not all that nice exactly and a lot of people frowned on it and dis-approved of that sort of thing. Like Jack.

'We can't have children and that's it. Not many people can now, and that's how it is. But we're lucky in so many ways. We can live a long, long time and we don't have to decay or grow old or get wrinkles or suffer all the aches and pains. We can stay active until almost the day we die – and that won't be for a long time, Alice, maybe not for another hundred and fifty years. So if you want something to love, let's get a puppy, or a kitten, and watch it grow. You can't afford to get attached to someone else's child. Not even a loaner for the afternoon. It just makes it all that much harder to come to terms with reality. You're just going on dangling out possibilities that can never be grasped. Or you end up like one of those people queuing outside some tawdry club place to see Miss Virginia Two Shoes, getting all tearful and sentimental over the antics of a fifty-five-year-old child. Do you see, Alice? Do you see?'

She saw. But she went her own way just the same.

And she didn't tell Jack anything. Mrs Davey glanced at her watch again. Twenty-five minutes gone. So soon, already. Twenty-five precious minutes. And Tarrin was far away, halfway up the oak tree. She suddenly wanted him near to her. She'd paid for him, after all, hadn't she, and he had gone too far away.

'Tarrin!'

He stopped climbing and looked down. She had got up from the swing seat and was looking up into the foliage.

'Would you like to come down now? Maybe you could play with the basketball.'

Sure, ma'am, yes, ma'am, whatever the customer pleases.

He began to descend. As he did, he wondered about her. She didn't just stay at home all day, did she? – what was there to do? She had to work, surely, if only to keep her mind occupied. She must have arranged to take the afternoon off so as to be alone in the house. What had she told them? Dental appointment, maybe? Visiting a friend?

Tarrin wondered if her husband knew. Maybe he didn't. Maybe it was her secret, her secret treat and her secret craving, to have a child for the afternoon. A real child, a real boy. Who would be expensive – but worth it.

The PPs were cheaper. You could rent a PP for half the rate Deet was charging. And some of them were pretty good too. And so they should be. They had years and years of experience behind them, of acting the child, of keeping the customer satisfied. Only some of them had been doing it so long that they had turned into imitations of themselves, caricatures almost. They had their routines off pat, but they were acting all the way. They laughed, they cried, they could be cute and sweet and cuddly to order. They could even turn on a tantrum, if that was what you wanted, and lie there yelling and screaming and acting spoilt and beating their fists and kicking their shoes on the floor until you gave in and handed over the chocolate bar which you'd said they couldn't have ever – and that was final, and otherwise there would be big trouble.

Yes, they could do all that. They could act the child better than anyone, but they had long since ceased to be children. They had the faces and the bodies of children, right enough, but they had the minds and souls of some strange new species that had never before existed in the world.

They had their admirers – just as Miss Virginia Two Shoes had hers – in crowds and droves. But they gave Tarrin the creeps, these children who were half a century old. And whenever Deet talked about getting the PP implant, it gave Tarrin more of the creeps than ever, the thought that Deet would want to turn him into one of them.

Of course, the operation was expensive, more money than a waster like Deet could ever dream of saving. On top of that, it was now illegal. And what child would willingly consent to be a child forever, anyway?

But a lot of things in the world were illegal, yet that didn't stop them happening. The law could forbid things, but it couldn't prevent them. There was always a corrupt doctor down some back street who knew some struck-off surgeon somewhere, who, for a small fee – well, no, for an extremely *large* fee – would be willing to do the PP implant to keep your child young and childlike forever, in this world in which a child was a rarity, and more precious than diamonds or gold.

And it was irreversible. That was the worst thing of all. There could be no change of heart, no changing your mind five years down the line and deciding that you would now like to grow up after all please, thank you very much.

The Anti-Ageing pills and the PP implant had come from rival research labs but were similar processes, both intended to prolong life and slow down ageing and decay. One eventually got the Food and Drug Authority's approval and the other didn't, for the Anti-Ageing merely slowed you down, but the PP halted you in your tracks and turned off the switch forever.

Some bright sparks had implanted first a rat, then a young chimpanzee, with the PP to see what would happen. The animals lived, but didn't develop. That began it. When the process started to be used on healthy children, the government made it illegal.

The lab eventually took the PP implant out of the chimp. It aged years in minutes and dropped dead of old age within the hour. At the post-mortem, its brain showed signs of advanced Alzheimer's and it had arthritis in all its limbs. Two hours earlier, it had been a youngster – a regular Peter Pan.

If Miss Virginia Two Shoes had her PP implant taken out, within two days she would have the face of a fifty-five-year-old. And who would come to see her then?

Tarrin shinned on down the tree, maybe a little too fast . . . 'Coming, Mum!'

'Careful now, careful!'

'Won't be a second!'

'Take your time now! Careful! I know what you boys are! Think you're indestructible, I know.'

'I know what you boys are.'

Only no one knows, Mum, no one knows, except that boy himself, how sad and how lonely only a boy nowadays can be. That's what people don't know about boys.

He scrambled on down. He was back on the lower branch now.

'No, Tarrin – don't jump from there. It's too high. Here – let me help you.'

Too late, he jumped. He landed fine, but pretended otherwise, deliberately stumbling and letting himself fall.

'Oh, Tarrin! Tarrin! Are you all right? What have you done?'

He was fine. He lay there, quite unhurt, as she ran to him solicitously, full of love and worry and care.

'Tarrin, Tarrin, Tarrin! You haven't broken anything, have you? You can still walk, can't you? Oh, you boys, you boys!'

He knew, despite her protests of concern, that she would be secretly disappointed to find him unharmed. As she hurried over, he reached out and picked up a sharp-edged stone which lay by the base of the tree, half hidden in the grass. He brutally dug it into his left forearm and dragged it down. It opened up a narrow cut about four inches long.

Blood instantly seeped out of it. Mrs Davey saw the blood at once. She didn't notice him drop the stone back into the grass.

'You've cut yourself! You've cut yourself! Quick. Come inside. Up to the bathroom. I'll see to it straight away!'

She helped him to his feet, the 'no contact' rule forgotten. This was different. This was an emergency. He limped as she helped him across the garden and back into the house.

'You're limping! Have you twisted your ankle?'

'No. Just a little, maybe. I'll be all right.'

'Oh, you poor thing. You poor, poor thing.'

'I'll be all right, Mum.'

'Oh, you poor, poor thing.'

She helped him into the house and up to the bathroom.

'Shall I take my shoes off, Mum?'

'Don't worry about that.'

He left small muddy patches behind him, shoe-sole sized, on the steps of the stairs.

'We'll go in here.'

It was the main bathroom. They probably had several. But this was the one with the first-aid stuff in it.

'Here, sit down here.'

He sat on the closed lid of the toilet. She took the first-aid kit from the cabinet and knelt down beside him.

'Now, this might sting.' She opened an antiseptic wipe and cleaned the wound. It stung. He made a face but didn't cry out.

'Sting?'

'A bit, Mum.'

'You're being ever so brave. You're a brave, brave boy.'

Mummy kiss it better.

He willed her to say it and he willed her to do it. And maybe she wanted to say and do it too. But it was a step too far, too real, too intimate. Even here, even now, they both maybe knew that it was all only pretend.

He wanted her to kiss his arm better, to hold him and comfort him and reassure him and to mother him. He suddenly wanted a mother every bit as much as she wanted a son.

There was a watch – maybe her husband's – which had been left on the side of the bath. It was probably one of several he owned. People had so many possessions. Tarrin glanced at the time. Only quarter of an hour left before Deet would come knocking on the front door.

She cleaned his arm with the antiseptic wipe and then watched to see if the bleeding had stopped. The wound was quite superficial, more of a scratch than a real, deep cut. Tarrin looked at it and wondered why he had done it – for her benefit, or for his? Or maybe it was a little of both.

She cleaned the cut again, wiping off the surplus blood. Then she took a sticking plaster from the first-aid kit and peeled its plastic paper backing away.

'You boys!'

Their eyes met – hers bright and smiling, amused but still concerned.

'You boys . . . honestly.'

'Sorry . . . Mum.'

They grinned as she peeled the plaster along the cut and held it tight to make it stick.

'OK now?'

'OK.'

'What about that ankle?'

He wriggled it around for her to see. 'Seems OK now.'

'Good.'

She threw the blood-stained wipe and the plaster wrapping into the foot-lever bin by the sink. The bin was shiny silver. It reflected a distorted image of the room.

'OK? Can you stand on it?'

He tried his weight on his ankle and did a little 'weight on the ankle' acting.

'It's fine.'

Stumbled.

'Sure?'

Recovered.

'It's fine.'

She supported him anyway, as far as the landing, then she let him take the banister rail.

'Manage now?'

'I can manage. Thanks . . . Mum.'

'There. Brave little soldier.'

Unable to stop herself, she ruffled his hair. He didn't mind. He rather liked it. He wished he could stay here, stay in this house forever, with this nice, kind lady, who surely had a nice, kind husband too. And they could be a family, and this would be home. Maybe he could suggest it. Maybe he could suggest to her that she could buy him from Deet.

Only there wasn't that much money. They were

well off here, the house told you that. But they wouldn't have the money to buy him from Deet. Deet said he wouldn't sell Tarrin at any price. But he would, for a big enough one. It was complicated too, the way Deet was about him, sometimes he really did seem to look on him as a real, genuine son. But most of the time he was just merchandise.

He was Deet's livelihood. If Deet sold him, even for a huge, huge chunk of money, the chances were that within three months Deet would be flat broke and busted. He could no more hold on to money than a man with greasy hands could hold on to eels. Deet didn't have the first clue how to save; all he really knew was squandering.

He must have made a small fortune out of Tarrin, but there was nothing to show for it. He could have bought a car, a house, had a place of his own and some money in the bank. But no, it had all gone on cheap motels and travelling and always moving on. It had gone on dead-cert racehorses which proved to be more dead than cert – horses that were supposed to have wings on their heels, but which only made crash landings.

It had gone on coffee-shop waitresses and ladies he had met in bars. It had gone on . . . well, Tarrin didn't really know what it had all gone on, but he knew that it hadn't gone on him. Or maybe only a little. He was always well fed, well clothed and in good health. But that was only Deet protecting his investment again.

And if Deet had his way, it would go on like this forever. If he could get the money together to pay for the PP operation, then he'd have a child and an income for life. And Deet might live another hundred and twenty years. Another hundred and twenty years of this. Of afternoons just like this one, or so similar as to make no difference.

Another one hundred and twenty years of such afternoons. Tarrin shuddered at the thought.

'Are you cold?'

'Cold?'

'You were shaking. You shuddered.'

'No, no.'

'Shock maybe. From the fall.'

'Could be, yes.'

They were back in the kitchen.

'Hot, sweet tea – that's good for shock.'

'I don't really drink tea.'

'A little more lemonade then?'

'That would be nice.'

'And a biscuit?'

He wasn't really hungry, but boys are supposed to be boys, and boys are always supposed to be hungry, even when they're not, and a refusal can often offend, and he wasn't there to disappoint the customer, so . . .

'Please, that would be lovely.'

'I, er . . . I baked them myself.'

Which meant he would have to eat two. Which was a pity, because he really wasn't hungry. But then he needn't eat so much later. Deet wouldn't mind.

'Not too thin, kid, but not too fat either. Not too skinny, not too chubby, that's not how they like them. Just about medium is the way to do it. That's what there's a major call for. Somewhere in the middle is about right.'

Deet knew the right thing for everyone, but didn't seem to know so much of it for himself.

'Could I use the cloakroom, please?'

She directed him to the downstairs cloakroom. He went to use it and made sure to run the taps a while afterwards so that she would know he was clean and had washed his hands.

'Don't go to the toilet in the customer's time, kid,' Deet had instructed him. *'They're paying for a kid's company, not to have him hiding in the john, so you remember that and hold on till after.'*

But you couldn't always hold on, sometimes you just needed to go, whether it was the customer's time or not.

When he returned to the kitchen, the atmosphere had changed. He entered to find Mrs Davey standing looking at the clock. Her face was sad again, her eyes full.

'It's all gone so quickly,' she said. 'All gone so fast.'

Then she seemed to notice the glass of lemonade and the plate of biscuits, as if she had only just seen them.

'Your lemonade . . . and biscuits. Come and sit down.'

'Thanks . . . Mum.'

Time to stop saying that now. Time to wind down. Better not call her 'Mum' any more. When the hour was nearly up, the word grew empty, it sounded hollow and false. It was like carrying on the party when everyone had gone home.

He sat at the kitchen table. He sipped his lemonade and reached for a biscuit.

'May I?'

'Please. I made them earlier. For you.'

She remained standing and watched him eat. She

42

took evident pleasure in it, almost delight. Why was there such a pleasure in watching a child do such a simple, everyday, necessary thing, such as fill his mouth with food?

'Hungry?'

'Little bit. Nice biscuits.'

'I made them myself.'

'They're lovely.'

'Thank you.'

'Really nice.'

She watched him finish it.

'Take another.'

'Be greedy.'

'Go on. Just one. I know what boys are.'

No, Mrs Davey, you're a good, kind woman, but you don't know what boys are. You know the myths and the stories and everything they are supposed to be. But you do not know what they are. I may as well say 'I know what Mrs Daveys are.' But you wouldn't believe that I did. You'd say how would I know, how would I ever know what it felt to be Mrs Davey, who wanted a family but who was barren, like almost everyone else in the world now, and whose husband was infertile, like so many men. How would I know? you would say. How could I understand the sadness, the loneliness and the pain involved in being Mrs Davey? And yet you tell me that boys will be boys, and that you know what boys are. How complicated we know we are, how simple and straightforward we think everyone else to be.

At her prompting, he took that second biscuit. He also glanced at the clock as he nibbled at the short-bread. Deet would be on his way back, coming down the street, maybe with that waitress's telephone number written on the back of his hand, or programmed into his mobe, maybe throwing that torn-up betting slip into a bin. He'd be coming down the road and then up the path and then standing outside the door looking at the second hand on his watch until he'd timed it so that exactly one hour was up to the very second, not one breath of time more or less. And then he'd ignore the doorbell – just so as to avoid any inaudible misunderstandings – and he'd raise his hand and brace his knuckles and he'd give it that old . . .

Rat-a-tat-tat!

'That'll be your father.'

Tarrin said nothing. It was simpler to let her believe what she wished.

'Is he your father? You don't look much like him.'

'No, he's not.'

Rat-a-tat-tat. Deet already growing anxious, afraid someone was getting something for nothing, something they hadn't paid for. If she didn't get to the door pretty soon, he'd have to levy a surcharge.

'Come in, Mr Deet. Sorry to keep you.'

No, everything was fine, just fine.

'Come in, he won't be a moment.'

'I'm fine on the doorstep, ma'am, just fine. So did you have a nice time together?'

'Wonderful, Mr Deet.'

'Good, good,' he smiled. 'Good, good.'

'He's a very nice boy, Mr Deet. A credit to you.'

'He is that, ma'am. Indeed he is. And it's plain Deet, ma'am, no mister about it. Just plain Deet, short and straight and that's how everyone knows me.'

'Well, here he is, ready to go.'

Deet was pleased to see that Tarrin was carrying a small package. The lady had given him a present there, a little bonus. Good, good. Very, very good. But then he spotted the plaster on his arm.

'What's that? What's happened there? What's that on your arm?'

'Oh yes, I'm sorry, there was an accident, I'm afraid.'

'Accident? An accident? What's this about an accident? If there's been any permanent damage I may have to—'

'It's OK, Deet. It's just a scratch. I just fell over, that's all.'

'Just a scratch?'

'That's all.'

'Maybe you should take him to the hospital just in case,' Mrs Davey said. 'In case of tetanus.'

'He's OK,' Deet said. 'He's had his injections.'

'Then that's all right.'

'Just a scratch, eh?'

Deet looked pleased and satisfied. He gave Tarrin a sly nod and an all-but-imperceptible wink, like they were both in something together and were pulling the wool nicely over Mrs Davey's eyes. He'd got cut so she could mother him. Professional stuff.

There was nothing to do but go now. There were just the goodbyes to be said.

'So what do you say to the lady, kid?'

'Thank you very much for having me, Mrs Davey.'

45

'Thank you for coming, Tarrin. I enjoyed your company immensely. And thank you too, Mr Deet.'

'That's just plain Deet, ma'am.'

'For bringing him along.'

'My pleasure entirely. And thank you too, ma'am, for being such a good customer and a prompt payer and all up front and such. You wouldn't believe the trouble I have with some of them, lousy would-be swindlers and cheapskates and what with Kidder-nappers all hovering and hanging and sniffing around and—'

'Deet!'

'Whassat, kid?'

'Maybe not right now?'

'What? Oh yeah. Right. Sure, sure. Got troubles of your own, no doubt, ma'am, without needing mine. OK. Well, nice to do business. Maybe another day sometime. We'll be back this way one time or other. You can always give me a call.' He reached for his wallet. 'Here, lemme give you one of my new business cards.'

He extracted one and gave it to her. Tarrin hadn't seen them before.

'Just picked them up,' Deet went on. 'Hot-lickety-split from the printer's. Still warm. Look at that, ma'am. Real class and genuine italics. My mobe number's right there, see. You just call me on my mobe any time you want.'

'Yes, maybe. Maybe I'll do that. Goodbye, Tarrin. And thank you.'

'Thank you, Mrs Davey.'

'If I could ever have a son, I'd want him to be just like you.'

'I wish you could be my mother, Mrs Davey. Truly I do.'

Deet smiled – that sly look on his face again.

'Don't he say the sweetest things, ma'am? You can tell he means 'em too. Which many don't these days, many don't.'

But Tarrin did mean it, with all his heart. He wasn't just trying to keep the customer happy like Deet thought – judging everyone by his own standards. No, he meant it, every word.

Mrs Davey's eyes were misting over. It was time to go, or stay and be embarrassed as she got upset.

'Better hit the road then, kid. On to the next. Business, business. No peace for the wicked, eh, Mrs D? Never a moment's rest. What it is to be popular. Not that I'd know myself – ha ha. Anyway, we'll be away.'

'Bye now. Bye, Tarrin.'

'Bye, Mrs Davey.'

'Bye, Mr Deet.'

'That's just plain Deet, ma'am. Straight Deet. No mister.'

'Goodbye to you.'

She hurriedly closed the door before the tears could come. They walked on down the path.

They were barely on the pavement before Deet reached for the parcel.

'So what'd she give you, kid? What's in the bag? What's the bonus? What've we got?'

'She gave it to *me*, Deet.'

'What if she did? What's mine is yours and yours is mine. We're both in this together. What'd she give you? Money? Toys? Something we can sell?'

'Deet . . .'

Deet stopped, disgusted. 'What's all this?'

'Biscuits, Deet.'

'Biscuits? She gave you biscuits? No silver keep-sakes? No souvenirs? Biscuits.'

'Shortbread. They're good. Home-made. Want one?'

'Nah.'

'Sure?'

'Keep them. Come on. We're due across town on another appointment. Come on, let's get a cab.'

They walked on down to the road intersection to see if they could flag down a taxi. Tarrin looked back once towards the house they had come from. Mrs Davey was standing in the living room, looking out of the big picture window. Tarrin turned and waved to her, and she raised her hand and waved back. He would have waved again, only Deet saw what he was doing and told him to stop.

'She's had her money's worth, kid. Why give them more than they paid for? They don't thank you for it. They don't give you nothing. Nobody in this world gives you nothing, kid, you remember that. You listen to your uncle Deet and you learn. Nobody gives you nothing.'

Tarrin held up his package. 'She gave me the bis-cuits,' he said.

Deet's lip curled in a sneer.

'Sure she did. And for whose sake? Yours? Or hers, to make herself feel all warm and lovely about herself? Yeah, biscuits, kid. That's about all you'll get for nothing. Biscuits and peanuts. Ha ha ha. *Taxi!*'

He waved and shouted at a black cab travelling on the other side of the road. The driver made a U-turn and pulled up alongside them.

'Where to?' he asked.

'I'll tell you when we're in,' Deet told him.

He opened the door and let Tarrin climb in first, then he followed.

'We want to go to the north side.'

'But I'm on my way home to the south side,' the cab driver said.

'Yeah,' Deet said, 'which is why I wouldn't tell you where we were going until we were in. And if you don't take us there, I'll report you for refusing a bona fide fare.'

The driver muttered to himself in a bad temper, but he drove on towards the address Deet gave him – Tarrin's next appointment, their next port of call.

As they drove, the cab driver's irritation seemed to evaporate. He grew interested in Tarrin and kept glancing at him in the rear-view mirror. Deet sat examining his new business cards, seeming pleased with the sight of his own name.

'That your kid?' the driver asked Deet.

'Sure he is. Why – anyone saying otherwise?'

'No, only going to say he seems like a nice kid.'

'Want to rent him?' Deet asked.

The cab driver bristled. 'Do I look like a kid renter?'

'Strictly legit,' Deet said. 'No offence. Just meant as family.'

'We rented one once, for an afternoon, me and the wife.'

'You don't say?'

'But she just got too upset after. It was worse than before.'

'Takes all sorts,' Deet said. 'Takes all kinds.'

'Must be nice, though, to have your own son – he is your son, right?'

'Somebody saying he isn't?' Deet asked.

But nobody was saying anything, and it remained that way for the rest of the journey, until the taxi dropped them off at the address of their next appointment. Deet offered to hold the biscuits while Tarrin went in and kept a Mr and Mrs Brunswick company. They were a friendly couple who lived in a high-rise apartment. They spent the hour playing board and card games with him and reading him stories. Deet passed the hour wandering the streets, looking in shop windows and finally sitting on a bench in a local park.

He opened the bag up and tried one of Mrs Davey's home-made biscuits. They were good. Better than shop-bought. He reached into the bag and had another. By the time he went back to pick Tarrin up, the shortbread biscuits were all gone.

3

The World's Revenge

Nobody knew exactly why it had happened, but it had happened all the same. Maybe it was the Law of Unintended Consequences, maybe it was nature just keeping itself in balance.

The Law of Unintended Consequences more or less stated that you could do things for the best, and the worst would come out of it. Or, on the other hand, with bad intentions, you might accidentally do nothing but good – or then, on the other hand again, do far more evil than you had ever originally intended. There was really no knowing. And who could have guessed that the price of long life for some would be no life at all for others?

It had started by everybody living longer, with often simple and general improvements in health care. Then, little by little, the general improvements had grown more specific, as the common killers of the elderly – the heart attacks, the cancers, the strokes – had been pushed aside. People lived healthier lives for longer and longer, staying active, remaining spry. Then the Anti-Ageing pills had come along, which most people took at around the age of forty, when they were available free from the government. So forty was about as old as you got, at least in terms of appearance anyway.

All that was going to kill you after that was an accident of some kind, or some freak illness against which nobody had been immunized. Then finally, at what had once been regarded as some impossibly great age, your system would surrender to time and give up the ghost, and not even medical science or Anti-Ageing pills could help you then. Your body would give out on you and you would die at some ripe old age of one hundred and twenty plus.

Some individuals had lived for over two hundred years. But they had a strange look about them – not in the wrinkles in their foreheads or their stooped backs, no, nothing of that kind, they were straight and erect as a forty-year-old. It was in their eyes. They seemed like people who had travelled in space and who had looked upon the immensity of the universe; eternity had moved into them, and taken up residence inside.

Yes, those were the two major killers now – unavoidable accident or the final collapse of a human body that had lived far beyond its allotted span. Oh, and sometimes there was a third cause – when people put an end to themselves because they had simply had enough. They'd wrung out the cloth; they'd tilted the glass back and swallowed the dregs and there was nothing left at the party to stay for. Once that kind of spirit had gone from you, it was hard to get a refill.

'Well, I'll be getting out now, kid,' Deet said. 'Maybe you'd better do some studying.'

He threw an Edu-Pack down on to Tarrin's bed in the cheap motel that was currently home. Tarrin saw that tonight it was geography.

'I'd go through it with you but I haven't got the time,' Deet said. 'So you'll have to do it on your own. But you're smart enough, kid, you'll understand it and, if not, get online with the interactive tutor.'

He pointed to the screen in the room. Most motels had them now, for the convenience of the customers. The only thing that distinguished the set from an ordinary TV was the QWERTY keyboard next to it. You could watch any one of the 549 channels, or you could surf the Net, or you could watch your choice of about fifty thousand online films (*a small charge will be added to your bill*).

'I'll maybe ask you few test questions when I get back,' he said.

But Tarrin knew he wouldn't. By the time Deet got back to his room next door, Tarrin would be fast asleep, having gone to bed long since. Or if Tarrin was still awake, Deet would be too far gone to make any sense. He would be slow and sluggish, or unnaturally cheerful, or – worst of all – sad and melancholy. Those would be the times when he would put his arm about Tarrin's shoulders and tell him that he loved him like a son and that he was a fine and wonderful substitute for his own flesh and blood.

It was all phoney, though no doubt he meant it sincerely enough at the time. It was the beer or the whisky talking. But really, it was no more than weeping at a sad film, and it wasn't even Tarrin he was feeling sorry for. It was himself, and the idea of himself as a man without family or loved ones. But had Deet been given family or loved ones, he would soon have tired of them and the responsibility, and he would be looking at airline timetables and checking out motel rates and thinking of moving on.

It wasn't as a son that he loved Tarrin, it was as a source of income. He loved him the way a miser loves his money in the bank, and he worried about him in the same way too – which is to say he worried that one day his source of income might vanish overnight, and then what would he do?

'Yeah, learn some geography,' Deet said. 'Then use the self-tester, or I might ask you a few questions when I come back, like I said, just to make sure you've been learning. People want a kid for the afternoon, but they don't want an uneducated one. So do some schooling.'

Tarrin often wished that he could have gone to school, but there were barely any left to go to. They were no longer an economic proposition, without the children to fill them. It was all individual tuition now or, for those who could not afford that, the Edu-Packs, which, if followed to the letter, brought you up to the required academic standard.

The schools stood empty now, ruined and derelict. Rats ran along the deserted corridors, spiders hung from the corners. The classrooms were quiet and eerie, with rows of empty chairs and desks facing a blank board.

One or two schools had been kept open as 'living monuments' and 'museums of childhood' and could be visited, just like any art gallery or stately home. Here was the sports hall, here was the chemistry lab, here was the assembly hall where five hundred children had once gathered every morning to hear the headmaster or headmistress make their announcements and speeches, trying to keep order as their listeners nudged each other and passed messages on scraps of paper and tried to make each other laugh, or fought the laughter back.

Venture outside and here was the sports field, the tennis court, the football pitches, the playground, where generations had learned to grow up, fighting their own personal battles on the way.

It was history.

'I'll see you then, kid.'

'OK, Deet.'

'And remember to keep the door locked and on the security chain and if anyone knocks, don't you let them in. Not even if they speak to you in my voice. Only let them in if they know the special knock, kid . . .'

'I know, Deet, I know.'

'And even if they speak to you in my voice and know the special knock, you look at them real careful through the spyhole first . . .'

'I know, Deet. I know what to do.'

'And even then, if they speak to you in my voice and know the special knock and even if it looks like me when you look in the spyhole, and even if they've got a good reason as to why they've lost their key, well . . . you still put the door on the chain, kid, when you open it, because you never know . . .'

'No, Deet, I know. You never know.'

'You never know what lengths they'd go to, these damn Kiddernappers!'

'Yes, Deet.'

'They're the worst of the worst, kid, and the lowest of the low. If you were to get lower than Kiddernappers, you'd be so low you'd never get back up again. You'd be crawling down there with the worms. You hear?'

'Yes, Deet.'

But people who win other people's children in card games, that's all right, Deet, is it? Tarrin wanted to ask. Only Deet had his sore points and got into something of a temper when pressed upon them. So Tarrin didn't ask him that question, not any more. But when he had asked him it in the past, he had never received a satisfactory answer beyond Deet getting angry and indignant and saying things like, 'You should be more grateful, kid, things I've done for you.'

Once Tarrin had asked him the most important question of all.

'Who did you win me from, Deet? Was it my dad?'

Deet had looked down at his shoes and had shaken his head. 'No, no . . . guess not, no.'

Even Deet would have thought that beyond the pale – a man who had gambled his own son away. It would have been bad business. Why gamble away the goose? Better to hold on to it and count the golden eggs.

'Who then, Deet, if it wasn't my dad?'

'Just somebody, kid, just somebody. I don't really know. Just somebody.'

'How old was I, Deet?'

'You were young. You were just a kid, kid.'

'Why don't I remember?'

'Told you, you were young.'

'How young was I?'

'Young.'

He'd never tell the whole story or even give anything away. But if it hadn't been his father who had gambled him away, who had it been? And where was his father? And his mother? And his home?

'Was I an orphan, Deet? Was that why the other person had me?'

'Might have been, could have been, he didn't say. I'm sorry, kid, I can't help you. The past is past, you've got to let go of it. Maybe your parents didn't want you or they needed the money and they let you go to another family, I don't know. All I know is I won you fair and square and I've got all the papers here, for guardianship and possession. And that's all you need to know.'

He did have the papers too. They'd been stopped quite regularly by the police, thinking maybe that Deet himself was a broad-daylight Kiddernapper. But once they'd checked the papers out, they had let him go.

'Forget it, kid, don't worry about it, don't let it bother you. Put it outta your mind.' Deet took a final look at himself in the mirror, and he seemed to like what he saw. 'Well, I'm away now, kid. You think over what I said to you about the PP implant and you and me being in business together for all our lives. You think about that while I'm out. I'm serious. It's a serious economic proposition. And remember to lock that door.'

But Tarrin didn't want to think about the PP implant. Not ever.

When Deet closed the door behind him, Tarrin

went and put the chain on it. He could hear Deet shuffling around in the corridor outside, waiting for the sound of the security chain being latched before he would go. He would return by the door to his own room, which interconnected with Tarrin's.

'I've done it, Deet!' Tarrin called through the door.

There was a muffled, vaguely embarrassed reply. 'OK, right, kid. Just lacing my shoe up.'

As if.

Then at last he was truly gone.

Tarrin looked around the room. It was like every other motel room he had stayed in, and there must have been hundreds of those over the years. It was bland, anonymous and soulless. It was the accommodation equivalent of fast food. It was a burger, that was what it was. It was like living in a burger. He had lived on them and lived in them for years – burger meals, burger rooms. It was a burger room with fries and cola and a spot of salad. Deet was a burger too – a burger person. He was fast food, ready to go.

A house would have been nice. A real room in a real home. A slow, home-cooked room in a home-cooked home. A fresh-fruit room, a home-baked room. That would have been nice, that would have been wonderful. But all the days of his childhood had gone like this – acting the part, acting the child, one or two hours at a time, a child for the morning, a child for the afternoon, bringing a taste of what it was to have a family to those who had none themselves.

Yet neither did he. That was the irony. Neither did he. He was as lonely as they were. He had nobody either. Just Deet. And sometimes that was worse than nobody. Nobody would have been a much better option.

Tarrin sat and opened the geography pack and started to read through it. He was good at geography. He should be. He'd been to enough places. He went over to the keyboard next to the screen and went online. He tested himself on what he had just learned and a 'Congratulations! 100%' message came up, along with some dancing cartoon rabbits, leaping for joy at his success.

Then he typed his name in and did a search. But there was nothing. Just as there was always nothing. But what did he really expect? A message saying, 'Tarrin – you are our long-lost son. Please contact us at this address so that we can take you home.'?

Fat chance. No chance at all.

He thought again of the DNA library. If he could just find the pattern of his own DNA, the fingerprint of his genetic being, and match that against all those in the national register, he might find a near and significant match. And a near and significant match might mean somebody close to him, a blood relative, a member of his own family, a brother, a sister, a father, a mother – anyone.

But he didn't have the pattern of his own DNA, nor the likelihood of finding it. Deet preferred him not to know. All it needed was a blood or a saliva sample and a visit to the lab, but he had neither the money to pay for it nor the means of getting there. Deet watched him like a hawk, and the only times he didn't watch him were like now, when it was dark, and too dangerous to go out – when the Kiddernappers were about. At this time of night most of the DNA labs would be closed anyway, except the late-nite pharmacy place in the centre.

'It's a question of demand and supply, kid,' Deet had told him, when Tarrin had first asked about the Kiddernappers and why it wasn't safe for him to go out on his own, not even in daylight to play in the park.

'When a thing's in short supply and high demand, its price and its value go up. And that's how it is with children. They're not being born like they used to be and no one really knows why. A few people can still have them – but they fetch high prices. So the temptation's there, see – you snatch a kid, you take them out of town, or across a border, you find some rich man whose wife is desperate for the children she can't have herself – and there you go. You've got yourself one of those well-paying, no-questions-asked deals. And the younger the kid, the better – no memory, see – won't even realize it's been taken. It'll love those parents that paid for it just like they were its own. So the younger you are, the more you're worth. Now, a freshly born babe in arms, kid, well, I tell you, you could get ten million for that, easy. Ten million and then some. A newborn babe's a *Mona Lisa*, kid, it's a work of art. It's a collector's item. Why, and if it was twins, you'd be walking so far down easy street you'd never need to turn back again for the rest of your long, long days. No eking it out from week to week, but living it high till the day you die. So you just be careful, kid. As long as there's kids, there'll be Kiddernappers. As long as there's a chance of money to be made, people will be out there making it.'

One thing puzzled him still.

'What about the papers though, Deet? How can even rich people pretend that kidnapped children are their own if they don't have the papers?'

Deet had snorted in disgust – in fact, had they been outside at the time, he would probably have spat with it.

'Papers! Kid, don't be naive! You think you can't buy papers? You think if you'd got the kind of money to buy a kid, that you can't find yourself some legal on the take and buy yourself some papers? They'll even issue you with a brand-new birth certificate in your own name and everything. They'll falsify the DNA records, the lot. Papers! The only paper you need in this world is the folding kind – the kind you keep in your wallet. Get me?'

He snorted again. 'Papers, kid, aren't mostly worth the paper they're printed on.'

Then he gave Tarrin a curious look, and he clammed up and wouldn't say another word or answer any further questions on the subject. But it was too late by then. The damage had been done, the thought had already been implanted in Tarrin's mind.

If you could buy papers and falsify records, then what about Deet's papers? What about Tarrin himself?

Had he been kidnapped himself once? Years ago? And would that explain the memories? The flashes from the past, of faces, of light, of fields of corn and the sound of birds and a dog occasionally barking?

I remember, I remember,
The house where I was born . . .

But were these real memories, or only the desire for memories, the longing for a recognizable past? Maybe they were things he had only invented, or random scenes taken from films he had once seen and had spliced back together in his mind to create the sort of past he would have wanted.

'Papers, kid, aren't mostly worth the paper they're printed on.'

Deet had never attempted to pretend that he was his father, though. He had always told him that he was no more than his guardian. And then, one night, when he had come back full of beer and high spirits, he had begun to boast about how he had won Tarrin in a card game, from a man who was a bad gambler and who had no other way to settle his debt.

Maybe the man who had gambled him away had been a Kiddernapper himself. That would make sense. Yes, it would. It would make sense of an awful lot – though it still wouldn't tell him where he had come from.

'I won you and you were my meal ticket, kid. I could have sold you, but that's not my way. Income and a steady living, that's what I was looking for. And we've been good for each other, kid, haven't we? Yes, we have, we have.'

Deet in one of his frank and friendly moods could be a mine of useful information. Even he occasionally seemed to feel the need to tell the truth, to offload the garbage.

For a long time there had been three of them – Tarrin and Deet and Miss Evangeline, who one day was going to be Mrs Deet, or so it was intended, at least so Deet kept saying, by way of hints and

62

understandings, if not in so many words. But Miss Evangeline got tired of Deet and his hints, which never actually came to anything. Or perhaps he tired of her. Or maybe it was the motel rooms and the fast-food burger life she had tired of. She was replaced in time by Miss Sandra and then by Miss Barbara-Sue.

Tarrin had been fond of Miss Evangeline, but he wouldn't let himself get fond of the others after that, for he knew that they too would stay their time and then be moving on, just like he and Deet were always doing – moving, moving, moving on.

At times he longed for the company of other children more than he even longed to discover some clue to the past. He saw them occasionally, but rarely got near. They mostly passed by in securely locked cars, with a minder sitting next to them or a security guard staring out from the back window.

Poor parents, who couldn't afford that kind of protection, instantly fled the city at the first sign of pregnancy, to take up residence in some remote cottage, in a farmhouse or a smallholding, where they could sleep at nights without a gun by the bed and a ferocious watchdog prowling the yard, worrying about an unannounced nocturnal visit from the Kiddernappers.

The early months and years of childhood were the worst in terms of risk and vulnerability, for they were also when the child was most valuable. Then the commercial worth of a child steadily diminished with age – just as Tarrin's own value was gradually diminishing – until one day you were grown up.

And then you weren't worth a damn thing to anybody. Unless they were mad enough to love you, of course. Once you had reached the age when you were not a child any more, the Kiddernappers weren't interested.

Tarrin gave up on his Net search and picked up the geography Edu-Pack again, but try as he did to read it, his concentration wavered.

It was the PP. Deet talked about it more and more now, about getting the PP implant. He never used to mention it at all, once upon a time, but now he talked about it at least once a day.

Deet could see his livelihood, his future, his life, all slipping away.

How was he going to live without a child to support him?

'A few more years, kid, that's maybe all we've got, then nobody's going to want you. You're going to be just one more nobody in a world of nobodies. The world's full of nobodies, kid, all with faces on them like stopped clocks. Just look around you and see it for yourself. People get to forty and they start to take the Anti-Ageing and then they all look the same – waxworks, kid, frozen smiles, plastic complexions. It's the world's revenge, kid, if you ask me.'

Tarrin hadn't asked him, but he looked at him with curiosity. 'What do you mean, Deet? The world's revenge?'

Deet had sat back in his chair and prised the ring pull off another can and had chuckled to himself.

'All the well-meaners, kid, all the do-gooders. All the medics and researchers who were going to transform it all – the whole meaning of existence, I'm talking about the whole mortal span, kid. You a Bible reader?'

'Not especially,' Tarrin said, though there was always a Bible in each motel room, one in every room he had ever stayed in, placed there courtesy of the Gideons, who financed the spread of the Word. He glanced at them occasionally.

'Nor me,' Deet conceded. 'But I've flicked through a copy every now and then, when I was sitting getting bored in some motel room or maybe couldn't sleep. It tells you in there, kid. The very words.'

'Tells you what?'

'Man's allotted span, kid, it's threescore years and ten. That's seventy years old to me and you, here in the modern world. We don't use expressions like "allotted spans" or "threescore" much, but a score is twenty and three of them is sixty and ten on top is seventy and that's about how long we're supposed to last. Anything above that is a bonus. But these well-meaners and do-gooders, all so proud of themselves with their awards for this and that and their Nobel prizes, what did they do, kid?'

'What did they do, Deet?'

'They fixed it so we could live longer. Little by little. Century by century, decade by decade. It was going to be the answer. A long, long, long, long life. Why, the way they were going to fix it, kid, we were even going to be immortal! We were going to live for-ever and never die at all! Ha!'

Deet knocked back a mouthful of beer and then spluttered a little.

'Hell, I'm going to choke to death! Hit me on the back, kid.'

Tarrin did.

'Harder.'

He gave him a good solid thump – there was feeling in it.

'Not too hard, kid. I'm OK now. What was I saying?'

'About living forever.'

'Oh yeah. Well, they couldn't quite do that. But they gave us up to two hundred years or more. That's threescore years and ten doubled, tripled even. Only if nobody was dying and people went on getting born, what was going to happen?'

'The world would get crowded, Deet.'

'Exactly, kid, sharp boy. I brought you up all right. The world would get so crowded we'd be standing shoulder to shoulder, we'd be swarming and crawling all over each other like termites in a mound. So what did the world do to rectify that situation, kid? To stop the trouble happening? What was the world's revenge?'

'It made people barren.'

'Sure did, kid. It made them infertile so they couldn't have any more kids, kid. The death rate fell, sure it did. And the birth rate fell right along with it. Ha! I like the world, kid. I like its sense of humour. I like the way it gets its own back on the know-it-alls and the stuck-ups and the well-meaners. They got us into this predicament and they can't get us out. What a deal! What a place!'

'Except for some people, Deet. They can still have children.'

'Some people, kid, some lucky, lucky people, can still have kids and no one knows why about that either. But are they lucky, kid? Are you lucky to have children when every childless person in this world

66

envies you and hates you for having them and would steal your children from you if they could? Is that lucky?'

He took another swig of beer and looked philosophical.

'It's a hell of a world, kid. You're better off as you are and not growing up at all. If there aren't so many kids around, make childhood last longer, make childhood last forever, kid. Don't ever grow up. You're better off with the PP, kid. I tell you.'

'But that's not nice – for the kid who has it. He . . . she might want to grow up.'

'Sure. That's why it's illegal, kid. But everyone knows you can still get it. And once it's done, well, the law just has to accept it or . . . or that would be punishing the victim, right? So they let Miss Virginia Two Shoes go right on dancing. And why not, kid? She's cute as a button, and she's got fifty-plus years of experience in that line of business as well. She knows more about it than any five-year-old. She's a professional, see, kid. She doesn't have fits and tantrums or lie on the floor and cry.'

'She's a fast-food kid, isn't she?'

Deet seemed to suddenly sober up. He put his can down and looked across the room at Tarrin.

'What do you mean?'

'I mean . . . I suppose I mean . . . you know . . . it's like . . . giving people what they want in a hurry . . . feeding them the easy way . . . no cooking . . .'

'No cooking?'

'Just . . . ready to eat.'

'You worry me, kid,' Deet said. 'Sometimes you sound too grown up for your own good. You'd

67

better not go talking to the customers like this when you're out on the hour.'

'I don't, Deet.'

'You'd better not, you hear?'

'I hear.'

'They don't want this kind of thing, kid, they want kiddy-talk.'

'That's what I give them.'

'Then you be sure you do, and keep it that way.'

'Yes, Deet.'

'You hear me?'

'Yes, Deet.'

'Sometimes I think, kid, that the sooner you get the PP, the better it'll be for both of us. Why, in five or ten years, you could learn to be a real professional kid.'

'I am a kid, Deet. I'm a child already.'

'I mean a proper one.'

'I am a proper one. I'm more proper than they are.'

'I'm talking about expectations, kid. Let's not cover that ground again. I'm just saying, if I had the dough right now I'd treat you to the implant and you could be a kid forever and ever, right till the day you die.'

'But, Deet . . .'

His eyes narrowed as he picked up his beer can again. 'But Deet what?'

Tarrin swallowed. He had to tell him sometime. Best to tell him now.

'I might not want to be a kid forever, Deet. I might want to grow up.'

'What for?'

'To be big. To do things – you know. Just to . . . be me . . . become who I am.'

Deet didn't say anything for a time. He just sat there, sipping and looking and sipping again. Then finally he shook his head. 'Nah,' he said. 'We'll get you the PP, kid. Soon as I get the money.'

'But I still might want to grow up, Deet.'

'What for?'

'I just . . . might . . . rather . . . I don't want to be a child all my life, in a child's body, but with some sort of grown-up's mind.'

'Wish I could be a kid again,' Deet said, opening another can. 'Someone to look out for you. No worries, no responsibilities. No bills to pay. You don't know when you're lucky.'

'But, Deet—'

'I ain't talking about it no more. I'm looking out for you, kid, that's all. There's a few years left in you, I reckon, and then you'll not be a kid any more. So we need to get it done before things start changing and your voice gets deep.'

'But you haven't got the money, have you, Deet?' he asked, afraid that somehow Deet might have acquired it.

'I know that, but I'm working on it and I may even be sitting here hatching out the master plan, even as I'm sitting here speaking and sipping on this beer. You leave it to your uncle Deet, kid, and he'll look out for you, just like he always has. Have I ever raised my hand to you, kid? Or even my voice that often?'

'No, Deet, no.'

'Ain't I more than your owner and legal guardian? Ain't I more like a friend?'

'Yes, Deet.'

'The best one you've got.'

'I never get to play with any other children though, Deet, nor the chance to make any friends . . .'

'You're hair-splitting. That's irrelevant. Have I ever let you down? Don't I get you work regular and make sure you get all your meals and your education?'

'Yes, Deet.'

'Exactly. And it'll stay that way once you've had the PP. Except that maybe, as time goes by, we'll be more of partners and I'll let you keep a little of your earnings back for yourself.'

'Thanks, Deet.'

'Won't that be nice?'

'Yes, Deet.'

'Well, I'm going next door to bed now, kid, but you don't have to worry as I'll be listening out for the Kiddernappers. They're not going to take you, kid. Don't you worry. None of them nasty Kiddernappers is going to take you from your uncle Deet.'

'Yes, Deet.'

'Whadda you say?'

'Night, Deet.'

'Night, kid. And brush your teeth. Keep them clean and white and shiny. The customers like that – clean, white shiny teeth on a boy. You can't do better than shiny teeth and shiny smiles for getting your foot in the door and grabbing those bonus bags.'

Then finally Deet would go to bed and snore

loudly until eventually he rolled over and the snoring stopped, and then Tarrin would get to sleep too.

The PP worried him. It was the thought that Deet really meant it. That he would have it done to him, whether Tarrin wanted it or not. Right now he didn't have the money. But what if one day he did?

Tarrin felt that he should get away, that he ought to escape. Only how? And to where?

There was no disappearing.

How did you hide in an ocean of adults when you were a child?

Sure, he could run, but where could he run to? How long before someone would find him? Deet. Or someone worse than Deet . . .

Who could he turn to? Where could he go? He didn't have a friend in the world. He didn't know anyone at all. For all the attention he got every day from the people Deet rented him out to, he felt as lonely as a bird in an empty sky. He felt so lonely sometimes, so desperately lonely. All he wanted to do was to sleep then, and never, ever have to wake up again.

It was another aspect of the world's revenge. One of those little ironies which had eluded Deet, for he had no profit or feeling resting on it. It was the fact that now that children and childhood were the rarest and most valuable things in the world, they had become almost intolerably unhappy and lonely and filled with fear.

Tarrin put on pyjamas and then went to the bathroom to squeeze some toothpaste on to a brush and to shine his smile. As he watched himself in the mirror, the song came back into his head.

There's a green land far away
Going to get there one fine day

That was all Tarrin knew of it. The opening words and a snatch of the tune and no more. He didn't know if it was a real song or something he had made up in his own mind.

Or something he had heard someone singing, a long time ago.

He had a memory; he could see the squint of sunlight in his eyes and a canopy being pulled over and then a view of the sky as from inside a tent with the flap slightly open. Then there was movement, a rocking motion, and the sound of a woman's voice singing that song, or maybe it was a hymn maybe, or a lullaby.

There's a green land far away
Going to get there one fine day

But was it an invention, or a true memory? And that woman's voice and that perfume and the squint of the sun and the blue of the clouds and the canopy of shadow, had they ever really existed at all?

Or were they just his imagination and thinking?

Thinking.

Of the wishful kind.

He left the bathroom, went to bed, put the lights off and soon fell asleep.

He dreamed of the sound of rustling leaves moving in a country breeze. He thought that in among the imaginary shufflings was the real sound of muffled footsteps from somewhere close by. He felt that there was somebody out there, out in the motel corridor, trying to tread quietly, going from door to door, from room to room, turning the handles, listening at the walls, searching for something, for somebody maybe – for a particular kind of someone.

Or maybe it was just Deet. Yes, it was probably only Deet in the adjacent room, on the other side of the interconnecting door. Deet wouldn't let anything bad happen. Deet had his investment to protect, his own interests to safeguard.

After a while, the sense of some nearby presence had gone. There was no one there listening or watching or waiting. No one at all. Sleep grew deeper, deep as a black ocean, and how pleasant it was to drown in it – for a few hours of merciful oblivion.

4

The Stranger

The stranger lay on the hotel bed still wearing his boots. It maybe wasn't big and it maybe wasn't clever, but he was doing it just the same. It was something he had always done – lain on the bed with his boots on. Not so much from slovenliness or even from a desire to affront the proprieties, but you just never knew, that was all, when you might have to get up on to your feet again and be on the move. Not in this line of work.

So there was no real point in a person taking his boots off until a person had decided that he was well and truly done for the day. And he hadn't reached that stage yet, even though the night was dark and the hour was late and the town was still.

He got off the bed, stretched and went to the sink in the bathroom and ran himself a glass of water. He had only recently come in from walking around the town. He had been a solitary figure, alone in the night.

It was a town of medium size, one of many he had stayed in over the years. It was not without its own distinguishing features and singular places and items of interest, yet all in all it was as anonymous to him as all the rest, and in the end they had all blurred into nothingness. He had got older doing this. Nearly seven years of his life had gone.

There were other men like him, women too, who lived this way and for the same purpose. Maybe their motives differed slightly, but their objective was the same – to find a child. To locate one, study its movements, get to know its routine, establish whom it belonged to, who was looking after it, what kind of security was in place, to assess the risk involved in attempting its abduction, and then, if everything looked right and the chance seemed worth taking . . .

To make your move.

But you didn't want to get caught. That was for sure. You didn't want to make any mistakes or go bungling anything or go picking yourself the wrong child.

It was an automatic life sentence for Kiddernapping, same as for being involved in PP implants. Society had to have some safeguards. The government couldn't have children being abducted and traded. So it was life automatic. And life meant life, and life was long, it was a long, long life sentence they gave you now. In some ways it was worse than death.

According to the hotel register, the man's name was Kinane. Whether this was true or not, who knew? He had used so many aliases in his life that perhaps he had started to use his real name by accident, having forgotten it for a while, and now maybe thinking that it was one he had invented or dreamed up.

He didn't much look like a Kiddernapper, but then what Kiddernapper did? Why should a thief look like a thief? Or a murderer like a murderer? And what did a thief or a murderer – or a Kiddernapper, come to that – look like anyway? They looked like anyone, could have been anyone, were anyone.

You didn't see them coming, that was the thing. Or you saw them coming, but they simply didn't look like the trouble they were. And by the time you realized who they were and what they were there for, it was all too late. Your child had gone. Your pride, your joy, the object of your love and affection, your life, your soul, your prize possession. He or she had gone. Probably never to be seen again. Gone to another town, another city, another country. Gone, gone, good and gone. Never to be seen again.

For somebody had stolen, and somebody rich had gone and bought, the one thing that money couldn't – or shouldn't be able – to buy. A child, your child. And now your little boy or girl was behind a security screen in a rich person's house, playing behind razor wire and looking out through bullet-proof windows, pining and crying for you. But if the child was young enough, it came to believe that two other people were its parents, and in time it would forget you, and not even recognize you . . . not even want you. And if, at some point in the future, it were given the choice of returning home or remaining with them . . . it would remain. For worse than the theft of the child was the theft of its feelings. They could even steal love in the end.

Yes, it was strange the way that money could purchase all the things that money couldn't buy.

But this was only true if the child was very young. The older ones never forgot. There was always a residue of memory in them, an image of home, of a mother's scent, a father's voice. The older ones took more convincing and persuading. So the rich people told them that there had been an accident, that their natural parents had died, that they had taken them in as poor orphans, and that all those stories about Kiddernappers were just that – stories to frighten little children.

Some of the Kiddernappers just took who they could and then tried to find a buyer. Others worked to order. Maybe someone wanted a little girl, twins, a boy and a girl, a blonde girl, a boy with blue eyes – for the customer had blue eyes too, and that way it would all look right and natural and nobody would ask any questions.

Others just liked to snoop around, to go from town to town, keeping an ear to the ground and an eye on the horizon and a finger on the pulse. They got to hear of a kid here, a child there, maybe one allowed a little too much freedom and independence, maybe one with a parent or a guardian who had let security slide a little, who maybe thought that their child was safe now and that this was a secure, respectable neighbourhood. Wrong. Wrong. Wrong.

But the thing to realize was that it didn't make you a bad person. That is, not necessarily. Just because you were a Kiddernapper, did that make you the scum of the earth? In some ways you could say you were performing a useful social service.

Sometimes there wasn't even any abduction involved. Sometimes the Kiddernapper was just the agent, the go-between, the man carrying an offer of money, which the parents were only too willing to accept.

Some people, able to have children, only had them in order to sell them to the highest bidder. *They* were the scum of the earth, if you wanted Kinane's opinion. Not the people who desperately wanted children and would give anything for them. No, it was the ones who would sell them, who would sell their own flesh and blood. They were the ones who should get a life behind prison bars, a nice, long one.

Kinane watched the television for a while, then decided that he would not go out again and that he may as well take his boots off, which he did. Then he undressed, washed, cleaned his teeth and got between the sheets of the bed.

It had been a satisfactory day, all things considered. He'd spotted a few marks, just one or two, but promising all the same, and it didn't look as if anybody else had spotted them.

He had been the only one trailing, as far as he knew, and that was how he liked it. You didn't want competition and two of you after the same kid. That was bad news for everybody and trouble all round. He'd just keep an eye out, that was all, and let things take their course for a day or so. He'd just keep watching, keep waiting, keep a low, discreet profile and a professional eye out.

He'd seen a girl that day, but it wasn't a girl that was wanted. It was a boy. A particular kind of boy. One of the dark-haired, dark-eyed variety. And he'd seen one, yes, indeed he had. He'd seen one at last, and he'd keep watching him, and maybe he might turn out to be perfect.

*

There were no appointments that morning and Deet knew that it wasn't healthy to keep Tarrin cooped up in the room all the time, so he took him out for some fresh air.

'A good, long, healthy walk, kid, that's what you need.'

If he was right in that, and if Tarrin needed a good, long, healthy walk, then Deet needed one more. He had a pallor about him, the result of a life spent out of the reach of the sun, in betting shops and bars, in clubs and motel rooms. Deet had the look of somebody who didn't like the light. He always seemed a little startled by it, as if it was causing him offence. He kept his sunglasses in his shirt pocket, ever at the ready for the first sign of blue sky.

They walked past a swimming pool and Tarrin asked Deet if they could go in swimming. Deet was as averse to water as he was to sunlight, but he could see the benefits of it, so he took Tarrin into a sports shop and bought him a towel and a pair of goggles and swimming shorts.

It took the shopkeeper a while to find the stuff.

'A boy!' he kept saying, over and over. 'I'll need to look in the back, sir. A boy, my, my. We've not had one of those in for a long time. I'll have to check the old stock. A boy. My, my. A boy.'

At length he found Tarrin a pair of swimming shorts that would more or less fit him. And length was the word. They hung round his waist and came down below his knees.

'They're the smallest we have, I'm afraid.'

'They'll do,' Deet said. 'They do, kid?'

Afraid that if he said no then he wouldn't be taken swimming at all, Tarrin nodded.

'They'll be fine,' he said, though he was worried that if he dived into the deep end, the shorts might shoot right off. Tarrin resolved not to dive at all. He'd just jump in and keep his shorts on.

'Got any goggles?' Deet asked. 'We got an appointment later and I don't want him red-eyed, like he's been bleating or something.'

'I'll see what we've got, sir.'

The shop owner found some swimming goggles. There were adult-sized, but he tightened them up and said they would probably do. Tarrin felt they would let the water in, but again he said nothing.

Deet paid and they walked out and back along the road to the public pool. Deet stayed with Tarrin as he changed, standing guard outside his changing cubicle.

'Damn Kiddernappers,' Tarrin heard him mumble. 'Can't even take a boy swimming but you're worried they'll snatch him right out of the water.'

While Tarrin swam, Deet sat on one of the benches at the pool side, glancing up from his racing paper every few seconds, making sure that the boy was still there in the water.

Apart from Tarrin, the pool was nearly empty. Once upon a time it would have been full up at that time of morning with parties of schoolchildren learning to swim. But today there were only a few adult swimmers. They smiled indulgently at the sight of a child, and one of them, a woman in her thirties, called over to Deet as she got out of the pool.

'Fine boy you have there. Fine boy.'

Deet smiled and nodded but he got pretty sick of it really, all the 'Fine boy you have there' stuff. It was like always hearing about the weather, over and over. There was nothing new about it that anyone could say to him and he was tired of hearing the old words endlessly repeated.

It was only when the swimmer had gone that Deet realized that he had failed to ask her if – as she was such an admirer – she might like to rent Tarrin's company for an afternoon. He should have given her a business card. He'd missed an opportunity there, which wasn't like him, not like him at all.

Maybe he was coming down with a cold, he thought. Good job he hadn't gone in with the kid swimming. It would only have made his cold worse. Not that he was certain he had one. But it was best to walk on the safe side.

Tarrin swam lengths for a while, and then, when the temptation became too great, he practised diving after all – first tying his shorts on tight with the waist cord. But it was no real fun on his own. He wished he had a friend, one to run with, race with, splash with, have some kind of fun with. The other swimmers just swam on, up and down, up and down, up and down forever.

He tried to see how far he could swim underwater and easily managed two widths. He rested then, and as he did he glanced at Deet, reading his paper, and he wondered again about the DNA and how he could get the money for a test. Deet wasn't mean, he bought him everything he needed, but he never gave him money of his own. And he was always with him too, except at night, when it was unsafe for Tarrin to be on the streets because of the Kiddernappers. That was the only time Deet would leave him, safely locked up in the motel room.

So Tarrin needed money and he would need to get away from Deet for a while. There had to be a way. But how could he do it?

The website he had looked at, the site of a nearby DNA tester, was asking for 500 International Currency Units. It wasn't that much. But how could he get it? Little by little, maybe. Maybe if the people he visited offered him a gift he could ask for money. Or would that seem grasping and rude? They might not want to give him money when they were already paying money to Deet for the pleasure of Tarrin's company.

He could tell them he was saving up for something . . . a present for someone . . . a present for Deet! For his birthday. No. Not Deet. Who in their right mind would ever want to give Deet a present?

For his mother. He could say for his mother. Flowers for his mother.

To put on her grave.

Surely any decent person would give him the money for that?

Then it occurred to him that it might be real, it might be true, his mother could be dead, his father as well. He might not see either of them ever again. Maybe they had died in an accident, or died of a new virus of some kind.

He might never find them, no matter how long he looked. Or perhaps he'd eventually only locate their memorials, the plaques recording their lives and their dates. Or not even that. Maybe they would have been cremated and their ashes scattered to the winds.

Tarrin wondered how long they had looked for him before they had given up. How long could anyone go on hoping? There had to come a time when you gave up hope, for the sake of your own sanity. Maybe they had given up a long, long time ago. Maybe they just thought of him as dead. Maybe that was easier.

'Hey, kid!'

Deet was calling and pointing at his wristwatch. It was time to go. Tarrin got out of the pool and went to the changing room. Deet hurried in around the other way and stood guard while Tarrin showered and got dressed.

'Bite of lunch then, kid, then off to the first appointment.'

'How many today, Deet?'

'Five today, kid. Busy, busy, busy.'

Five. Tarrin's heart sank. It was too many. Each visit was only an hour, but it was still too many. Three Tarrin could manage without difficulty. But even four was hard. It was hard to smile, hard to be pleasant, hard to be, for sixty short minutes, the perfect child that somebody had never had, to fulfil the desires of a lifetime.

'I'm only a kid, Deet,' he had said to him once.

'That's why they want you,' Deet had answered.

'I mean, I'm bound to disappoint them. I can't be perfect, Deet. I don't know what they imagine kids are like, but I don't think it can be me.'

'You'll be OK, kid.'

'It's having to make them happy, Deet. It's so

hard . . . to be what they want you to be all the time. I'm just a person, Deet. I get tired and fed up and ratty and . . . you know.'

'Stick with it, kid. We're making good money.'

Deet just didn't understand. Didn't know, and didn't understand. And wasn't really interested.

'So what do you want for lunch, kid?'

Tarrin wanted a sandwich. A home-made sandwich, with cheese and crisp cucumber slices, and a glass of freshly squeezed orange juice.

'What say we get a burger?'

'What say we don't get a burger, Deet? Just for a change.'

Deet's mouth dropped open. He had never heard Tarrin talk like that before. 'Whadda you mean, kid? You mean pizza?'

'I thought maybe we could have a sandwich, Deet. For a change.'

Deet gave it all of five seconds' consideration, then shook his head. 'Nah. We'll get a burger. You know where you stand. Let's get a burger and a cola, kid.'

So that was what they got.

The dog walkers were out in force in the park. Almost everyone had pets. Cats and dogs were the favourites – child substitutes. Small, baby-sized dogs were the most popular: pugs and terriers and Pekinese. People fussed over them and scolded them in an affectionate way when they barked too much or bothered someone.

Tarrin felt people's eyes on him as he and Deet crossed by the ornamental lake. He had never got used to being stared at and there was no respite from it. He, like every other child, was an object of intense scrutiny and curiosity.

'What do you think you're looking at?' he wanted to shout. But if he'd started that, he'd have been shouting all day.

They walked past a closed-up nursery school. The Red House Nursery, a faded board outside it read. There was some play equipment rusting and decaying on the overgrown lawn. Once the garden would have echoed with the sound of children's voices, now it was silent. Once the walls inside the nursery would have been decorated from floor to ceiling with childish pictures of the sun and the sea, drawings of red houses and blue skies. Now the walls were bare. Now the place was as silent as a mausoleum.

The lack of children meant that thousands of people had been left without occupation. So many businesses had closed – factories making toys and children's clothes, cartoon makers, film makers, publishers of educational works and books for children. Teachers were made redundant, schools and maternity units had closed down. Any children born now were born at home – with a midwife in attendance, who had possibly never even seen a birth before, except on video.

The sales of skateboards, Rollerblades and mountain bikes plummeted, as did demand for computer games, footballs, music downloads and a hundred different gadgets.

Zoos and theme parks were often empty of visitors for hours, even days, at a time. The roller coasters collected dust; the log flumes were dry; the animals stared out from behind the bars of their cages. Maybe a solitary soul came by to stare at the animals staring out, feeling sorry both for them and for himself. Eventually all but a handful of theme parks closed down. Many shops went out of business as sales of sweets, snacks and confectionery plunged. There was no school-run. No school buses. No school parties to take to museums and science centres and city farms.

There were no gangs either, running riot in the streets or hanging around the shopping centres, riding on the trolleys, chewing the fat and smoking what they weren't supposed to. Nobody went to the beach to make sandcastles, to ride the dodgems or the donkeys, to play the arcade machines at the end of the pier, to beg for more ice cream and another stick of rock.

It was quiet. No shouting voices, no shrieks, no laughter, no fights, no bullying, no sounds of games, of balls bouncing, of people calling, just calm, sweet silence. Only it was not as sweet as it should have been. It was too silent, at too high a price. It was almost like the loss of birdsong – the vanished sound of children. Yet some people preferred it that way: calm, staid and orderly, and the world a grown-up place.

'Where do we have to be, Deet?'
'You'll see when we get there.'
Tarrin hoped it would be a rich house. Maybe he'd be able to get the 500 units in one go. Then he could get his DNA tested, get a map of it from a blood sample, then get it matched up on the national database and . . .

Maybe he could find them, his family. Maybe they

were still alive, his mum and his dad. Maybe they
were still hoping, maybe they were even still looking
for him. Maybe.

He could hope, anyway. He could do that much.
Where there was life there was hope, and where life
was long, hope was long too.

'Ready, kid?'

'I'm ready, Deet.'

'You didn't finish your burger.'

'I wasn't really hungry.'

'After all that swimming?'

'I swallowed some pool water and it filled me up.'

'Not finished your fries either. Something wrong
with your fries?'

'To tell the truth, Deet – I'm sort of tired of fries.'

'Tired of fries? I never heard of a kid before who
was tired of fries.'

'Well, I am, just a little bit.'

'Maybe we can have a pizza tonight.'

'OK.'

'That be good?'

'Yeah, that'll be fine.'

'See, I look after you, kid, don't I? Eh?'

'Yes, Deet.'

'Don't I look after you?'

'Yes.'

'Don't I, kid? Take you swimming and get you
burgers and pizza?'

'Sure.'

'I look after you.'

'Right.'

'So what's wrong, kid? Cat got your tongue?'

'You look after me, Deet.'

'That's it, kid. That's what I do. So come on now, let's us get to work. Time we made us some money.'

It was the 'us' that puzzled Tarrin. It always had and it always would. The 'us' and the 'we'. In what possible way were 'we' getting to work? What work did Deet do?

Tarrin didn't wish to be rude about him, but surely, looked at in a cold, objective light, Deet was nothing but a parasite. He was nothing but a great big flea. Nothing but a giant bedbug who had made Tarrin his pillow and the world his bed.

5

Birthday Boy

Deet's knocking on the door didn't bring anybody to
it, so, much as he didn't care to, he had to press the
bell. It probably rang somewhere, deep within the
bowels of the house, but as far as Deet and Tarrin
were concerned, where they stood by the white-
painted front door, the chimes maintained a dignified
– even indifferent – silence. They just had to stand
and wait.

'There's money here, kid,' Deet said, nodding saga-
ciously as he took in the porch, the flower beds, the
trees, the lawn, the tennis court and a building which
no doubt housed the swimming pool.

'Money here in sack-loads,' he said, and he nodded
again, in confirmation of his initial opinion, as
though he were some kind of an expert on wealth, a
connoisseur of it. He almost seemed to roll the taste
of it around in his mouth, as if it were wine.

'Money here, kid,' he said again, as if Tarrin
couldn't see that for himself. The house was big,
detached and stood imposingly in landscaped gardens.

'Got it all, see, kid,' Deet said. 'Got it all.' Then his
envy turned to one-upmanship, to an inner satisfac-
tion that no matter how rich these people were,

they didn't have the one thing that only Deet could supply.

'That is, they got it all, 'cept one thing.'

Tarrin knew his cue. He knew just what to say. 'What's that, Deet?'

'You, kid. You. Kids. Children. And that's why we're here.'

But he was wrong. As he saw the moment the door opened. His jaw dropped and his face assumed an expression of shocked surprise. The door had been opened by a well-dressed, slim-built woman, who was plainly on the Anti-Ageing and had been for some time. She had cold-looking skin, with the faint sheen of frozen time upon it. There was a slight artificiality to her appearance too, as if a skilled plastic surgeon had done a pretty good job, but had been unable to disguise the fact that he had done it.

The woman could have been any age between forty-five and a hundred. She was immaculately dressed in casual designer clothes. A smell of expensive perfume wafted from her. And next to her stood a child. A boy. About Tarrin's age.

'Mr Deet . . .'

Deet was so surprised, he didn't even bother to correct her on the niceties of his terms of address. He didn't explain that it was straight Deet, pure and simple, with no mister attached. He just stood there and gawped and took several seconds – a long time for Deet – to regain his composure.

'G-good afternoon, ma'am. Mrs . . .' He checked his notebook of phone numbers and appointments. 'Mrs Weaver, I believe.'

'That's right.'

Then he couldn't help but comment. 'You've got a boy already.'

As though she had no business wanting two.

'That's right,' she said. 'I have. We have. My husband and I. This is Paul. And this is . . .?'

The two boys were staring at each other. They were of more or less equal age and height and build, only Paul was blond, and better dressed, and he seemed to have acquired that same odour of wealth, of money, that permeated the gardens and the house and its owners. The whole place was redolent of affluence and security.

'This is . . .'

'I'm Tarrin,' Tarrin said. He spoke to the woman, not to the boy. The boy was looking at him with a rather cold, hostile, even vaguely malicious expression.

'Tarrin. That's a nice name. Well then, Tarrin, this is Paul. And Paul, this is Tarrin.'

If the adults had been waiting for the two boys to shake hands, they were disappointed.

'Hi.' Tarrin nodded.

'Hi,' Paul grunted back, keeping his hands firmly in his pockets.

'Well, won't you come in, Mr Deet?'

'Well, I . . . my custom is mostly to leave you to it, ma'am. To make myself scarce for the duration of the . . . eh . . . appointment, and to reappear at picking-up time. But . . .'

'We're a little isolated here. I don't know that there's really anywhere for you to go.'

Deet had been thinking that himself when the taxi had dropped them off. There was no betting shop nearby for him to pass some time in, no cafe or greasy spoon where he could spend an hour over a cooling cup of coffee, telling the waitress how good-looking she was and what potential she had and how she should have been in showbiz. (And not exactly saying, but letting her get the impression, that he was an agent, or a film producer, or a director of some kind.)

'Well, that's very kind of you, ma'am.'

'You can take a seat in the kitchen with cook, if you like. I'm sure she'll find you something and that the time will soon pass.'

Inwardly Deet bristled at this suggestion. It seemed to put him on a level with the hirelings and the underlings and the servants in the hall. Which wasn't how he saw himself, no sir. He was the wheeler, the dealer, the supplier, the man with the upper hand. But what the hell – he could swallow his pride this once, if it meant getting a free cup of coffee, and maybe a slice of cake along with it.

'That's very kind of you, ma'am. I'll take you up on that then, if I may.'

'Please. Won't you both come in?'

They went inside and, as the door closed behind them, Tarrin saw that the hall was decorated with streamers and balloons and that there were cards on the hall table and on the window ledges, and that a string of letters had been draped above the stairs. They spelt out the words 'Happy Birthday Paul!'

So that was it, he thought. That was it. It was the other boy's birthday. And Tarrin was his present.

Deet saw the sign too. 'Celebrating, ma'am?' he asked. 'Is it a birthday occasion?'

'Indeed it is, Mr Deet. Did my husband not explain when he made the arrangements?'

'It slipped his mind or it slipped my hearing, ma'am,' Deet said, having recovered his usual swagger. 'But either way is no difference. We're here for you and it's your hour and whatever you want to do with it.'

Mrs Weaver looked at him. 'Two,' she said.

'Two?' Deet went pale.

'Two hours. Wasn't that the arrangement?'

Deet got out his pocket book and checked the booking. 'I only have you for one, ma'am.'

'We specifically asked for two. One is hardly enough, is it, for the boys to get to know each other, to play together . . .'

'Quite so, ma'am, quite so, it's just . . .'

'I hope you're not going to disappoint us, Mr Deet.'

Deet saw that she was taking a sealed envelope out from the drawer of the hall table and he realized that he was going to be paid in cash, which was just how he liked it – no cheques, no records, nothing for the tax office to get its hooks into.

'No, ma'am. Don't you concern yourself about that at all. If it's two you wanted, two it is.'

Tarrin stared at Deet, a pleading look on his face. *Not two hours, Deet,* it said. *Not two hours. One's enough, isn't it?*

It was odd that for so long all Tarrin had wanted was the company of another child, but now that the prospect was a reality, all he desired was to be out of the place as soon as possible. He didn't like the look of Paul in the slightest. He felt panicky and his chest was tight. He didn't like it that he had been brought here as a birthday present, a birthday treat, that he was there to be played with, to do as the other boy wanted for two hours.

Tarrin had longed for the company of another child on the basis of their being equals. That was what he had dreamed of, not this – of being some rented companion, there to please another child, to do his bidding, almost some kind of servant.

'Deet,' he whispered, 'I don't feel well. I want to leave.'

But Deet made a point of not even looking at him.

'We do have other appointments,' he said to Mrs Weaver. 'But I'll just get on my mobe while I'm sitting in the kitchen and rearrange things with our other customers, or clients, as I call them. That'll be no problem at all, ma'am. Absolutely no problem.'

So Mrs Weaver handed him the envelope, and then she called for Maria, her cook and housekeeper, to come and take Mr Deet to the kitchen and to give him a cup of coffee if he wanted, and maybe a slice of her famous sponge cake – which made Maria smile, and she led Deet away.

'Enjoy yourselfs, boys,' he said as he went. 'And play nicely now,' he said to Tarrin, with a slightly nervous note in his voice, and an edge of warning to it.

Now, don't you screw up, kid, his eyes told Tarrin, and Tarrin knew full well what they were saying, but he pretended not to have noticed anything, his face remained impassive, quite blank, professional.

Deet followed Maria to the kitchen. He had the

forbearance not to open the envelope and count up the money in Mrs Weaver's presence, but as soon as he was out of her sight he slit the envelope open with his thumbnail, and then, while Maria made him coffee and cut the cake, he surreptitiously counted the notes and was pleased to see that he had been paid in full, plus a little extra. He put the envelope away in his inside pocket and patted it once or twice, every now and again, just to confirm that it was still there, and that Maria hadn't stolen it from him by some sleight of hand.

'Lovely cake,' he told her. 'Great coffee.'

He would have gone on to tell her that she had missed her calling in life and should have been in showbiz, but Maria was plainly anything but a would-be film star and they would have both known immediately that he was lying – which was one person knowing too many.

So they talked of other things.

'That their own kid?' Deet asked Maria. 'The boy there?'

She grinned and shook her head. 'They bought him,' she said,

'Recently? Or a while ago?' Deet asked.

'From a baby.' She nodded.

'From new, eh? Mother sold him?'

Maria shrugged. Maybe she knew, maybe she didn't; if she did, she wasn't telling, if she didn't, she wasn't about to express an opinion.

Her silence was enough.

So they'd bought him from a Kiddernapper, Deet thought. For all their money and their big, big house, they were no better than he was. For all Mrs

95

Weaver's fine, fashionable clothes and her sweet perfume, her hands were tainted too.

'Nice house,' Deet said. 'Nice coffee. Nice cake.'

'Good,' Maria said. 'Glad you like it. Have some more?'

Deet wasn't hungry, if anything he was overfull. But he wanted to get in her good books, so he pushed his plate over.

'If I may. Too delicious to refuse.'

She smiled and cut him a handsome slice. Deet noticed that another cake was sitting on a wire rack. But that one hadn't been cut yet. It was the boy's birthday cake, with his name and his age displayed upon it in blue icing.

Pink for a little girl, blue for a boy.

Deet knew people said it didn't have to be that way, but it usually was. There was no reason why a boy couldn't have pink or a girl have blue, but mostly people stuck to the traditions, no matter how liberal and enlightened they pretended to be.

> *My old granny used to say*
> *In her old-fashioned way*
> *Pink for a little girl*
> *Blue for a boy.*

Deet smiled to himself. He'd been a child too, hadn't he? He remembered things; he had a history, a past, memories of better days, of innocent times. Yes, he'd been a boy himself once, just playing and not caring about much really, not with any notion of what kind of man he might grow up into.

'I don't suppose,' he said to Maria, 'you know . . . how much they paid for him.'

Maria looked at him, shocked and affronted. 'Of course I don't know. And why would I tell you?'

'No offence. No offence. Just wondering.'

The plan had been formulating for a long time, and now Deet could see how to make it work. People said you couldn't have your cake and eat it. But you could. Or you could if you had two cakes – your own, and somebody else's. One to eat and one to keep. But how to get somebody else's cake, if they wouldn't give it to you?

Only one way possible. Only one.

Yes, Deet had an idea for how to get the money – to pay for the PP implant, to get the kid done once and for all, and to make him into a money-spinning kid forever. In fact, there was only one way in which he could ever hope to raise the kind of money for such a costly and illegal operation.

He could see just how to do it.

Deet rubbed his hands together, as if his palms had been made itchy by a money spider walking all over them.

'Could I trouble you for another cup of coffee, Maria?'

She poured him one from the pot.

'Well . . . so what would you two boys like to do?'

The three of them were in the living room. Tarrin was perched uncomfortably on the edge of a sofa, with the look of a boy on his best behaviour about him. Paul was standing by the window, scowling at both Tarrin and at his mother, as though none of this had been his idea and he had never wanted any of it, and it had all been her doing.

Which maybe it had.

People buy what they can afford, even when it is not necessarily what they want. The Weavers could afford a child for the afternoon as a present for their own son on his birthday, so they had arranged it, and the present had arrived.

He's probably afraid, Tarrin thought. Afraid and nervous. He's used to being the only boy and doesn't like me being here. It makes him worried, jealous, insecure. He's used to being the only one and he likes it that way. They probably persuaded him that it would be a good idea to have another boy to play with, and he said yes, but now I'm here, he doesn't want me, it suddenly doesn't seem like such a good idea after all.

Two hours though. Two hours booked and paid for. They had to get through it.

'So . . .' Mrs Weaver's smile was starting to look glassy. Maybe she'd had a picture in her mind of two happy brothers playing together, but things weren't working out quite like that.

'I know!'

Tarrin was glad that somebody did.

'How about we play in the garden!' she said.

This was the parental 'we'. There was the royal 'we', when kings and queens said such things as 'We are not amused' – meaning 'I don't think that's funny.' That was when 'we' meant 'me'.

The parental 'we' was when 'we' meant 'you'. So 'How about *we* play in the garden?' meant 'How about *you* play in the garden? While I sit here and do something else.'

'Sure,' Tarrin said, trying hard to seem cheerful and enthusiastic. 'Shall we play in the garden, Paul?'

'I suppose,' he said.

'It's a lovely day,' his mother reminded them. 'You can play for a while and then we'll cut the cake.'

'I suppose.'

For a boy with a birthday in a house full of cards and presents, Paul didn't seem that happy about much.

'There are plenty of things out there,' Mrs Weaver said. 'The swing, the slide . . . there's tennis, basketball, or you could play with the super-soakers.'

'Yes, let's do that, eh, Paul?'

'OK.'

Mrs Weaver opened the big patio windows, the ones which went from floor to ceiling, and enabled them to step right out into the garden.

She led them outside.

'Well! I'm going to sit here and watch while you play.' Then she remembered something. 'Oh, wait . . . no, you both carry on. I'm just going in to get the video camera. We'll want to remember this, won't we, Paul? It'll be something to look back on.'

She turned back into the house and left the two boys alone together in the garden.

Tarrin felt uncomfortable. He didn't like this place, he didn't like this boy, Paul, or the way Paul looked at him. He just wanted to be out of there.

Now, don't you screw up, kid.

He remembered the look on Deet's face and knew

that if he did screw up, Deet would be angry and life would be miserable until Deet got over it.

'You want to play with the basketball, Paul?'

'If you like.'

'It's your birthday.'

'I said if you like.'

'OK. Shall we shoot at the hoop? Take turns each?'

Paul didn't say no, so Tarrin picked the ball up and bounced it around a few times on the paving slabs of the patio, then he aimed and shot at the hoop which was fixed to a side of the garage.

The ball went in and trickled through the net and fell out again.

'You were too near.'

'Sorry?'

Paul was scowling at him. 'I said you were too near!'

'Was I?'

'Yes.'

'Where should I shoot from?'

'There.' He pointed to a line.

'Here?'

'Yes.'

Tarrin picked up the ball and went to throw it again.

'It's not your turn.'

'Sorry. I thought you meant you wanted me to take it again.'

'It's my turn.'

'Sorry, Paul. There you go.'

He lobbed the ball over to Paul. But the boy made no effort to catch it, and let it bounce right past.

'What's up?'

'You were supposed to pass it to me.'

'I threw it over to you.'

'Did you?'

'What do you want me to do? Put it into your hands?'

Paul didn't answer. Tarrin went and got the ball and handed it to him.

'There, then. OK?'

Paul said nothing. He half-heartedly aimed the ball at the hoop and threw it. He missed.

'Aw, bad luck.' Tarrin picked the ball up.

'What do you think you're doing?'

'Isn't it my turn?'

'No. It's mine. I get another.'

'Oh.'

'Well?'

'OK.'

He handed him the ball. Paul took it and walked a few steps nearer to the hoop.

'Excuse me.'

'What?'

'I think you're over the line, Paul.'

'What?'

'You told me I had to shoot from behind the line. Well, I think you're over the line.'

'No, I'm not.'

'Well, it just looks it to me.'

'You don't say.' He lobbed the ball upwards. This time it went into the hoop.

'Hey, good shot.'

'I don't want to play any more.'

'Don't you want to play?'

'No.'

Tarrin caught the ball as it rebounded and aimed it at the hoop.

'I said I don't want to play any more!'

Tarrin aimed and threw. The ball went in.

'I said I didn't want to play! I didn't want to play! You're not allowed to play!'

'Something wrong?'

Mrs Weaver had returned. The camera was in her hand. 'Something wrong, Paul?'

'He was cheating.'

'I'm sorry?'

'He was cheating.'

'I don't think I was, actually—'

'You were! Don't contradict me! You're just rented! This is my house!'

Tarrin coloured. His hands balled into fists. He leaned over, his face close to Paul's face, his mouth by his ear.

'Don't you talk to me like that. You say that again, I'll kill you.'

He whispered it so that Mrs Weaver wouldn't hear. But Paul heard. His eyes narrowed and he glared back. For a second Tarrin thought that he was going to spit in his face. 'You spit at me I'll spit right back.'

'Is something the matter, boys?

Mrs Weaver walked forwards, an uncertain smile on her face. She had no experience of this, of quarrelling children. She didn't know how to deal with this at all.

'How about playing a different game?' she suggested. 'How about a go on the climbing frame and the slide? Why don't you show him how to climb up the climbing frame, Paul?'

'I know how to climb up a climbing frame,' Tarrin muttered.

'Sorry?'

'Nothing. That would be nice.'

'Go on, Paul. Go on.'

Paul seemed pretty proud of his climbing prowess. He went up first while Mrs Weaver pointed the camera at him. But when Tarrin shinned up after him with equal ease, suddenly his climbing skills didn't seem quite so outstanding after all.

Maybe all these talents, which he had been told and persuaded to believe were so special by his parents – the parents of an only child, and the only family on the street – were quite ordinary abilities after all.

After the climbing frame, they threw a ball to each other from separate ends of the garden. Things were OK as long as Mrs Weaver was there, at least they were tolerable, but when she went back into the house to see if the cake was ready for cutting, or, if not, how much longer it would be, the game immediately ended.

'Aren't you going to throw it back?'

Paul didn't even answer him. He took up a tennis racket and began to hit the ball against the wall of the house. Tarrin stood and watched for a time and then picked up a racket himself.

'I didn't say you could play.'

Tarrin threw the racket down on the path.

'That cost money.'

'So?'

'Pick it up.'

Tarrin didn't move.

'I said pick it up.'

Tarrin folded his arms.

'Do as I tell you. You're only rented. I own you. For two hours. So pick it up.'

'Pick it up yourself.'

Paul raised his racket and swiped at Tarrin's head. Tarrin felt a stinging blow against his ear and the side of his face.

'Ow!'

Before he could think or even stop himself, he retaliated. He struck out with his fist and punched the boy back, in the same place, on the jaw, just below his ear.

'Ahhhhh!'

The cry was out of all proportion to the injury, but Paul sank to the ground, holding his face.

'Ahh! Ahh!'

Mrs Weaver ran from the house. 'What is it, Paul? What is it?'

'He hit me. He hit me. The hired boy. He hit me!'

Mrs Weaver nearly dropped the camera. She stood staring at Tarrin, as if he were a dog turned unexpectedly vicious. She took a step backwards towards the house.

'Mr Deet! Mr Deet! Mr Deet! Come quick! It's your boy!'

Deet appeared in seconds, still chewing and swallowing, cake crumbs around his mouth.

'What is it, ma'am? What is it?'

'He hit him! He hit my son!'

Deet didn't really know what to do either. 'Hit him? What did he do that for?'

'It's all right, Mother.'

It was Paul who spoke. They stared at him, wondering what he was going to say. What other outrages had been committed?

'I hit him first.'

He seemed proud. Proud to have started the fight and equally proud to have received as good as he had given. He actually grinned at them all.

'I hit him first. Right, Tarrin?'

As surprised as the adults, Tarrin nodded, wondering what could be the catch. 'That's right. Right.'

'We were only playing – right? And it went a bit too far.'

'Right.'

'Sorry we got you outside and got you worried for nothing.'

'But your head . . .'

'I'm all right, Mum. He's all right too. Aren't you?'

'Sure, sure, I'm all right.'

'Well, I really don't know, Mr Deet.'

'Boys, ma'am. Messing around. Boys'll be boys. Same the world over. Get 'em together, they start messing around and rough-housing. Don't know what they're doing. All part of the fun of it, I'd say. Part of the birthday fun.'

But as he spoke, Deet gave Tarrin a sour, recriminating look, quite the reverse of what he was saying.

'Well, I don't know . . .'

'Boys'll be boys, ma'am. Take my word on that.'

'Well, if you're sure . . .'

'We're OK, Mum. Come on, Tarrin. You want to play on the tennis court?'

'I might beat you,' Tarrin said in a low voice. 'What then?'

'You won't beat me. I'm good at it.'

He was right. Tarrin didn't beat him. The game was a draw. But winning or losing no longer mattered. The fight had broken the ice between them. All that mattered was to play.

Deet returned to the kitchen. Mrs Weaver filmed the tennis match, then took the boys in for drinks and cake. The birthday cake was cut in the kitchen and they all sang Happy Birthday – Maria, Mrs Weaver, Tarrin and even Deet. He sang loud and lusty and slightly off-key.

When the time came to go, Tarrin asked if he could use the bathroom, and he was directed upstairs to one on the landing. He used the bathroom, washed his hands and then, as he made to go back downstairs, he happened to glance through an open door into one of the bedrooms.

He saw temptation there.

It was Mrs Weaver's bag. It lay open upon the bed. In the bag was her purse, which was open too, and plainly visible inside it were folded banknotes. She must have filled Deet's envelope from this wad of ready cash, to pay him for the hire of Tarrin for the afternoon, and then had left the bag on the bed.

Tarrin hesitated. He didn't want to steal, but what choice did he have? How else could he ever pay for a DNA trace?

And they had so much here, so much.

While all he needed was five hundred.

Tarrin went into the bedroom. He could hear voices downstairs. Deet and Mrs Weaver talking about boys being boys, and her saying that she had got some good footage on the video camera and that maybe we should all do this again, and Deet agreeing – as of course he would, for it meant more money.

The thick, heavy carpets swallowed the sound of his steps. Tarrin came to the bed. He reached out and took the purse. There was a roll of eight, maybe ten, 500-unit notes. She'd never miss one. Not one. Never.

He peeled one away, put the roll back into the purse and thrust the stolen money deep into his pocket.

Deet's voice called up the stairs.

'What you doing up there, kid? You taking a bath or something?'

He hurriedly left the room and walked out into the corridor just as Maria appeared on the landing, carrying a basket of laundry. He couldn't be sure if she had seen him come out of the room or not, but he acted as if she hadn't – confident and unabashed – and he went on down the stairs.

'Well, there he is now. We'd best be on our way. So what do you say, Tarrin?'

'Thank you, Mrs Weaver. Thank you for having me.'

'Our pleasure, Tarrin. Thank you for being here.'

The boys didn't shake hands, but they nodded to each other.

'Bye, Paul.'

'Bye.'

'How's the ear?'

'It's OK. See you again maybe.'

'Yeah. Great. Happy birthday.'

'Thanks.'

Then they were back out in the street and Deet was hurrying Tarrin along as he looked around for a taxi.

'Come on, kid, we're behind now. I didn't know she was wanting two hours. It's screwed up everybody's appointments. I had to rearrange it all. We'll be working till seven in the evening now.'

We, Deet? *We'll* be working?

'Come on, kid. Cab over there. Taxi!'

They got in. Deet gave the driver the next address and settled back into his seat.

'So what did you punch him in the ear for?'

'He hit me first. You heard him. He said so. I was provoked, Deet, defending myself.'

'Well, next time don't retaliate. It's bad for business. Just walk away, or do like the man said and turn the other cheek.'

Tarrin said nothing. He looked out of the window at the passing cars. He slipped his hand into his pocket to make sure that the 500-unit note was there. It was. He would have loved to have taken it out and looked at it. But Deet would have seen it then, and have asked where it had come from, and would have soon figured it out, even if Tarrin refused to tell him, and he would have given Tarrin a lecture on the morality of stealing.

Then he would have taken the note from him, put it into his own pocket and kept it for himself.

They drove on across town. Tarrin kept thinking of Paul's life, his house, his family, his safe and settled environment, and could not help but to compare it with his own.

Then he thought of Maria, Mrs Weaver's cook and housekeeper, and how, as he and Deet had walked away, he had looked back at the house, only to see her staring after them, looking down at them from a bedroom window, with the basket of laundry in her arms.

Deet slid across the seat, so that he could talk to Tarrin in confidence.

'You know, kid,' he said, 'you know I'm always looking out for you, don't you?'

'Sure, Deet, sure.'

'But I'm never content with things as they are. You know that too, kid?'

'Yes, Deet. If you say.'

'I'm always planning, always scheming, always thinking two moves ahead.'

'Right.'

'Which is what I'm doing now, kid. Plans for the future, I'm talking about. You and me. And it's your future I'm thinking of, kid. Yours more than anything and what's going to become of you when you get too old to be a kid any more. Plans, plans, plans.'

'Right, Deet.'

'So you hold the faith, kid. No matter how weird things might get and how strange they might become, you have faith in your uncle Deet. He'll always be there for you – right?'

'Right.'

'I'd tell you more only I can't, because the fact of you even knowing could be all wrong and dangerous for you. Right?'

Tarrin had no idea what Deet was talking about and wasn't even sure that Deet did. He just liked the sound of his own voice sometimes and the drone of his own thoughts.

'Right, Deet. Right.'

'You'll see, kid. All in good time.' Deet tapped his head with his forefinger, like he had Einstein in there. 'I'm planning here. I'm planning.'

'OK, Deet. Thanks for telling me.'

'Just keeping you in the picture.'

They drove the rest of the way in silence, Tarrin thinking that more than ever and more than anything he needed to get away from Deet. Yet where was he to go?

In a world almost without children, where could he hide?

Tarrin didn't like it when Deet talked about what he was planning. Deet's plans usually meant pleasure and reward for one person, and one person only. And unpleasantness and trouble for everyone else.

'You didn't need to hit him though,' Deet said later, still brooding over the fight.

'He hit me first, Deet.'

'Bad for business,' Deet said. 'Maybe he did, but it's bad for business. Hitting the customers, kid, it's just not businesslike. It simply ain't professional.'

6

The Match

Deet bought a takeaway pizza on their way back to the motel that evening.

'Got one with some vegetables on it,' he said. 'Looking out for your health, see, kid.'

He was some nutritionist all right.

They sat and ate in silence. While Tarrin was getting some water to wash it down, Deet went to his room and rifled through the stack of Edu-Packs. He came back with one entitled History and threw it down on the bed.

'As it's late, don't worry about it too much,' he said. 'Maybe do just half an hour. Education's OK, kid, but it'll only take you so far. Look at me and where I've got today, and I don't know much history. Nor much physics nor chemistry either. But I'll tell you what I do know, kid – which side the bread is buttered on. As long as you know that, you'll be OK. You've got to work out which side the bread's buttered on and how to apply the jam. Because there's people out there with all sorts of education who can make all kinds of fancy things. But they can't all make money, kid. And it's the only thing worth making. And if anyone tells you otherwise, ask them how they propose to live without it. So you listen to your uncle Deet, now. You'll find it's an education in itself.'

Yes, Tarrin thought, maybe it is too. But he didn't think it in quite the way Deet intended.

The money Tarrin had taken was burning a hole in his pocket. He was conscious of it there all the time, seeming to radiate its own heat. He was frightened that it might fall out, or that he might accidentally pull it out, or, worse, that Deet's mobe would ring and it would be Mrs Weaver, calling him, saying, 'I'm sorry to ring you, Mr Deet, and I really don't intend for this to be taken the wrong way at all, but after you and Tarrin left this afternoon, I went up to my bedroom and looked in my purse and there seemed to be a sum of money missing. And I remembered that your boy had been upstairs on his own briefly, and Maria said that she had seen him standing by the door of the bedroom, and so I just wondered . . .'

But it didn't ring. It remained mercifully silent.

Go out, Deet.

He willed him to go.

Go out, Deet. Run your hand across your lips, like you always do, and say, 'Mouth seems a little dry tonight, boy. Whistle seems a bit dry too. Better go out and wet it a while, I reckon. So you be good now and keep the door latched, and don't open it to anyone, no matter how respectable they look through the spyhole, because it could all too well be a Kiddernapper. You hear me now?'

Say it, Deet. Say it and do it and then go. And as you go, say, 'Don't go staying up too late now, kid, or watching TV or playing on the computer there.

112

Just finish your studying and then twenty minutes in front of the screen and then wash and brush and into bed. OK, kid? OK? And if I don't see you later, then I'll see you in the morning. And by the way, I'm thinking of us moving on soon, kid. It's time to move on. It's all worked out for a while round here. We'll find another town in a day or so. A good kid's always wanted somewhere. A good kid will never go begging.'

Say it, Deet. Say it and do it and go.

Deet stood, almost as if responding to nothing other than the force of Tarrin's wishes. He ran his hand across his lips –

'Mouth seems a little dry tonight, kid . . .'

Ten minutes later Deet was washed, changed and ready to go.

'Keep the door shut tight, remember.'

'I know, Deet. The Kiddernappers.'

'They're around, kid. Believe me. They might not always look the part. But they're around.'

At last, Deet was gone.

Tarrin waited. He gave him a minute. One, two, three. He gave him five. Deet didn't come back. Then he took the money out and held it to the light.

Five hundred. It would pay for it all. The blood or saliva test, the DNA analysis, the match with all other database DNA profiles.

It would buy him the information. It might buy him the name and address and the whereabouts of his family, their area of origin, his place of birth. Knowledge and information – more precious to him than any amount of money.

113

Money *isn't* everything, Deet. Not at all. In some ways, it's the least.

It was dark now and Tarrin hadn't been out at night on his own ever. He'd never once been allowed out alone in the darkness.

> *Watch out, watch out.*
> *There's a Kiddernapper about.*

Was there? Was it true? Or was it just grown-ups making you scared with their own fears?

Only one way to find out.

Tarrin laced his trainers and then found the room key. There were two. Deet had taken the other one with him. The key was plastic, the size of a credit card, with a magnetic strip on the back.

What if Deet got back before he did?

No. He'd be gone for hours. He'd be in a pool hall somewhere, putting his money on the side of the pool table, wanting to play the winner of the game that was going on. Or he'd be in a bar, telling the waitress that she should be in motion pictures and letting her believe that, somehow, he could get her there, right where she truly belonged.

Say he'd forgotten something though. And he came back. Just as Tarrin was leaving. He'd need to have a story ready, about thinking he'd seen something, or hearing a suspicious noise.

Tarrin gave him another five minutes. But Deet didn't return. So he undid the security chain, peered along the corridor and saw no one. He let the door close silently behind him, then he made his way to the motel entrance and slipped out into the night.

Kinane stood and stretched himself and went to the window. It was dark out, but the night was fine, warm and even a little humid.

He decided to go out and take the air, and then, when he had walked for a time, buy himself a meal somewhere, maybe in some small Italian place. He liked Italian food, always had. Not too spicy but always flavoursome.

It had been an unproductive day. He'd strolled around the city streets and had even wandered out into the suburbs. He'd seen a few kids, as he ambled around, but they had all been under close surveillance, and anyway they hadn't been right. They'd all been girls, which wasn't what he was looking for.

It was a long game. You needed patience and a reserve of money to carry you through the lean, empty times. You'd think you'd found what you'd been looking for, but then you'd realize you hadn't, so you'd go on looking, spreading the net wider and further, believing that sooner or later it would happen. It would all be worth it when the right one turned up. You could barely put a price on a thing like that. Finding the right kid, it was pay day.

Of course, others were looking too; there was always the competition. You had to be one step ahead of them. One step ahead of the opposition, and one step behind your prey. You just had to have better reflexes, better instincts, you needed to know where to look.

Anyway, it was dark now, and it was late. He could relax and clock off for a while and start looking again tomorrow. There weren't going to be any kids around, not at this time of night. Not alone and unattended. If there were any kids out tonight, they'd probably have gorilla-sized minders and be hand-cuffed to them.

He checked his appearance in the mirror and, finding nothing offensive about it, he made sure that he had his wallet in his pocket before leaving the room and walking down the two flights of stairs to the street.

Tarrin had the address of the DNA bureau, and it wasn't far, but just being out in the night made him nervous. What if someone tried to snatch him off the street? What if he ran into Deet? Deet would go ballistic. Maybe he should invent another story and have it ready in advance, just in case he did run into him. He could tell him that someone had tried to break into the motel room and he had climbed out of the window and run.

Only it would be obvious that he hadn't climbed out, because when they returned to the motel, the windows would all be shut tight from the inside.

Then he saw him. He saw Deet, right there, inside a bar across the street. There he was, halfway along, perched on a stool. He had a beer in front of him, and he seemed in good humour. He was talking to a woman sitting on the stool next to him. It seemed like they were getting to know each other and were enjoy-ing each other's company. Deet leaned close and whispered something into the woman's ear and, whatever he had said, it made her laugh, and it made him laugh too.

Tarrin stood watching. He knew that Deet couldn't see him. Not even if he turned to the window and looked out. Deet wouldn't see who was out in the street; he'd just see his own reflection and that of the woman beside him.

A man and a woman walked past, arm in arm, maybe on their way to the theatre or to the cinema.

'Look, a boy there on his own.'

He caught the man's voice as he spoke to the woman. He heard her tutting and saying something about the parents and how if she were lucky enough ever to have children in a million years she wouldn't be letting her boy out on his own in the dark, dark, dangerous night, no sir, no way, no fear.

He realized he ought to be moving. He took a last look at Deet, who seemed to be happily planted in the bar for a good long while yet. He was beckoning the barman over and ordering refills for himself and his new lady friend. And he was paying. The woman glanced at the roll of money Deet peeled a bill from as he threw a note down on the bar top to pay for the drinks. She moved her stool a little closer and put her hand on his arm.

Why didn't Deet ever save some? Tarrin wondered. He could have had a house, a home, a wife; they could almost have been some kind of family by now.

But no. Deet was a waster, born to move on, a regular rolling stone, and not a scrap of moss on him.

Tarrin turned away and hurried on along the street to the first, the second, the third intersection, and

117

then he turned right. He walked past a small Italian restaurant. Two couples were going inside for dinner and as they opened the door the smell of food wafted out; it was the smell of basil and garlic and freshly made tomato sauce. It was nice, mouth-watering.

But Tarrin hurried on.

The DNA bureau was still a quarter of a mile away. He passed a long parade of shops, most of which were still open. It was a cosmopolitan quarter here, a place where all races and nationalities seemed to have found a home from home, and they had kept their own tastes and had brought their likings with them.

There were late-night grocery shops, shops selling halal meat, almost side by side with kosher butchers and vegetarian restaurants and launderettes. There were off-licences stocked with drink, and newsagents selling win-a-billion cards, and gadget places selling all the latest mobes, which could make calls, play vids and do almost everything for you, except eat your dinner.

Tarrin wasn't afraid here. Not where it was busy and where it was light. People, as a whole, had a loathing for Kiddernappers and there was an almost universal revulsion towards them. It was the worst thing in the world to steal a child from its parents. All decent people knew that, and had they been witness to any attempt to snatch a child, they would have intervened on the child's behalf.

Nevertheless, people stared at him as he hurried along. One or two of them shouted.

'Hey, son – you OK?'

'I'm OK.'

'Where's your dad? Where's your parents?'

'I'm OK.'

'Who's looking after you?'

'I'm OK, thanks. Thanks for asking, but I'm OK.'

'OK. Well, hurry home now.'

'That's where I'm going.'

'There might be Kiddernappers about.'

'I know. I'll be careful. I'm OK. Thank you. But I'm OK.'

He hurried on, his hand gripped tightly round the money he had stolen from Mrs Weaver's purse.

I'll pay you back one day, honest I will, pay you back as soon as I can. I'll get your address from Deet's pocket book and put the money in an envelope and post it to you. I will, honest, I will. It wasn't stealing, just a loan. I couldn't ask first if I could borrow it, but it was just a loan. I'll pay you it back – one day. I just needed it, you see. I had no choice. I just needed it more than you did.

The DNA bureau was just around the next corner now. But instead of increasing his speed, Tarrin stopped. He realized where he was. He was standing right outside the small theatre dedicated to the life, times and talents of Miss Virginia Two Shoes.

The place looked more glamorous than it had ever done during the day. There were neon lights and illuminated pictures, spotlit by hidden bulbs. They showed Miss Virginia Two Shoes in full flight, dressed in her cutest costumes and dancing her best steps. In one picture she was dressed up like a Hollywood film star, in fake diamonds and furs. She was made up to look like a grown-up, which was

119

strange when her major attraction was that of being a child.

Tarrin stopped to look at the pictures. The light matrix display flashed out its message:

Miss Virginia Two Shoes. Fifty-Five Years
Young and Still Dancing.
Everybody's Favourite Girl.

He fingered the money in his pocket. He would dearly have loved to have bought a ticket and gone inside. He wanted to see what the PP had done to her. The process held a macabre, eerie fascination for him. He was as much attracted by the idea of being a child forever as he was repelled by it.

It had occurred to him too that PP not only stood for Peter Pan, but for something else – Pied Piper. The man who had got rid of the Hamelin rats – but the townspeople wouldn't pay him his due, so he played his pipe again and this time it was the children of the town who were mesmerized by his playing, who followed him and were spirited away. Never to be seen again.

PP. Peter Pan was good and friendly, a warm happy ideal, the best of childhood, freedom without responsibility. But the Pied Piper, that was different. That represented lives lost and abducted, parents dispossessed of their children, deprived of ever seeing them grow up. The PP implant robbed them of that, and left instead the artificiality of Miss Virginia Two Shoes, her youth as good as pickles in a jar.

Yes, Tarrin thought, maybe that was what she was in the end – a kind of dancing pickled onion.

Tappity-tappity-tap.

He could hear the sound of her dancing. He looked around, wondering where the noise was coming from, then he saw a fan, the vents of which opened and closed, opened and closed.

Tappity-tappity-tap. Then the vents closed, silence, then they opened, *tappity-tappity-tap* again.

It was tempting to pay the money and go in. She sounded almost as pretty as she looked, so light and quick on her feet. Then she began to sing. He pressed his ear to the vent to hear her.

'On the good ship Lollipop . . .'

Then the vents closed. Then opened again.

He listened a while to her singing. He would hear a bar of the music, then the vents would close, then they would open and he would hear another bar, and then finally he heard applause.

She was a good singer. There was clapping and whistling and shouts of 'Encore!'

The pictures made her look so sweet too. She was everyone he had always wanted but had never had, all somehow rolled into one – mother, sister, and sweet girl next door. She made him feel warm and wanted.

Yet she repelled him too.

Fifty-five years old and still dancing. Everybody's favourite girl.

To be fifty-five and still have the face and body of a girl – it was creepy, repulsive.

Tarrin vowed then that he would never ever have the PP. Not even if Deet tried to force him. He'd run away first and take his chances with the

121

Kiddernappers. He'd rather grow old. He'd rather die.

He walked on. He came to the corner, made another right, and then there he was, outside the DNA bureau.

It was still open. As he knew it would be. All the inner-city bureaux were emblazoned with neon signs reading '24/7 – 52/12'. They never closed and they offered everything. Not just DNA testing but general health checks, prescription dispensing, blood monitoring, checking of cholesterol levels, eye tests, hearing tests, you name it.

Tarrin pushed the door open and walked in. The place was empty of other customers right at that moment, but there was a friendly-looking young woman behind the counter, wearing glasses and dressed in a white lab coat. She didn't really need to wear the lab coat, the boss just liked it that way. He felt that the sight of a white coat was reassuring for the customers. It was what they needed to see. It made things look clean and cool and professional.

'Hi.'

'Er . . . hi.' Tarrin looked up at her, wondering if she was really as young as she seemed, or if she too was on the Anti-Ageing.

No. He didn't think so. She didn't have the look about her. She was genuinely young. About twenty, he reckoned. Friendly and nice.

'Hi. You out on your own tonight?'

'Er . . . yeah. Yeah.'

'OK.' She could see he didn't want to be asked those sorts of questions. 'So how can I help?'

'I'd like a DNA profile, please.'

'Of yourself?'

'Yes. Profile, match and trace.'

'You know that's five hundred units?'

'I know.'

He took the note out and laid it on the counter. He was embarrassed to see that it was crushed and crumpled. He had scrunched it up into a ball without knowing it, he had been holding on to it so tight.

He made an attempt to smooth the note out. 'Sorry.'

'That's OK.' She took the money and put it in the till. 'OK. Give me your hand.'

He placed it, palm upwards, upon the counter.

'Index finger – OK?'

'OK.'

She put on surgical gloves, then she wiped his finger with an antiseptic wipe; next she took a small device with a sharp metal point to it, pressed it against the plump part of his finger, warned him that . . .

'This might hurt for a moment.'

Then clicked the top of the device. The point shot into his finger, almost immediately retracted and, a split second later, a tear of blood came out.

'Will that be enough?' he asked.

'Sure,' she smiled. 'It'll do.'

She picked the drop of blood up using a thin glass capillary tube. She then transferred the blood to a test tube in a rack.

'OK. Just get you a plaster.'

She put a sticking plaster over the spot on his finger, but it had already stopped bleeding.

'OK. Just take a seat.'

123

'Will it take long?'

'Few minutes.'

He sat on a chair by the counter and watched as she took the test tube with the drop of blood in it, added some liquid to it and then placed it inside a large white machine.

'Does that do it all?'

'It does.'

'Can I watch?'

'Nothing to see, I'm afraid. It all happens inside.'

She started the machine and it droned faintly as it went into motion. There was nothing for Tarrin to do but to wait.

The woman leaned her elbows on the counter and smiled across at him. He saw that she had a name badge on her white coat, reading Julia.

'Trying to trace your folks?' she asked.

'Kind of.' Tarrin nodded, not sure how much personal information he could risk giving away. She seemed nice enough though.

'You not with your mum and dad now?'

'No,' he said. 'I'm with Deet.'

'Deet?'

'He won me in a card game.'

Julia laughed. 'You're kidding me.'

'No. He won me. That's what he says.'

She didn't laugh any more. 'That's terrible. That's awful. Can't you get home?'

'Don't know where I came from,' Tarrin said. 'Don't know how old I was when he won me. Or who I was. Or if I had brothers and sisters. Don't know anything at all. That's why I'm here.'

'Can't you go to the Child Bureau?'

'They can't do anything. Deet's got proper papers. He's my legal guardian. The Child Bureau can't help.'

'That's terrible.'

'That's why I'm here.'

The machine pinged and came to a stop. From the printer attached to it a strip of paper slowly emerged with Tarrin's DNA profile upon it. Julia held it up.

'There it is. That's you. Your own genetic fingerprint. That's how and why you're unique. Nobody quite like you in the world.'

'Can you try to match it for me? On your database.'

'Sure. How close do you want?'

'As close as you can get.'

'OK. I'll try for parents and siblings, aunts and uncles, round about there.'

Tarrin nodded. He felt nervous now and apprehensive.

'OK,' Julia said. 'I'll put it through.'

She fed the DNA profile into a scanner that transferred the codes into the computer memory. Then she specified the parameters, hit the search button and waited while it hunted for matches.

Tarrin was standing now, and all but leaning over the counter.

'Any hits?' he said.

She shook her head. 'I'll widen the parameters a little for you,' she said, 'then keep widening them till we get a match.'

She hit the search button again. And again.

'Any hits now?' Tarrin said.

She nodded. But she didn't seem happy for him. Her face was tight-lipped, a little sad.

'Something wrong, miss?'

'No. Not exactly.'

'What then?'

'No, no . . .'

'It is hitting?'

'Yes, it's hitting.'

'It's found them then? Has it? Has it found them? My family – are they on there? Has it found them, miss? Please, has it? Has it found my mum and dad?'

There were tears in her eyes – he could see them misting over.

'What's wrong, miss, please, what's wrong?'

'Wait. Just wait.'

'Aren't there any hits? Isn't there anyone like me? Aren't there any hits? Is it my DNA? What is it?'

'Just wait. It's stopped now. I'll print them out. You'll see. Just wait.'

She instructed the computer to print the hit file. The printer surged into life. Tarrin watched as a sheet of paper came out. He watched as the words upon it slid along. There was a name there . . . there was a name . . . a name . . . and a whereabouts . . . a place of origin . . . a last-known address . . . maybe even a telephone number . . . maybe even . . . even a photograph . . .

There was a name! Yes. There was a name. A name, a name, a name, a name. Of someone who shared his structure, his genetic make-up, a leaf, a branch, a twig, a stem, a trunk of his own family tree.

But then he saw why the assistant had been so sad for him.

It was because beneath the name was another

name, and another after that. And another too, all the way to the bottom of the page. And after the page was another page, and another after that, and another still, and another, and another, and another.

'Can't you stop it! That's too many. Can't it stop?'

'Don't you want them all?'

'There can't be that many, there can't! No!'

Still they kept coming, name on name, page on page.

'The machine's gone wrong. It can't have matched me properly. The machine's gone wrong.'

'I'm sorry, I'm really sorry.'

'But what can I do?!'

Finally the printer stopped. There must have been a hundred printed pages lying in the tray. And on each page a hundred names. A hundred hundreds. Ten thousand matches.

'There are more. I've just stopped it printing.'

'How many more?'

'Quite a few.'

'Can't you narrow it? Narrow the search?'

'That's as narrow as it will go for you on the database.'

'But . . . all these people . . . how can they match me?'

'I'm sorry,' Julia said. 'It's the way we are. We're all totally unique and individual, sure, but that's a full hundred per cent of our DNA. But over ninety-nine per cent of it, we share with other people. Why, ninety per cent of our make-up we even share with other animals. These names are the closest matches we have for you.'

Tarrin's stomach knotted up with the sickness of

disappointment. 'But how can I ever get through all these names?' he said. 'How can I? It's just impossible. I just can't do it.'

'Can't you try . . . maybe one of them . . . maybe if you chose at random . . .'

But Tarrin just stood there, not listening to her, hopeless, despairing.

It was just another lie. The advert had said they could trace your folks. That was what they said. Match you up and trace your folks. But they didn't say there would be that many relatives, so distant and so numerous. It was another lie, just another lie.

'I'm sorry . . . look . . . maybe you just expected . . .'

Too much, yes, too much.

'I was hoping for you. Hoping there might just be a few. There are sometimes. No more than two or three pages. I was hoping it would be like that.'

Tarrin turned away from her and stared out at the street.

'It doesn't matter,' he said. 'It doesn't matter.'

'I'm sorry.'

'It doesn't matter.' He tried to fight back the tears. 'I'll never find them now,' he said. 'Never.'

But he wasn't really talking to the woman, just thinking out loud.

'I'll never find them, never find them or know them or see them. Never know who they were or where I came from and where I belong. I'll never know. I hate this world. I hate what everyone's done to it. I hate them all for all wanting to live and never to die and let someone else live and have the life that they had. I hate them. I hate them. Why do they all have to live so long? Why can't they give someone else a turn? Why?'

She had come from behind the counter. She stood by him and looked out of the window too. He could see her reflection there with his own.

'No one wants to die, I guess,' she said. 'When it comes to it. Nobody wants to die. And nobody does now, not for a long time.'

'And nobody gets born . . . the world's revenge.'

'What?'

'The world's revenge. Only why does it have to avenge itself on me? I didn't do anything. I never did anything to anyone. All I ever wanted was to go home. But how can I, when I don't know where that is.'

She saw that there was nothing she could do. She did all that she could, which was simply to stand there with him, staring out into the night.

At length he rubbed the tears from his face with the sleeve of his shirt.

'I'd better go back,' he said. 'Or Deet might come home.'

'Do you want to take this?' she said, indicating the sheaf of paper with all the printed names.

'How can I? He'll find it. What use is it anyway? All those names. It's hopeless. It's no use.'

Without saying anything more, Tarrin opened the door and hurried from the shop.

Julia remained at the window and watched as the boy disappeared along the street.

Tarrin plunged on into the night. He hurried, but he didn't run. If he ran, it might attract attention to him, which he didn't want. He just had to get back before Deet did, that was all. He had no idea how Deet might react if he came back to find him missing. He would assume the worst, that he had been taken, that Deet's lifetime meal ticket had gone. And then for his meal ticket to walk back in through the door, just as Deet was about to start hunting for him, well, he might be moved to tears of relief and gratitude, or on the other hand he might erupt like a volcano.

Deet had never raised his hand to him ever, not once. Not even when full of beer. Drink had the tendency to make him meek and maudlin and sentimental about himself. No, Deet was a waster, but he was wasn't a violent man.

But there was no telling what even the meekest of men might do when he feared that he had lost his meal ticket.

A voice called from the shadows.

'Hey, kid. What you doing out on your own there? Hey, kid, it's you I'm talking to.'

Tarrin hurried on, back the way he had come, back past the neon-fronted theatre which was home to Miss Virginia Two Shoes.

'*Animal crackers in my soup . . .*' she sang.

The vents of the fan pulsed closed again. Her song was momentarily curtailed.

Tarrin walked on, checking that he wasn't being followed. He wasn't. It was OK. There was nobody there. He'd be all right. Deet wouldn't be back yet. He'd still be in the bar, drinking. Tarrin glanced at his watch. Deet never got back this early. Never.

He retraced his steps, passing the same shops, the same continental grocery stores. One shopkeeper was

130

starting to take the fruit in from the outside displays, getting ready to close the place up. He passed the small Italian restaurant, and hurried on.

He didn't see the man at the window table who was gazing out into the night, sipping at a double espresso as the finishing touch to his meal.

The instant he saw the boy walk by, the man swallowed the dregs of his coffee and, without even waiting for the bill, threw a sum of money down upon the table, which he rightly felt would be enough to cover the cost of the meal and then some.

Before anybody could even attempt to stop him, or wish him goodnight, he was out of the door.

'Hey, son. Hey, hold up there. Don't rush there. I need a word.'

Tarrin heard, he turned, saw the man following, put his head down, walked faster, pressed on.

'Hey, son. Just a minute, please. Just a word now. I don't mean any harm.'

Sure you don't. Kiddernappers never did. Never meant you any harm at all, until you stopped, and then they grabbed you and the chloroform patch was over your mouth and your nose and you were breathing in unconsciousness and the next thing you knew you didn't know anything.

He speeded up. The man kept pace with him, but he didn't get nearer or close the gap.

Deet. Deet would help. He'd run into the bar or bang on the window. He could explain why he'd left the motel room later. He'd think of some excuse. None of that mattered. Deet would make the man go. Tarrin knew he would. Of the two evils, the one ahead of him and the one behind, Deet was the lesser.

'Come on now, son. I just want to talk to you. I just need to see your face.'

Kinane could have grabbed him right there and then, but there were people around, too many people. It was too much of a risk. Some have-a-go hero would intervene and before you knew it the cops would be there.

If he could just get the boy alone.

They came to an intersection. The boy ran across against the lights. Car horns blared, drivers shouted.

'What are you doing, kid! Trying to get yourself killed?'

No, no. No, no. Quite the opposite.

Kinane ran too. He got the same treatment. Car horns and squealing brakes and people shouting.

The boy had increased the distance between them. He kept on running. He sprinted a few hundred metres but then slowed and seemed to hesitate outside some bar. He appeared to look inside but, not finding what he wanted there, he began to run again.

Kinane was gaining. He was maybe not as young or as fast, but he had stamina and strength. His hands were large, his fingers thick and strong, like a farmer's. He had stamina. He wouldn't give up.

He drew level with the frontage of the bar the boy had stopped by. Curiosity impelled him to slow down too and to glance inside and wonder what the boy had been looking for. Nothing he could see. Nothing special at all. Just a bar like any bar.

When he looked up the road again . . .

The boy had gone.

Vanished.

In that fraction of a second. The time it had taken him to glance into the bar and then to look back again. He had gone.

Kinane ran on. He stopped by an alleyway, looked down it, investigated. It was a dead end. The boy wasn't there. He went back to the road, taking his time now. If the boy was hiding, he would find him. But if he had truly run on, he wasn't going to catch him.

Not tonight anyway.

But that didn't matter. He had seen him, that was the thing. At least now he knew where to look.

'Goodnight, boy,' he whispered. 'Maybe I'll catch up with you tomorrow. I'll find you. You stay around much longer and I'll find you.'

But staying around much longer wasn't in Deet's plans.

Deet's plans were for moving on.

But then again maybe that didn't matter, for everybody who moved on left some traces of their going behind them. If there were two things that Kinane knew something about, it was patience and hunting; they just seemed to go together. Kinane was the kind of man who knew how to wait – a long, long time.

7

Moving On

Tarrin slid the key card into the lock and, as he entered the room, he felt fear in the pit of his stomach; he was all but resigned to the inevitable sound of Deet's voice demanding, 'And where the hell do you think *you've* been, kid?'

But it didn't come. Deet hadn't been in the bar, but he hadn't returned yet either. He must have gone on somewhere else.

Tarrin quickly undressed. He went to the bathroom and brushed his teeth, then got into bed and turned off the light. But he couldn't sleep. It was the thought of the other man, the stranger, the one who had come after him, and the sound of his soft, friendly voice, intoning, 'Come on now, son. I just want to talk to you. I just need to see your face.'

He'd never seen a Kiddernapper before, not a real live one. He'd been warned about them more times than he could remember, and he'd heard about them even more, but it was the first time he had come face to face with one and the threat had turned into actuality. The most astonishing thing about the man was how human he was. He had hardly seemed like a monster at all. But maybe that was the lure, the clever enticement, the trickery of it all.

Tarrin also couldn't sleep because of his disappointment. His hopes of finding his family had gone. He kept thinking of the names, the page after page of them, and the printer spitting them out, one after the next, all the great long list of impossibility. He had naively expected two names or so. He thought he would just get the names of his parents, right then and there, just like that, culled from the database, maybe even with a current address and a telephone number, or, failing that, at least a time and a date and the place of his birth.

Nothing so easy.

Then he remembered something he had seen in the bureau. He had to smile to think of it, the irony of it was so bitter and cruel and yet so funny too.

It was one of the names on the list. He had seen it as it had slid out of the printer.

It was Deet.

Charles Randolph Deet.

He shared a partial DNA profile with somebody called Deet.

It was laughing or crying time. Take your pick. Or time for both maybe. He could barely believe it. What if it was the same Deet? And they were somehow related. Two leaves on different branches of the same immense family tree.

What if he told Deet? What would he say? 'I always knew it, kid, I always knew we had a bond. Didn't I always tell you I was looking out for you, just like a father, didn't I say that?'

Yes, it would be just one more fine feeling for Deet to take advantage of.

'All the more reason for us to stick together, kid, all

the way to the end, to set up as real partners – in a "family business" as it were. All the more reason to get the PP implant, kid, and then we'll be walking our way down easy street the rest of our days.'

Tarrin heard voices out in the corridor. He listened. It was Deet, whispering something, and then there was a woman's voice. She laughed softly at whatever he had said.

Tarrin heard the door to Deet's room being opened, then he heard the voices murmuring to each other and people making the sort of sounds they do when they are trying too hard to be quiet.

He saw the light come on under the door. Then he heard Deet say, 'I'll just check on the kid, make sure he's still in there and hasn't gone walkabout with no Kiddernappers.'

The door opened a fraction, Deet's head peered round, his face silhouetted by a sliver of light. Tarrin shut his eyes tight and kept his breathing soft and slow. He heard the interconnecting door click shut before he opened his eyes again.

'He's OK,' he heard Deet whisper. 'Like a babe. In fact . . . come to think . . . you're quite a babe yourself.'

The woman giggled. 'Oh, Deet – you're so charming, you know. You're so . . . I don't know . . . such a gentleman.'

Tarrin almost sat up in surprise. Deet? Charming? And a gentleman? Maybe they were both drunk, maybe that was it.

He closed his eyes and put his fingers in his ears. When he took them out again, the room next door had fallen silent. He felt tired now, more than tired,

136

shattered and exhausted, tired out by the fear of the Kiddernapper and the disappointment of the DNA test.

'I'll never find them now,' Tarrin thought again. 'Never, never find them.'

He felt himself sink into sleep. He began to dream of the green fields again, and the long summer lane. He saw the white-painted fence and the branches blowing in the wind, and the clouds and the blue patches of sky. He heard the buzz of the insects and felt the warmth of sunlight on his face. Then he felt himself rocking, and there was a sweet, clean smell in the air, and a woman's voice singing.

> There's a green land far away,
> Going to get there one fine day.

One fine day.
Then he was asleep.

When Tarrin woke, Deet was in the room, pulling back the curtains and letting the light stream in.

'OK, kid? So who's the sleepyhead? It's nine o'clock, kid. Let's get some breakfast.'

Tarrin sat up and rubbed his eyes. 'Deet . . .'

'Yeah?'

'Is there someone else here?'

Deet looked at him, tense, suspicious, then he relaxed. 'No. Just us. Why?'

'I thought I heard someone, during the night.'

'Did we wake you? I just had a friend come back for coffee.'

'Oh.'

'But they've gone now.'

'Oh, OK.'

Then he noticed that Deet was taking the suitcases out and was starting to pack.

'What are you doing, Deet?'

'We're moving on, kid, we're moving on.'

'Again? But—'

'It's all worked out here, kid. We'll come back another day, but it's all worked out for now.'

'But—'

'But what, kid?'

'I don't want to move again, Deet. We're always moving.'

'Why not, kid? One place is as good as another. So let's go see it. And besides . . .'

'What?'

'There's better opportunities . . . elsewhere.'

'What do you mean, Deet?'

'You'll see, kid. I've got plans. Ain't I always telling you that I'm looking out for you and that I've got plans? Well, they're working out, kid. As you'll see.'

'But, Deet . . .'

'Come on, kid.'

He threw his clothes at him. 'Get clean, get dressed, get packed, get fed and then let's get moving.'

'But, Deet . . .'

'What?'

Tarrin wondered if he should tell Deet about last night, about the man who had come after him, the Kiddernapper. But to do that would have meant confessing that he had gone out, and that would need an

138

explanation as to why. Unless he lied, concocted some story, said the Kiddernapper had come to the door of the room while Deet had been out, or had peered in through the window. No. It would all get too complicated. It would get all tangled up like a ball of string. It was best to tell the whole truth or say nothing. So nothing it was.

As Tarrin dressed, Deet's mobe rang in the other room. He answered it and Tarrin could hear his voice rising with indignation.

'No way, lady! No way! I don't like your tone, ma'am. I have to tell you that I don't like your tone! Well, you do that. Yes. You do.'

The call ended and Deet came back into the room.

'You hear that!' he said. 'Accusing us of stealing! A five-hundred-unit note gone missing from her bag she says, and accuses us of taking it. It makes me sick, kid, I don't mind telling you. People like that with all that gravy. Got so much they couldn't even count it all if they tried. Ringing up accusing a person of dipping his bread in the sauce. And they wouldn't even know what a hard day's work was if it fell on their heads.'

Tarrin felt that was equally true of Deet, but said nothing.

'They make all this song and dance about a simple five hundred that must have fallen down the back of a drawer somewhere. Accusing poor people who're just trying to make an honest living.'

Tarrin wasn't too sure about the 'honest' either.

'Well, I told her kid, I told her. Told her just what to do!'

Tarrin felt guilty, yet relieved too that Deet had

stuck up for him and did not suspect him. Deet would never have stolen from a customer himself, Tarrin knew that. Overcharged, diddled, deceived and conned, maybe. But blatantly steal, no. It would have been too risky, too much of a chance of permanently losing his reputation, and all his customers along with it.

'Told her what to do. Told *her*!'

Deet threw a few more clothes into his suitcase and he was packed.

Kinane woke in his room that morning to find himself lying on top of the covers, still dressed and in his boots. He rubbed a hand across the stubble on his chin but didn't bother to shave it. Instead he went straight out and returned to where he had last seen the boy the previous night, carefully retracing his steps. He hung around the area for a while, and he explored the nearby streets. Quite what kind of clue he was looking for, he didn't know, but he would recognize it when he found it.

The bar the boy had stopped to look into was closed and quiet. Inside a woman was going around vacuuming the floor and then polishing the tables. Kinane watched her through the window, until she noticed him staring and seemed to get nervous. So he left her to it and moved on.

After walking around a while, and on the point of giving up, he turned a corner and saw the frontage of the Rapid Link Motel. It was a motel chain he knew and, indeed, he had enjoyed its hospitality himself, on many occasions and in many different cities. It was cheap and clean and functional and nobody asked you any questions. Some of the motels were fully automated and you could check in using a credit card, be issued with a card key, be served (or rather serve yourself) with a pre-packed breakfast, and be gone the next day without seeing or talking to a soul.

But Kinane wanted a soul, an ordinary, simple, trusting soul. Somebody he could talk to.

He found him pushing a mop around the reception area, cleaning the grime off the tiles.

'Hi there.'

'Hi.'

'Did you want to check in?' the man with the mop asked.

'No, I'm all right. Just looking for someone.'

'Oh yeah?'

'I was told there was a kid to rent here.'

The janitor stopped mopping the floor, took a handkerchief from his pocket, and started mopping his forehead.

'Kid to rent?'

It was only a guess. Kinane had no means of knowing. But he calculated that no proper parent would let a child out alone at that time of night – not with people like himself about. So maybe he was a loaner, and you didn't loan your own kids out, so that made him belong to someone else, like someone making money out of it, which would mean always moving on, which would mean a motel, which would mean . . .

'You want to rent one?'

'My wife,' Kinane said.

'Oh?'

141

'It's our anniversary and we were never able to have any of our own . . .'

'Who is able?' the janitor said, putting the handkerchief away and leaning on the mop, glad of an excuse to stop and take a breather.

'So I thought it would be a nice surprise.'

'Well, there was a kid here earlier with a man – said he was his father – only they checked out.'

Damn it. For a moment Kinane felt anger and annoyance. He'd been wasting time looking in the wrong places. He should have got here an hour, two hours ago.

'I don't suppose you'd have a number?' he asked.

'No, don't believe so . . .'

The janitor went behind the check-in desk. 'Ah – yes, I have. Yeah, there it is. He left a card, see. Number's right on there. Name of Deet.'

'Can I copy it?'

'Take the card, mister. He paid in full. I don't need it.'

'Thanks.'

'You're welcome.'

Kinane took the card and left. He walked straight back to his own hotel, packed, paid his bill, and went down to his car in the basement car park.

He headed out of the town and drove a few miles into the countryside, to where the ground was high and clear of trees.

Reception would be good here, which was what he needed.

Then he sat and he waited. There was no point in doing it yet. Give them a while to arrive at where they were going to, then do it. He didn't want to arouse any suspicions by calling the number too often or too soon.

To pass the time, he turned the radio on and listened to some music. Then, growing restless, he got out and locked the car and went for a walk over the fields. After a while, he stopped and stretched and looked about him. It reminded him of somewhere – the fields, the recently ploughed earth, the pattern of the ploughing, where the blades had cut into the soil making deep, parallel incisions. It was geometric and somehow satisfying.

Did a good job here, Kinane thought, as he surveyed the fields around him. The plough lines were straight and regular. Even in the corners of the fields, where the tractor had had to turn, the plough tracks were smooth and round, like the curves of letters of the alphabet. He walked on, resolving to go as far as the brow of the next hill, but there was another hill beyond it, with the promise of a better view. So he just went on walking.

He walked for several hours. By the time he got back to the car, he was hungry and thirsty, so he drove on to a village and found a shop where he could buy some food and drink. Then he drove on to the top of another high hill, where again there were no pylons or phone masts or trees. He took out his mobe and set it into the cradle of the Sat-Sys which he owned, and which had cost him several thousand units.

Now he took the card the man from the Rapid Link Motel had given him, and he keyed in the number printed upon it. Then he waited for Deet's mobe to ring. Only it didn't ring. It had been turned off.

'The big city,' Deet said, somewhat unnecessarily, as it was quite evident what it was. 'The big smoke.'

Tarrin leaned his head against the window of the train and looked out. Deet usually preferred the small towns, the provincial capitals. Small pools suited a kind of fish like him. Tarrin wondered why they had left them for this great ocean of tarmac, brick, concrete and shining glass.

'You can work a place out, kid. You can overstay your welcome. You come to a place, you're a novelty. You stay a while, you're not a novelty no more. You stay a while longer, they get tired of the look of you. In the end they either don't even notice you, or they do, but they don't like what they see. Either way is no distinction. The best way is moving on.'

But it still wasn't like Deet to head for the big city. He said himself that the place made him feel nervous.

'Only needs must, kid. It's where the money and the chances are. It's where the deals are done. Where the movers and the shakers do the shaking and the moving.'

They arrived at the mainline station and Deet wasted no time in getting them a cab and giving directions to another Rapid Link Motel – one not too far from the bright lights and the brash, expensive places.

'Big-city prices, kid,' Deet said. 'They can't be avoided. If you want to be here, you just have to pay them. When in Rome, pay the Romans . . .'

Once settled and unpacked, Deet insisted on taking Tarrin out to buy him a new set of clothes. They rode the Pod into the centre, to a street of designer shops. They found a shop that specialized in small sizes. They were good clothes too, expensive. But no doubt Deet had his reasons for spending the money.

It was later on, at about five o'clock, and they had stopped for burgers, when Deet announced that they had an appointment.

'I'm taking you round to see someone later, kid. It's someone somebody put me in touch with and they've got a proposition. So I want you to be on the old best behaviour, kid, as we're going round to millionaire's row, see, and we don't want no crumbs on the carpet or no elbows on the table – you get what I mean?'

'Not exactly.'

'This is a big chance, kid, a major opportunity. Now, I can't say too much, only you got to remember that no matter what happens, you keep faith in your uncle Deet.' He winked. 'You hear what I'm saying?'

'I hear what you're saying, Deet, but—'

'Just remember that, kid. I'm thinking about your long-term future, see. So, no matter what happens tonight, you just remember that. You got me? Just remember that your uncle Deet wouldn't turn his back on you – OK? And even when I'm not there, I'm still there – you get what I'm saying?'

There were times when Tarrin wondered why Deet couldn't simply say things instead of asking him if he got what he was saying. Maybe Deet was so used to bending the rules that he couldn't be straight now even if he tried to be. He could only hint at things, point vaguely at unspecified intentions, wink and nod. But to be specific – he couldn't seem to manage it. He was like some antique floorboard, warped and buckled and crooked, which just simply couldn't be nailed down flat any more.

'Only that's the thing to remember, kid – got me? Your uncle Deet wouldn't abandon you. He's playing the long game, right? He's working to the plan. However it goes this evening, you hold on to that.'

'How what goes, Deet? Where are we going? What's going to happen?'

'We'll just have to see, kid. Just have to see. I don't want to make no commitments or promises, as it might not turn out that way. Just have faith, kid, and we'll just have to see. Come on then. Let's get going.'

They returned to the hotel, where Deet not only insisted on Tarrin showering and getting dressed in the newly bought clothes, but he shaved and showered himself and put on his dark grey special-occasion suit.

'Pack an overnight bag too, kid,' he said. 'A tooth-brush and things, in case we decide to stay over.'

But Deet didn't pack an overnight bag for himself. Which made Tarrin wonder. But he was so used to wondering about Deet and his motives and intentions that he couldn't feel surprised. And he was so used to not getting any straight answers that he didn't even bother to ask questions.

It was nearing seven when they left the room. Deet flagged down a cab and gave the driver an address. The traffic was still heavy from the evening rush, so they sat back and just had to tolerate the journey, though maybe Deet found this harder to do than

Tarrin, as his eyes kept wandering to the meter as it clocked up the fare.

Deet took his mobe from his pocket. 'Switched off,' he said. 'When did I do that?'

He turned it back on, checked his messages and texts and put it back into his suit.

The cab had taken them to an expensive and fashionable area of the city now, and Deet's earlier promise of a visit to 'millionaire's row' was proving not to be unfounded. They were in a street of tall Regency houses, each several storeys high, with valley gutters and slanting roofs and elegant sash windows.

'Arm and a leg, kid,' Deet said. 'That's what it would cost you to live here. And that's just renting. To buy a house here – well, you'd need the kind of money that money just can't buy. Number eighteen, driver.'

The taxi stopped. Deet paid the driver and led the way up some steps to the door of number eighteen. It was, like all the other houses, large and imposing, with double-fronted windows. As was his way, he knocked on the door and eschewed using the bell. His tactics seemed to work, as footsteps could soon be heard from within, as if hurrying down some stairs.

And then Deet's mobe rang.

'What the—' He snatched it from his pocket. 'Perfect! Just perfect timing!'

He glanced at the mobe screen to see the number of the caller, but the screen was blank. Number withheld.

'Hello? Who is it?'

But no sooner had he answered the call than whoever was making it cancelled the call or was cut off.

'What the—'

The door was opening. Deet hastily turned the mobe off and stuffed it back into his pocket. He just had time to whisper, 'Best behaviour, kid. Best behaviour,' before the door was pulled open and a man appeared upon the step.

'Mr Deet, I take it?' The man was plainly a servant, or a personal assistant of some kind.

'Just plain . . . yeah . . . I guess. Mr Deet, and . . . this is my boy.'

'Please come in, Mr Deet. Mr and Mrs Hartinger are expecting you.'

'Glad to hear it,' Deet said. He followed the man inside. 'Come on in, boy, and wipe your feet,' Deet instructed. Tarrin did as he was told and the door closed behind him.

But he noticed that Deet hadn't wiped his own feet. And the man who had let them in noticed it too.

The call had been short, but it had been all that Kinane had needed to pinpoint the exact location of Deet's mobe. The Sat-Sys gave him its precise coordinates. It was accurate to within a few metres.

Kinane noted down the coordinates, and then he fed them into the car's navigator, so that it could work out the best, the shortest and the most traffic-free route for him. It did so within a few seconds and Kinane saw that his destination lay towards the capital, to its very vibrant and beating heart. He

148

slipped the car into drive and pulled away. He was briefly held up by a herd of cattle, which were being taken from their field towards the farmyard and milking parlour across the road.

Kinane watched the cattle pass, their full, milk-swollen udders swinging, their broad, black shoulders and their mottled black-and-white flanks moving slowly past. Their tails jerked, swatting at insects, and each cow had a yellow plastic earring with a number upon it, for identification.

'Evening, ladies,' he mumbled, and he smiled at their curious faces and at the large eyes which turned towards his car.

He pressed the button to lower the window, and the smell of the cattle invaded the car interior. It was warm, rich, the scent of animals mingling with the perfume of summer grass. It was an odour of milk and breath, of earth, of skin, and even of the cow muck which steamed on the road, but which had its own, not unpleasant fragrance.

The stockman who was driving the animals across the road apologized for the hold up.

'That's OK,' Kinane said. 'No hurry. Just let them take their time.'

He didn't mind them really, not at all. He knew where he was headed. Five minutes wouldn't matter.

'Good yield?' he asked the stockman.

'Pretty good,' he said.

'GMs?'

'No. Pure stock.'

'Fine-looking animals.'

'Thanks.'

'Reminds me of home.'

149

'You a farmer?'

'Not for a long time. Was once though. Long time ago.'

'So what do you do now?' the curious stockman asked.

'I look for things,' Kinane said.

'There money in that?'

'There can be, I believe,' Kinane told him.

'Then I hope you find what you're looking for,' the stockman said, as the last of the cattle went through and he closed the gate.

'Me too,' Kinane nodded. 'Me too.'

He waved to the stockman, who raised a finger by way of acknowledgement and farewell, and he drove on.

The car navigator gave him the shortest route to the city. He took it, and within twenty minutes was rolling along a five-lane freeway, with thousands of other cars.

An overhead speed camera flashed as he drove under a bridge.

But it wasn't for him. It was another motorist, there in the overtaking lane, who was foolishly streaking by at over ninety miles an hour, maybe even clocking the hundred.

Kinane kept strictly to the speed limit. He couldn't see the point of doing otherwise and of making trouble for yourself. In that respect, if no other, he was a law-abiding citizen. It was the tortoise and the hare, and it was going slow that got you there or, at least, taking it steady did.

So he took it steady and he drove on to the east.

He'd be in the capital by nightfall. He knew exactly where he was headed.

This time, yes, this time, he might get lucky.

8

Padded Cell

The room was large and high ceilinged; there were two sofas to sit on, several well-upholstered easy chairs and, in a corner, by a window, was a grand piano.

Deet looked around admiringly.

'There's money here, kid,' he whispered, though Tarrin could see that quite plainly for himself.

Deet went on looking at all the signs of affluence – the expensive furniture, the paintings on the wall, the thick carpets, the deep, comfortable sofas. This was the place to be, he told himself, these were the kind of people to do business with, this was where the money was, and he deserved to be right there with it.

Tarrin went to look at the piano.

'Don't touch nothing, kid,' Deet warned – quite unnecessarily, for Tarrin had no intention of touching anything. He knew how to act in other people's houses. He had been in enough of them.

He was intrigued by the book of music which sat on the grand piano.

'*Waltzes and Preludes*', the cover read, 'by Richard Hartinger'.

Tarrin walked away from the piano and went to look at the bookcases. They filled one wall, all the way from floor to ceiling; there was a ladder in place to take you to the top.

There was a line of books on one of the lower shelves, which was just about at Tarrin's eye level. He read the titles, none of which meant anything to him, but he saw that the author's name was R. Hartinger. He wondered if it was the same Hartinger who had written the waltzes and preludes and, if that was so, was he also the same R. Hartinger as the man whose house they were in, and who they were waiting to see?

He moved on, to look at some of the paintings on the walls. In among those by other artists were some abstracts and some more conventional landscapes and portraits. They had all been executed by one R. Hartinger.

Then Tarrin looked at Deet and wondered what he was up to. Deet was sitting on the edge of his chair – though he could have easily sunk back into it and let the comfort and softness swallow him up. His hands were together and he was digging the thumbnail of one hand into a fingernail on the another. He looked tense and nervous and vaguely untrustworthy. But, then, he always did.

Deet saw Tarrin looking at him, and he winked.

'This could be our big score, kid,' he whispered. 'So don't worry about nothing. Whichever way it happens or whatever how it seems. You just have faith in your uncle Deet and remember he's always looking out for you. Right?'

Tarrin nodded. He sat down opposite Deet on one of the sofas. He could have easily sat next to him, but he didn't want to.

'How long do they want me for, Deet?'

Deet gave a thin smile. 'That's the big question, kid. That's the big, big, question.'

'An hour?'

Deet grinned, but didn't explain why it was funny. 'Could be, kid.'

'Longer?'

'Could be longer. Have to see.'

'For the whole evening?'

'Maybe.'

'Why'd I need to bring an overnight bag, Deet?'

'Just in case, kid, that's all.'

'Did they ring you up, Deet?'

'Stop asking so many questions, kid. It's all in hand. You don't need to worry.'

'Deet . . .'

'What?'

Tarrin thought better of it. 'Nothing.'

He sat and waited, thinking it was odd, though, that they had only been in the city a very short while and already they had a customer. It was almost as if Deet had brought him to the city specifically for him to come to this house, on this evening.

Tarrin felt uneasy. The new clothes felt constricting. His hands were clammy.

A door opened and a man and woman entered. They were both tall, both well dressed and elegant. They were both on Anti-Ageing and there was no telling how old they were. They could have been fifty. They could have been a hundred years older than that.

'Mr Deet . . .'

'Mr Hartinger . . . how are you, sir?' Deet stood

154

and tried to surreptitiously wipe his hand on the seat of his trousers before extending it for Hartinger to shake.

'Good to meet you, Mr Deet,' Hartinger said, though the expression on his face and the language of his body didn't quite live up to the warmth of his words.

'And this'll be your good lady, I'm sure,' Deet said, proffering the hand to Mrs Hartinger now.

She barely touched it before letting it go and murmuring, 'Mr Deet . . .'

'Can we offer you a drink?' Hartinger asked.

Deet could have done with a beer, but didn't feel it was appropriate to ask for one somehow, so he just sat back down and said, 'We're fine.'

But Hartinger preferred Tarrin to answer for himself. 'And this is . . .?' he said.

Deet got back to his feet, realizing that he had missed out on the full introductions.

'This is the kid,' he said. 'Kid – stand up . . .' though Tarrin was already standing – 'this is Mr and Mrs Hartinger.'

'And you'll be Tarrin?' Mrs Hartinger said.

'Yes,' Tarrin nodded.

'How do you do, Tarrin,' she said. She put her hand out. He took it hesitatingly. Their fingers touched, then she moved her hand away.

Mr Hartinger nodded to him. 'Please,' he said, 'sit down. Would you like a drink of some sort, Tarrin?'

He asked for some lemonade. He could feel Deet's eyes boring into him. But he was thirsty, and they had offered.

His drink was poured, and then Hartinger gave a

drink to his wife and took one himself and they sat across from Deet and Tarrin, the four of them forming a square.

'What would you like me to do?' Tarrin asked. He felt the silence and their scrutiny to be oppressive.

'Do?' Hartinger said.

'Yes.'

'You have a repertoire?'

Tarrin looked puzzled.

'An act?'

Mrs Hartinger smiled. 'We don't require you to do anything at the moment, thank you, Tarrin. At least nothing other than to be yourself. Why do you ask? What do you usually do?'

Tarrin looked to Deet for help, but none was forthcoming. He felt himself colour with embarrassment, but he didn't know what he was embarrassed about.

'People ask me to do things sometimes,' he said.

'Tell us,' Hartinger said. 'For example.'

'Things that boys are supposed to do.'

'Like?'

'Run and play. Go out in the garden. Climb a tree. Get dirty.'

'Get dirty!' Mrs Hartinger laughed, exchanging an amused look with her husband. 'Get dirty! Imagine that. They pay you to get dirty!'

Deet didn't like the way the conversation was going. He felt out of it too, and wanted to get back in.

'He doesn't get that dirty,' he said.

'Oh, it's all right, Mr Deet, we really don't mind how dirty he gets. I'm sure it all washes off. It's just . . . the idea.'

'It's what people like, ma'am,' Deet explained. 'What they expect in some ways. They've read it in the old books that boys are always up to mischief and like to climb trees and get dirty. So I say to him, "You do what people want you to, kid. We're here to keep the customer happy. So if they want you to get dirty, you get good and dirty."'

'Hmm,' Mrs Hartinger said. 'And what about girls?'

'People don't expect them to get so dirty,' Deet said. 'In fact, they expect them to stay pretty clean on the whole. I don't have no girls myself, but I know people in that line of business. What people expect from girls is mostly to get dressed up, or maybe do a little baking or home-making or play with dolls.'

'How strange,' Mrs Hartinger said. 'I loved climbing trees when I was a girl.'

'People don't want things as they are, ma'am,' Deet said. 'They want them as they used to be in those good old days, they want things like they ought to be.'

'It seems to me,' Hartinger said, 'that they don't want a real child at all.'

'Some truth in that, I dare say, your honour,' Deet said. He felt that calling the customer 'your honour' never did any harm. 'No, I guess they don't want a real child, as a real child is problems and trouble – or can be. No, they just want a child for the afternoon. Just a child for the afternoon, to act like they do in the old storybooks, and then to go away.'

'Well, that isn't what we want.'

'I realize that, ma'am,' Deet said. 'I said to the kid even before we came in here, these are people of

157

quality and class here. They don't want no kid for an afternoon. They either want more than that or they don't want nothing at all.'

Tarrin looked at Deet. He had said no such thing.

'Does the boy know, Mr Deet? Have you explained it to him?'

'Not as such, ma'am,' Deet said. 'Not as such. I thought it best to have a sit-down first and for us all to see how we liked the looks of each other and to go on from there.'

There was a brief and uneasy silence. Tarrin felt the first deep pangs of misgiving. Hadn't explained what to him? What was going on? What was Deet up to?

'It's all right, Tarrin,' Mrs Hartinger said. 'Don't look so worried.' She seemed to regard him with some amusement. 'We wouldn't do anything you wouldn't agree to. It would have to feel right for you as well.'

'Whh . . .' Tarrin felt his voice cracking, which made him feel ashamed. He cleared his throat and began again. 'What . . . do you mean exactly?'

'Ma'am!' Deet prompted him.

'Ma'am.'

Mrs Hartinger looked across at her husband. Tarrin looked at him too, wondering how he had found the time and the talent to not only compose music but to write a shelf-full of books and to paint a wall-full of pictures.

'We're looking for a son, Tarrin,' he said.

'Or a daughter,' Mrs Hartinger added.

'Yes. A child. And not merely for the afternoon. We know they're expensive but, well, we have the money, and everything we need and want we have, and there's precious little else to spend it on . . . so we thought . . . a child . . .'

'We've looked at several,' Mrs Hartinger said.

'And some of them were promising.'

'But maybe not quite what we were looking for.'

'So we've yet to decide.'

'And then, while making enquiries, we heard of Mr Deet – and yourself, of course – and so we asked him to call.'

A strange chill went through Tarrin. It was the way they were talking about him, almost as if he wasn't there, as though he were just another commodity, the latest in a long line of luxury purchases they were thinking of acquiring.

They were shopping around. And he was part of the merchandise. Would they buy this model, they seemed to be asking themselves, or would they get that one? Which colour would they have it in?

Was Deet going to sell him?

He felt sick.

He turned and stared at Deet, his brows arched in puzzlement and enquiry.

Deet?

It made no sense. Deet had always said that he was the golden goose. That you didn't sell the goose that laid the eggs. So why had he changed his mind? Without any consultation or discussion?

Tarrin was growing up, that was why. Another few years and he would be just like everyone else. And what then? What would he have? How would he live? Deet would abandon him. He'd be on his own.

Deet was selling him now while he could still get

a good price. Children were expensive but, plainly, the older they got, the less expensive they became, until finally they grew up and were worth nothing at all.

Tarrin looked around the room. The Hartingers and Deet went on talking, but he wasn't listening any more. He looked at the furnishings, the decor, the antiques, the knick-knacks. Everything was perfect. Everything was in the best possible taste.

In a corner chair, asleep on a cushion, he noticed a large, fluffy Persian cat. It must have been there all the time, breathing so softly that you could barely hear it. It woke now and opened its eyes and stretched itself, standing on the cushion and arching its back. It was sleek and well groomed, pampered and cared for.

That's what I'll be like.

Yes. He looked at the Hartingers. They were elegant, well groomed, languid, well cared for, almost feline themselves.

They want another cat.

And I'm the cat they want. They say they want a real child, but they don't know what a real child is. There's more to it than food and warmth and shelter. That's part of it, but only a part of it.

It was a whole lot more complicated than that.

The Persian cat jumped softly down from the cushion, walked across the room and climbed on to Mrs Hartinger's lap. She smoothed its fur and after a minute or so it began to purr with contentment.

They'll expect me to purr too. And if I don't, and when I don't, they'll be disappointed.

Deet! I don't want to stay here! Deet!

160

But Deet just went on making small talk.

Deet, I can manage an hour or two at a time, being what people want me to be, but I can't do it always, not all the time, not twenty-four hours a day. I have to be myself.

At least with Deet he could be himself. Once the day's work was over, he could be himself again.

I can't be with these people, Deet. I can't be what they want me to be: nice and clean and tidy and well behaved and no trouble at all, to purr when I'm patted, to miaow when I'm hungry.

I'm not a pet, Deet. I'm not a pet.

The conversation intruded into the panic of his thoughts.

'Well, maybe I should leave you a while to all get acquainted,' Deet was saying.

No, don't go, Deet. Don't go.

Then Tarrin thought of all the times he had wanted to get rid of Deet, to escape from him, for him to simply drop dead. But now he wanted to hold on to him tightly, to run with him, far from this house, to go back to the hotel and the life they knew, the Edu-Packs and the burgers and being a child for an hour or so every afternoon, and always moving on.

'Why don't you make yourself comfortable here, Mr Deet, and pour yourself a drink while we show Tarrin around the house.'

Deet eyed the drinks cabinet optimistically. It seemed to him to be pretty well stocked, with some single-malt whiskies, the kind that would set you back a lot.

'If that's OK with you.'

'Of course. Tarrin, would you like to see the house?'

He nodded and stood up, doing what was expected. The Hartingers stood on either side of him and escorted him out of the drawing room. They began by taking him down to the basement, to show him the cellar and the old-fashioned things there. Then they worked their way up through the house. Mrs Hartinger's arm dangled at her side, next to him. After a time he realized that she wanted him to take her hand, to hold it the way she must have thought a son held his mother's hand.

He didn't want to hold her hand though. Deet had always told them that they weren't to hold his hand. No contact. They knew that. And even if it was different this time, it still seemed false to do so, artificial. She wasn't his mother anyway, and no amount of hand-holding would change that.

She must have sensed his reluctance and she moved her arm away. It was early days yet. Time would make all the difference.

'And this would be your room.'

They opened the door to a room which had everything in it. It was a child's room, painted in a pale, neutral cream colour; it was full of things to play with, books to read, a computer, a television. You'd be pampered in a room like that. It could have done for either a boy or a girl.

'Do you like it, Tarrin?'

'Yes, it's lovely. It's very nice.'

Nice like a doll's house, nice like a luxurious prison.

They walked on along the corridor, then back

down to the drawing room. Deet was lounging on one of the sofas now, with a large glass, half full of whisky, in his hand. He seemed quite at home.

As they entered, he held the glass up.

'I took up your offer, your honour,' he said.

He waved the glass, as if to say, 'Cheers!' and drank half of it down. He put the glass on a small table, setting it carefully upon a coaster.

'So,' he said, 'how did we all get on?'

'I think we got on admirably,' Mr Hartinger said, and Mrs Hartinger nodded. 'Wouldn't you say, Tarrin?'

What could he say? That all he felt towards the Hartingers was a great, overwhelming indifference? It wasn't that they were bad people, they were probably very nice. He just didn't want to be with them, that was all. He wanted to go home, back to the hotel. Hotels and motels had been home for so long, they were where he felt safe, where he wanted to be. But this house seemed too clean and tidy, almost clinical and sterile. He wanted some untidiness, some dust, to see Deet's empty beer cans on the floor.

'Yes, we got on fine. It's a lovely house.'

'We like him, Mr Deet. He seems like a very nice boy – polite, well mannered, not at all loud, clean . . .'

We'll take it.

We've given the car a spin, and we like it, so we'll take it!

Was that really all he was? Just merchandise, to be bought and sold.

This isn't right, Deet. You know it's not right.

The cat came up to him and would have jumped on

163

to his lap, only he folded his arms and moved his body aside so that it couldn't. It padded off and jumped up on to Deet.

'Hey! Nice pussy cat!'

Then Tarrin remembered the overnight bag. Deet had left it in the hall.

'Pack an overnight bag, kid. Just in case.'

Just Tarrin though. Not Deet. He hadn't packed an overnight bag too, had he?

He didn't mean to leave him here tonight? Not tonight? Surely not? It couldn't all happen this quickly, this abruptly . . .

'Well, we'd be interested, I think, Mr Deet. We'd need to talk it over between ourselves first.'

'Of course you would, ma'am, naturally you would. Only, if I may give a word of advice here, it might be best not to take too long on that, ma'am, as I have to tell you that there are other interested parties.'

Deet, you're lying again. He was trying to push the price up, maintain the interest, force a quick decision.

But the Hartingers saw straight through him. They were too sophisticated, too wealthy, too experienced. They hadn't made their money by being taken in by the likes of Deet.

'Well, naturally, if you've already made other commitments, Mr Deet . . .'

He backed off, afraid of losing the business now. 'No, no, didn't say that, didn't say that . . .'

He got to his feet. 'Say we leave you to think it over? To sleep on it.'

'Fine. Let's do that.'

Tarrin felt as if reprieved on the night of execution.

'You've got my number.'

'We'll be in touch tomorrow.'

'And how about you, Tarrin? Any questions?'

'Yes. Did you write all these books and this music and paint all these pictures?'

'Yes.'

'How?'

'Life is long, Tarrin. It must be filled. For the first fifty years I was a musician, then I wrote, now I paint.'

'You just learned?'

'You can learn to do almost anything if you have enough time. And we have.'

The Hartingers' personal assistant, or butler, saw them out. Tarrin was careful to remember his overnight bag.

'We'll get the Pod,' Deet said, plainly unwilling now to spend more money on cabs, 'but first let's grab a burger.'

They walked a mile to burger country. There were no burger bars where the Hartingers lived, just quiet wine bars and five-star restaurants. Deet and Tarrin sat across from each other at a small table. Tarrin didn't feel hungry and just picked at his meal.

'What's up, kid?'

'Are you going to sell me, Deet? To those people?'

Deet looked pained.

'Sell you? Kid, would I sell you? After all the time we've been together? You – who's been like my own kid to me. Would I sell you?'

'You're not going to sell me then?'

'It's not a question of selling, kid. It's more a thing of finding you a good home now. This kind of life

165

you've had, always moving and never settling, you deserve a little better than that now.'

'But what about you, Deet?'

'I'll be fine.'

He didn't seem to want to talk about it, but Tarrin persisted. 'What about the goose laying the golden eggs, Deet?'

'OK, kid, I'll be straight with you. How much longer you got? A few years, tops, and then no one'll want you any more. You won't be cute enough. You'll be too tall, too grown. So what do we do? Well, there's the PP implant which'll keep you a kid forever, but I don't have the money for that. So what do we do? Either we find you a good home now, or I go on renting you out till you get too big to rent out. And then what?'

'What, Deet?'

'Parting of the ways, kid, has to be. I can't feed you if you're not bringing anything in. I'm not a charity, kid. When you get too big to be rented out, well, you'll just have to look after yourself.'

'What'll I do, Deet?'

'Get a job, kid. Same as the rest of us.'

'What can I do?'

But Deet just shrugged. 'If you'd have the PP, you could go on being a kid forever. You'd always have the money then.'

'But I don't want to be a kid forever.'

'Then you have to grow up and face the world, kid. If I get you in with the Hartingers, you've got a head start. They're old. They may be on Anti-Ageing, but even they won't live forever. Who're they going to leave all their stuff to? Might be you. Get them to like

166

you – a little more each day. Get them to love you, kid, make with the cute stuff and the winning ways while you're still a kid enough to do it. Then they'll keep you, even when you grow. See, it's like cats and kittens, kid. Everyone loves a kitten, but not everyone likes a cat. Or sheep and lambs. Lambs are cute and pretty, but a sheep – nah.'

'You mean they might not keep me when I get big?'

Tarrin looked down at his barely touched meal. The prospect of growing up seemed daunting. What would he do? Deet hadn't shown him how to do anything, apart from be a child. Who would help him? Where could he turn?

Maybe the Hartingers might not be so bad after all. They seemed good, gentle, kind, rich and generous. Maybe he could make a life there.

It might not be so bad to be a cat.

'It's you I'm thinking of, kid, that's what you've always got to remember,' Deet said. 'Don't you want those fries?'

'I'm not hungry.'

'Got to eat something, kid, keep your strength up.'

'I'm not hungry tonight, Deet.'

Deet ate the fries for him.

'Deet . . .'

'Yeah?'

'What'll you do?'

'Me do?'

'Yes.'

'What do you mean?'

'When I'm gone.' As far as Tarrin could see, if Deet wasn't renting him out to people, he'd be without an occupation.

'Oh, I'll get by, kid.'

'But what?'

Deet grinned. 'Oh, I'll think of something.'

Maybe he'd win another kid in a card game.

Then Deet hunched forwards in his seat, made sure they couldn't be overheard, and he got all confidential.

'Look, kid,' he grinned, 'I can't tell you no more than I'm telling you, because if you know more than's good for you, you might accidentally spill the beans. But you take it from me that Deet's looking out for you, and if you go to the Hartingers', kid, don't be surprised at what happens – OK?'

'But what, Deet? What will happen?'

'I can't tell you, kid. If you don't have the open can of beans you can't go spilling them, so it's best I don't give them to you. But you just remember that your uncle Deet's looking out for you. You got that? Your uncle Deet's looking out for you. And even when you think he's forgotten you, well, he won't have. I'll be looking out for you, kid, whatever happens. And even when I'm not there, I'll still be there. You get me, kid? You get me?'

Tarrin didn't, but he nodded and said, 'Sure, Deet, right,' just to get him to stop talking.

Deet wiped his hands on a paper napkin and said they should go. They returned to the hotel and Tarrin did some studying while Deet took a shower and changed his clothes.

He came into Tarrin's room to announce that he was going out for a while. It was the usual bedtime story.

'Keep the door locked, kid, and don't answer to

anyone knocking, not even if it's the maid, saying she's come to turn the beds down and put a chocolate on the pillow.'

'OK, Deet.'

'Got to mind out for those Kiddernappers, kid. Don't want the Kiddernappers to get you.'

'No, Deet.'

'That's right. You listen to your uncle Deet. Now don't stay up all night studying.'

'No, Deet.'

'That's right. Studying's OK, but you can do too much of it.'

Deet went out, carefully closing the door behind him. Tarrin heard his footsteps receding along the corridor.

Tarrin ran a bath and lay in the hot, soapy water, looking up at the ceiling. He wondered how much Deet was selling him for, how much the Hartingers would be paying if they decided they wanted him after all. He could imagine the haggling and the bargaining and Deet starting off by demanding some outrageous price, way beyond his market value, and the Hartingers coolly declining and making a more reasonable and sensible offer.

Tarrin felt he was still worth a lot though. He'd bet anything on that. He grinned to himself, strangely pleased.

It almost made him feel wanted.

9

Deal

Kinane parked the car and looked around. It was a rich street of rich houses, all with security lights and surveillance cameras, with alarms linked to the police station, or to some security patrol, and more than likely all with double- or triple-locked doors, fastened shut with mortices and deadlocks.

It didn't look like the right sort of place really, not for somebody who stayed in the Rapid Link Motel, who rented a kid out for a living and went under the name of Deet.

Kinane checked the coordinates again, which the scanner had given him. Well, this was where Deet had been standing when he'd answered his call, somewhere around here, give or take. The Sat-Sys scanner was normally accurate to within five metres.

Must have been loaning him out again, Kinane thought. He squinted out of the window and wondered which of the houses it might have been.

Maybe he ought to try ringing, get another fix on him. But it was risky, hanging up and arousing suspicion again. A man like that would know all the tricks. He wouldn't want to lose his livelihood. He'd know straight away that someone was trying to get a position on him and he'd buy himself a new mobe in no time.

But then, if he had a customer here, and if the customer was a rich one, he might come back.

'Yeah. He'll be back.'

Kinane said it out loud. Sometimes he talked to himself just to hear another human voice. He'd spent far too many years alone now and beyond asking for a coffee, reserving a hotel room, or stopping at a petrol station to buy some fuel and a newspaper, he barely spoke to anyone.

'Yeah. He'll be back all right. Just a matter of waiting.'

Which he was good at.

Kinane sank down in the seat a little and turned off the car's sidelights. He knew he couldn't stay there too long; if anyone saw him, they'd get suspicious, and would want to know why he was sitting there in this rich street in his travel-weary car. He knew it was unlikely that the kid would reappear that night, but he just wanted a rest for a while. He'd take five minutes, then he'd go off and find a cheap room somewhere; he'd come back in the morning to keep an eye on the place.

Wonder how much he's worth, he thought?

He did a quick calculation. The kid had to be worth a good million, million and a half, maybe even two if he didn't grow too quickly.

Two million.

At that price somebody else had to be after him too. Kinane couldn't be the only one.

He tilted the rear-view mirror and looked back

along the street. A car was approaching, driving slowly, on sidelights only.

No, he couldn't be the only one – not at two million.

The car drew up beside him. The driver glanced briefly in Kinane's direction as he passed, maybe curious as to why he was parked there and sitting in the dark.

Flies to the honeypot. Bees to the flower. There'd be others, sure as God made the little green apples, and the red ones too.

The car drove on, came to the end of the street and turned off to the left. The driver had looked harmless enough, but so what? A Kiddernapper could be anyone.

Yes. Might be a woman, even, the competition.

This one, for example.

He looked ahead. Coming towards him was a woman walking a Pekinese, which she had on a retractable lead. She was well dressed, affluent, respectable. She looked like she meant no harm to anyone. But she gazed around her as she walked too, keeping her eyes on the windows of the houses, looking in wherever they hadn't yet drawn the curtains. Was she just being curious, or neighbourly, or . . .

Looking for something?

A rocking horse in the window? A high chair? A toy left on display? A doll sitting on the sill? Some stickers fastened to the glass? A child's painting, resting on the mantelpiece? A photograph, hanging on the wall?

Maybe she wasn't just a woman walking a dog.

Maybe she was a Kiddernapper, looking for clues, for evidence of occupation, for traces of a child.

She walked on, the click of her shoe heels disappearing into the night.

Kinane looked at the large, imposing house directly across the street from him, wondering if it was the one. If so, it was going to be a hell of a place to break into, Kinane thought. How do you get into somewhere like that? More importantly, how do you get out of there with a kid in your arms, especially an uncooperative one who didn't want to go? A live kicking and biting one? Screaming too, if you'd let him.

No. You'd have to use the chloro for a job like that. Even then it wouldn't be easy. Be better if you could just talk him into going with you. Tell him there was a green and happy land somewhere and you were going to lead him to it, and all he had to do was to trust you and to take your hand or follow your trail.

Fat chance.

What kid was going to leave the comfort of a house like that to go walking around the night with a stranger?

Maybe you could snatch him in the street. Coming out of the door, going back in. Or lure him out, maybe.

Yeah. Yeah.

The kitten. It had worked before, might work again. Come along with the kitten, leave it outside, get the kid to hear it mewing, out the kid comes.

He goes to pick the kitten up, you pick him up. He's in the boot of the car before he knows it, and poor little kitty goes on mew, mew, mewing, and doesn't stop till somebody comes running out and shouts:

'Where's the boy gone?!'

Yeah. The kitten might work. It was crude, it was basic, it was not subtle, but you didn't want to turn your nose up at it. It could still work. It was always new to somebody. There was one born every minute – or there had been, once.

Kinane grinned a thin and mirthless smile, thinking that there weren't many innocents left. People sure got wily with their long, long lives and more devious with every year. Yes, the rich got richer and the crooks got more crooked. The longer you did something, generally speaking, the better at it you got. A 150-year-old burglar, still in possession of his health, faculties and memory, was some burglar.

But then, a 150-year-old detective was some policeman, too. So perhaps it all evened out.

In the end.

Whenever that might be.

Rare, precious and innocent were the world's children.

'Childhood is a rare and precious thing, you know,' so Kinane's old teacher had said once. Little did she know. She hadn't known the half of it. And yet, how right she had been.

Kinane glanced in the mirror again, this time to look at himself. His skin was lined and showing signs of age. Nothing above the normal maybe, but he'd been getting one or two curious looks.

'Hey, man, not taking the Anti-Ageing yet? It'll stop you getting older, but it won't bring your looks back. Better take it soon, before you end up looking like a piece of leather.'

People looked at you, not rudely exactly, at least not yet, but they thought you were strange if you let yourself get too wrinkled before taking your Anti-Ageing pills.

In fact old, lined faces were as rare as the really young ones. And nobody much liked the look of them.

'Oh gross! Disgusting! Will you take a look at *that*!'

He remembered the voices, the opinions of the spectators looking at the photographs in the Museum of Age and Childhood. He'd gone there once to kill an afternoon. There were photographs from long ago, of grandmothers and grandfathers, with faces like dried, cracked mud. Their lines were deep, their eyes were milky, their necks were shrivelled and their skin sagging.

But now people died with the same faces that they had had maybe one hundred and sixty years before. Over a century and a half of time and experience had gone by, and not left a single mark on them.

That was what the Anti-Ageing pills did – they stole the paint from the tip of the brush, the graphite from the pencil – time went on moving over the paper, but made not a single mark. The canvas and the parchment remained blank.

Personally, Kinane preferred to see people's faces decorated – that is with a little make-up on them, the kind of make-up that only time could apply.

A police car cruised along the street. Kinane slid further down into his seat, disappearing from sight, before sliding back up again to watch the patrol vehicle turn the corner.

Time to go maybe.

He started the engine and put the car into drive.

It was a long time to pay day, in this line of work. He could go months and years without finding what he was looking for and obtaining what he wanted.

But then, when you considered that a baby taken from a pram could bring you a cool, icy, six million, it was worth learning the art of patience, and the art of perseverance, and the arts of watching and waiting.

Even the art of going quietly away.

And the art of coming back.

Deet must have returned some time in the early morning. Tarrin hadn't heard him come back, but he heard him now as he woke in his bed, for the sound of Deet's snoring came drifting through from the other room.

Tarrin got up, tiptoed to the interconnecting door and quietly closed it. He didn't want to think about the Hartingers any more, so he went and put the television on low and watched the children's cartoons. There were hardly any children left to watch them, but the television companies went on putting out repeats regardless. Adults watched them instead – in the same way that adults could be seen playing on the swings in the park or making themselves sick and dizzy on the roundabout, spinning recklessly round, sometimes even flying off and hurting themselves, scraping their elbows and knees.

When I was a child,
I spake as a child,
I understood as a child, I thought as a child:
but when I became a man, I put away childish things.

Well, that may have been true once, back in those Gideon Bible days, but it was true no longer.

Deet woke about an hour later. He stumbled into Tarrin's room, in need of a shave, a shower and a change of vest.

'Just freshen up and I'll be with you, kid,' he said. 'Then we'll get some breakfast.'

He went back to his own room and Tarrin heard the shower run. When Deet reappeared he looked and smelt a little better. There was the scent of antiperspirant, aftershave and toothpaste, all mingling into one minty pine-tree odour.

'OK. Let's find a spoon, kid,' Deet said, leading the way out to the street.

He meant a greasy-spoon, a workmen's cafe of some kind, where they heaped the rashers of bacon up high, and where they still served a full fried breakfast, with sausage and eggs and fried potatoes and mushrooms and great mugs of tea.

'This'll do.'

They went inside the first place they found. Deet asked Tarrin what he wanted. He asked for eggs and beans. The Hartingers were still knocking on the door of his thoughts, but he wouldn't let them in.

'Am I working today, Deet?' he asked.

Deet gave him a sly look. 'Ain't arranged nothing yet, kid,' he said.

'Oh?'

177

Deet usually had something fixed up pretty quick.

'I thought we'd just wait and see for a day,' Deet said. Then he winked. 'The Hartingers,' he said, 'see if they take the bait.'

Tarrin ate his eggs and beans and drank his orange juice.

'You know, Deet,' he began, 'if you'd saved the money I'd made, instead of spending it all—'

'You don't know nothing about finance, kid,' Deet snapped.

'No, I was only going to say—'

'Well, you don't need to.'

'That we could be quite well off by now, Deet, and have a place of our own, you know, like our own house, a real home, and be like a family . . .'

'You've got family. I'm your family, ain't I?'

Tarrin could see he was getting angry and knew he should let the subject drop, but he went on, just the same.

'I only meant, Deet, that it would make more sense to save some. Because, as you say, I won't be a kid forever, and then what?'

'You leave all that to me, kid,' Deet snarled. 'And button your lip.'

Tarrin turned away to look out of the window. The capital seemed much like any other city to him, there was just more of it, that was all – though maybe that did make a difference to the way the people in it acted – they seemed to talk faster, move quicker, be more impatient, in more of a hurry.

'Hey, look, Deet.' He pointed across the street. There was a billboard of unlit neon lights, the kind of

178

thing that would come alive at night but which was dead and dreary during the day.

'Well, what do you know! Miss Virginia Two Shoes has got a rival.'

It was a club. Underneath the black neon tubes was a poster printed in fluorescent inks on a luminous background.

Miss Davina 'Bo-Bo' Peep, the poster read. *The cutest thing on two legs.* And there was a photograph of the prettiest girl you had ever seen, prettier even than Miss Virginia Two Shoes, all dressed up in ribbons and bows.

'Forty if she's a day, kid,' Deet said. 'Been playing the circuit for years.'

Tarrin stared at the picture. It seemed impossible to believe that the girl in the photo could be forty years old. She looked so sweet, so pretty, so young.

'She's had the PP, Deet?'

'You betcha,' he said. 'And you think of the money she's making.'

But before Tarrin could really get around to thinking about all that and to working out whether any amount of money was worth having to be in a child's body until the day you died, Deet's new mobe rang.

'Mobe's ringing, Deet.'

'I can hear it.'

'Why did you get a new one yesterday?'

'Free upgrade.'

'Can I have the old one?'

'No. They kept it. Now, shh! – I'm answering!'

It could only be one person. There was only one person to whom he had so far given the new phone number.

'Mr Hartinger, good morning. How are you, sir? Yes, indeed it is. Deet speaking. No, not Mr Deet, sir, no necessity for that. Just Deet, it is, straight Deet, not formalities, no titles. Just straight Deet will do when people are making the cheques out. Ha ha! That's right. My little joke.'

Tarrin winced. He always cringed at Deet and his little jokes and at the ingratiating way he talked to people who had money, as if trying to both wheedle and to bludgeon his way into their affections and their finances.

'So, Mr Hartinger, and what can I do for you, sir? I'm assuming this isn't just a simple How-dee-do call, though if it is, it's more than welcome. Or maybe there's a question or two you forgot to ask last night. Some details you might need to be apprised of.'

Deet winked at Tarrin again, as if to say, 'The fish is on the line, he's taking the bait, we've got ourselves a live one.'

'You've discussed it? Well, I'm glad to hear that, sir. Both you and your good lady? Well, that's a good thing to do, if you don't mind my saying, a joint and mutual decision. Avoids future friction, I always think, and makes for the more harmonious relationship.'

He winked at Tarrin again.

'So you're still interested, sir? And you'd like to make an offer? If he's still available? Well . . . I guess he is, just about . . . though right at this moment, sir, I have to say that I'm fielding calls. Fielding calls, Mr Hartinger. Other interested parties, I have to say, who've made offers themselves. But I told them I wouldn't accept nothing nor put pen to any paper until I'd heard from you.'

Deet covered the mobe with his hand and whispered gleefully, 'I'll get him to push the price for you, kid.' He winked again, as if Tarrin ought to be pleased about this – that not only was Deet selling him, he was trying to get the top price for him too.

Tarrin went cold. He felt a deep inner rage.

'What about me, Deet?' his mind screamed. *'What about me?'*

I won't go, he told himself. *I won't go. I won't go and live with those people in that great big house. I won't go.*

Then he looked at Deet, at the stubble on his chin which no razor ever quite removed, at the grease on the plate in front of him, at the sly expression on his face as he negotiated with Hartinger, and he thought that if he didn't go, then this was the alternative. This was it.

'Well, that sounds like a fair price to me, sir . . .'

I want to go home, Deet. Can't I go home? Do you know where my home is Deet?

Deet always got angry when he asked him that. No idea, kid. Don't know. Couldn't say. Couldn't help you there.

Where's my real home, Deet?

This hotel is home. What's wrong with the hotel? You oughta be grateful. It's a nice room. It's got a TV with five hundred and forty-nine channels and a Gideon Bible by the bed. What's wrong with the room?

Do I have a mum and dad, Deet?

Sure you did. One time.

What happened to them, Deet?

Couldn't say, kid.

You must know. Didn't they love me?

Sure they did.

Did they sell me then? Why did they sell me if they loved me?

Maybe times were hard, kid. Who knows. Or maybe they didn't sell you. Maybe it was a car crash and an orphanage affair.

Are they dead, Deet?

I don't like to upset you kid, but who knows, who knows?

How did you find me, Deet?

Told you, kid, won you in a card game.

Seriously?

Yeah. Sure.

Who was I with then?

Some rich guy who thought he was good at cards.

Not my dad?

He wasn't your dad, nah.

So how did I come to be with him?

I don't know, kid, you're going too far back for me now.

Can't we try to find them, Deet?

Past is gone, kid. Forget about it. Think about the here and now.

But if the past was gone, why did the dreams still come? Dreams of the sunlight filtering through the trees. Dreams of a woman, dreams of a man? Dreams of the scent of freshly mown grass and the sound of cattle lowing in the fields? If the past were truly gone, why did it keep returning?

I remember, I remember,
The house where I was born . . .

'OK, Mr Hartinger, we have ourselves a deal, sir. I'll be round to shake hands on it and to bring the kid over some time this afternoon. I'm sorry? How does he feel about it? The kid? Oh, he's delighted.'

Deet grinned at Tarrin and winked, mouthing, 'You're delighted, aren't you, kid?' He winked again. Then he fixed a time, said cheerio and finished the call. He put the mobe down on the table, took up his knife and fork and cut into a sausage. It had gone cold and globules of fat had congealed upon its surface.

'It's done, kid,' he said. 'We sold you.' He speared some sausage into his mouth.

Tarrin sat there, shocked into silence and incredulity.

Sold me? Sold me?

But you can't sell me, Deet.

You can't sell me. I'm a human being. You can't sell a human being, Deet. Not a human being.

Deet took another bite of his sausage. He waved the bit that remained on his fork in a gesture of appreciation. Deet with a sausage, it was like a connoisseur with a bottle of fine, vintage wine.

'Hmm. Good sausage, kid,' he said. 'Just how I like them.'

You can't sell me, Deet, Tarrin's mind went on repeating. I'm a human being. You can't sell me.

But apparently he just had.

183

10

Souvenir

After breakfast, Deet took Tarrin around a couple of shops where he bought him a new toothbrush and a notebook and pen.

'To remember me by, kid,' he said, though the pen was not really expensive. 'I dare say I'll be calling by every now and then to see how you are and that no one's mistreating you, but I won't be outstaying my welcome. They'll be wanting to bond with you, no doubt about that, and won't want too many mementoes of the past coming by – such as myself. But just remember, kid, that out of sight don't necessarily mean out of mind and that I'll still be watching out for you.'

He winked his conspiratorial wink again. Tarrin was sure that Deet was up to something. He just didn't know what, but he knew better than to ask, for Deet would just clam up and tell him nothing. Whereas if he didn't ask, he might let something slip before they got to the Hartingers'.

They returned to the hotel and Tarrin packed his few possessions. He still felt numb, a little frightened and apprehensive at the prospect of change. In Deet, there was the comfort of familiarity, but Tarrin knew in his heart that he had never loved the man, barely even liked him a lot of the time.

'Well, I'll miss you, kid,' Deet said, as he checked around the room, making sure that Tarrin had everything. 'It's been a long haul and a long road and we've seen some good times, but even the best of friends must part and so it is with you and me. It's a good home you're going to, kid. There's money there and they'll look after you. So don't you disappoint them, as I don't want any complaints or anyone demanding any refunds. Just go with the flow, kid, and you'll have a ball. So let's put that happy face on and we'll go do the deed.'

Deet gave him a playful punch on the shoulder. And that was it. They left the hotel and got a cab to millionaires' row.

They didn't see the man in the car, parked a short way down and across the street from the Hartingers' front door. They didn't see him as he watched them get out of the taxi, watched Deet pay the driver, watched curiously as Tarrin pulled a bag and a small suitcase out of the taxi after him – as if he had come to stay somewhere for a while.

The man watched as they walked up the drive to the Hartingers' house and as the door opened and they were admitted. He watched the door for forty-five minutes, after which time it opened again and Deet came out alone, calling goodbyes to those within, and folding up what looked like a cheque and putting it safely away into his wallet. Then he stood a while, looking up and down the street for a cab. Seeing none, he began to walk. He walked right past the car the man was sitting in. The man raised a newspaper as Deet approached, but Deet paid him no heed. As Deet walked by, the man looked at his face and didn't much care for what he saw.

He sat in the car for a long time – longer than was safe, but he had to risk it – waiting for Deet to return to collect the boy, waiting for the boy to come out. Eventually it grew dark, and still Deet did not return.

'He's not coming back,' Kinane thought. 'He's sold him.'

He sat there wondering how he could ever break into the house, with its cameras and alarms and security. It would be difficult, but anything was possible – at least it was when there was enough at stake.

It had been an awkward and a stilted farewell, with Mrs Hartinger anxious to see the back of Deet as quickly as possible, but not wishing to seem ungracious by urging him to go, or by making such remarks as, 'Well, we musn't keep you, Mr Deet,' and 'Well, thank you for bringing Tarrin round . . . I'm sure you must be busy.'

The business side of things had been taken care of by Deet and Mr Hartinger, who were ensconced in the latter's study. Deet made a pretence of admiring the paintings on the walls, while all the time keeping a close eye on the words and figures Hartinger was writing in his chequebook.

When Deet was satisfied, he handed over Tarrin's documents and the two men shook hands.

'Well, he's yours now, and I'm sure you'll give him a good home.'

'We will, Mr Deet, rest assured of that.'

'He couldn't do better, I'm thinking,' Deet said.

'Nice surroundings, good address, educated people . . .'

'We'll do our best for him, Mr Deet.'

'Which is why I'm letting him come to you,' Deet said. 'It's his future I'm thinking of, his welfare. I've only ever wanted the best for the boy, and you can offer him things that I never could – home, security, family. That's what a child needs.'

Hartinger would dearly have loved to tell Deet exactly what sort of a lying, parasitic, self-serving hypocrite he thought he was. But there was doubt in Hartinger's mind as to his own actions. If Deet had sunk low enough to sell a child, then what had Hartinger done in buying him? Or could he excuse his behaviour on the grounds that he was indeed in a position to offer Tarrin a better future and a better home?

'Well, I'll just say a quick goodbye to him, if I might, then I'll be on my way.'

Hartinger would have preferred it if Deet could have contented himself with just the second of these two actions, but he could hardly refuse his request, so he led the way to the drawing room where Tarrin and Mrs Hartinger were – as Deet put it – 'getting acquainted'.

'So how's it going, kid?' Deet said. 'You getting to know your new ma? She's a good one, kid, I can tell you that. She'll love you like you were her own. Ain't that so, ma'am?'

'We'll certainly do our best to give Tarrin all the love and care he needs, Mr Deet,' Mrs Hartinger assured him.

Deet spun the moment out for a while, and he even

managed to get a little moisture into his eye when it came to the final parting of the ways. But however upset he was to part from his charge, the cheque in his pocket seemed to console him.

'Bye then, kid. You be happy.'

'And you. Bye, Deet.'

As he turned to go, Tarrin felt his own tears begin to fall. He wanted to run to Deet, to put his arms round him, to beg him not to leave.

Don't go, Deet. Please, don't go!

But even as the tears fell, he recognized that what prompted them was not any real love for the man, just a sense of loss of the past, and a fear of the future.

Then the butler arrived, and Deet was gone, walking out of the drawing room, going along the corridor, then the front door was heard to close. Tarrin hurried to the window just in time to see Deet walk down the steps to the street.

He saw the way he scrutinized the cheque, the way he put it away safely in his wallet, the way he put the wallet away and patted his pocket, the way he walked on without a backward glance.

Suddenly Tarrin didn't feel so sad after all.

'Tarrin . . . Tarrin?'

'Sorry, I was just thinking . . .'

'Would you like to get settled? In your room?'

'Yes, OK.'

'Are you OK?'

'Yes, I'm all right, ma'am.'

'Please, Tarrin . . .'

'Yes, ma'am?'

'Mum – I'm your mother now – aren't I? And

you're our son. Mum and Dad. Can you call us that? Is that OK? Mum and Dad?'

'Yes, of course . . . Mum . . .'

She smiled. 'And Dad.'

Tarrin smiled too. He even seemed to stand straighter, visibly to grow in stature.

They weren't really 'Mum and Dad', of course, and they never would be. But the desire to please was ingrained in him, after so many years of doing nothing else. That was why he was there, after all, to keep the customer happy.

For the first few days Tarrin buried himself in books. His new room was full of them.

Deet hadn't liked books much. 'I don't trust them,' he'd said. Though he liked the cinema. 'Give me the visual image, the motion picture, any time. I'm not saying the camera can't lie, of course it can, it lies all the time. But books lie too. And if you need all those words to say something, there's something fishy going on. If a man needs five hundred pages to tell a lie, what kind of a lie is he telling? A film isn't like that. Someone arches an eyebrow on screen, and that tells you a whole lot about him, but in a book it would take three pages, and a stack of punctuation.'

Tarrin worked his way through the books. He read about families and schools. He read about people whose parents had split up, of children who had run away from home, who didn't get on at school, who were poor, who were picked on, who had to struggle against terrible odds and adversities, but it all worked out somehow in the end.

189

But there was no one like him. Which was maybe no bad thing either. Because he didn't want to read about anyone like himself. He didn't wish to be reminded. He wanted only to forget, to disappear for a while into that book-filled graveyard, to be buried there, to haunt the headstones, to never come back to life.

The Hartingers were tactful people and they didn't bother him much for the first few days. They just saw to it that he had all that he needed and that he didn't go hungry or short of company when he wanted it. They made polite conversation with him when they all sat together round the table at meal times. They were fine, kind, gentle, considerate, sophisticated people.

And yet . . .

Tarrin didn't know what it was. But it was some immense, uncrossable gulf, like one of those canyons that they had in adventure films, with a rickety old rope and wooden plank bridge stretched perilously across it, and sure to break the moment anyone put their weight upon it.

It was a gulf of time.

The Hartingers were both over a century old. Their own childhoods were so far away now that they could remember little about them, or how it had ever felt to be truly young.

So they were nice, very nice. And yet, whenever Tarrin came across the blue-grey Persian cat, he felt that, yes, that was just what he was too – an acquisition, a must-have, he was something that would look nice around the house – a pet.

He noticed that when Mrs Hartinger picked the cat

up, she would say, 'Floo-Floo come to Mummy now. Floo-Floo come to his mummy.'

Then he would remember that she had asked him to call her 'Mum'.

So there was Tarrin and there was Floo-Floo – different species, yes, but both household pets, one a cat, one a boy.

After allowing him a few days to settle in, Mrs Hartinger took him out in the car to have him measured for some new clothes.

'I know you can still buy the odd thing off the peg,' she said. 'But there isn't much to choose from, so it'll be nice to have something made.'

So she took him to a tailor.

Then they arranged for tutors to give him lessons.

'Did you actually learn anything while you were with Mr Deet, Tarrin?'

'Yes. He used to buy me Edu-Packs. He said I ought to study. He said people didn't want to rent a kid for the afternoon if he was going to turn out to be pig— that is – if he was going to turn out to be ignorant.'

'Good, well, we're not completely starting from the beginning then. But we'll get a few tutors in, to smooth off those rough edges, shall we say. Do you play the piano?'

'No.'

'Would you like to learn?'

He didn't know. 'Er, yes. I guess.'

'Good. We'll start lessons for you next week.'

'OK.'

'And we'll have to get you your injections. Did Mr Deet take you for your injections?'

'I'm – I'm not sure. Yes. I think he did.'

'We'll get you a health check anyway and, if you need them, we'll get you your injections. Which reminds me, I must arrange to take Floo-Floo to the vet. He needs his injections too.'

Over the course of the next two weeks, a routine developed. Tarrin would wake, have breakfast, and then a tutor would come to take him through a particular subject, or the piano teacher would arrive to take him through his exercises and scales.

Mr Hartinger might go to his office to take care of his business, or he might stay at home and paint in the room he had turned into an artist's studio, while Mrs Hartinger might go riding in the park with some friends. She kept a horse in a nearby stable. It seemed strange to find such a place in the middle of town, but there it was, at the end of a mews. She took Tarrin with her to see her horse once or twice. He liked it. He liked the smell of the stable. It reminded him of his dreams, and of the green land, far away.

In the afternoon Tarrin might be left to himself or taken out somewhere – always under the secure supervision of the Hartingers' personal assistant, Bradley. This was not because the Hartingers didn't trust Tarrin, but because of the risk from Kidder-nappers. And they had paid so much for him too. Mr Hartinger noticed from his bank account that Deet had wasted no time in cashing his cheque.

They took him to parks and to old playgrounds. They bought him a bike, and he rode it along the river bank, with Bradley jogging alongside.

But all the while Tarrin was watched, though he would never have known it, and Kinane would focus the binoculars upon him from a safe, inscrutable distance, waiting, just waiting for the moment to be right.

In the evenings the Hartingers began to take him out with them.

'If you could wear your suit tonight, Tarrin . . .'

'Yes, Mum.'

'There's a good boy.'

Which were the very same words she used as she stroked the mane of her horse, or as she lifted Floo-Floo up from the cushion, trying to extract his claws from the cloth.

There's a good boy. There's a good boy.

They got dressed up and went to concerts, to theatres, to some interesting and to some very long and very boring evenings.

Occasionally they would have friends round, and they would show Tarrin off to them. He was expected to be – if not amusing – at least polite, which he invariably was. He sat at the dinner table with all the adults, only his glass was full of juice or water rather than wine. But he passed the dishes and the basket of rolls and he answered the questions he was asked, and although he went to bed early he was often still awake enough to hear the guests leaving. He heard their voices, their thank-yous and farewells and their 'You must come round to us one night.' Sometimes he heard Mrs Hartinger say in a low, theatrical whisper, 'So what do you think of our boy?'

'Oh my, isn't he heavenly! Isn't he just so . . .!'

Or, 'He's so cute, so charming. But do tell, dear – even if I am being nosy – how much was he?'

Just as they had maybe once asked about Floo-Floo, 'So cute, so charming. Does he have a pedigree? And by the way, where did you find him, and how much did he cost?'

Tarrin lay awake then, feeling more alone than he ever had, even wishing that Deet would come back for him, or at least come and visit. The times he and Deet had had together began to seem like good ones. True, Deet had only thought of him as the goose that laid the golden eggs, but at least he hadn't mistaken him for a cat.

'They just wanted me,' he thought, 'like they wanted something they saw in a shop window. I was expensive, and they could afford me, and they thought I would look nice, and they didn't have one. Only they do now. And here I am.'

Sometimes he thought of running away, but of course he still didn't have anywhere to go. He kept thinking of that green land far away, but he knew neither where it was nor how to get there. It was probably only a dream, not a proper memory, just some small light of hope that his imagination had conjured up to make the dark more bearable.

One day Mrs Hartinger asked what he would like to do, and he said that more than anything he would like to have a friend to play with.

'A friend . . . well . . .'

Mrs Hartinger looked doubtful. 'We don't actually know anyone with children as such . . . unless . . .'

She brightened up and went away to make a phone call. When she returned she announced that she had arranged for 'a little friend to come around on Sunday afternoon'.

194

Tarrin looked forward to it for the rest of the week, but when the 'friend' finally came he proved to be what Tarrin had once been, a child on loan for the afternoon. Only he wasn't even really that. Not a proper child. He was a PP. He'd had the implant. Tarrin knew it immediately, though the Hartingers had no idea.

He asked him when they were out in the garden together, supposed to be having fun doing what boys did.

'How old are you?' Tarrin asked the boy.

'Whaddaya want to know for?' he answered aggressively.

'You've had the PP, haven't you?' Tarrin said.

'Whaddif I have? And whaddif I haven't?' the boy/man said – and he shoved Tarrin with his hand.

'They'll be watching,' Tarrin warned him. 'Probably even videoing everything, for the album.'

'Whaddif they are?' the PP boy said. 'They'll think it's just boys being boys and doing a bit of rough stuff. So do you want to play or don't you?'

'Tell me how old you are,' Tarrin said. 'Or I'll fall over and cut my knee and tell them you did it and you won't get paid.'

'I could lay you out, kid,' the boy/man said. 'With one good swipe.'

'Just tell me how old you are.'

The boy sighed. 'OK. So I'm sixty-six. What about it?'

'Sixty-six?'

'OK, I lied a year. I'm sixty-seven. How did you know I wasn't a kid?' He nervously touched his face, worried that his skin was ageing.

'It's not that,' Tarrin said.

The boy looked relieved. 'It's what then?'

'The look . . .'

'What look?'

'In your eyes.'

'I don't have any look in my eyes. Now let's start playing like we're supposed to, or they'll think I'm not earning my money.'

So Tarrin threw a ball around and had a game of catch with the boy. But it was only because he felt sorry for him.

Just before their time was up, Tarrin said, 'Will you tell me something?'

'Whaddaya want to know?'

'What's it like – always to be a child?'

'It's just great, kid,' the boy said. 'Just great. The best thing in the world. OK? Happy now?'

Then the afternoon was over. The boy had to leave. He had another job to go to.

'Well, Tarrin, did you have fun with your visitor?'

'Yes, thank you. It was very nice.'

'Did you play together nicely and have lots to talk about?'

'Yes. Yes, we did.'

'Well, that's good. It must be nice to meet other children.'

'Yes, Mum.'

'Perhaps we'll do it again one day.'

'Yes.'

'Or if you want to save up your pocket money, you can always have somebody round yourself.'

'Yes.'

'Well, I'm going to go out now and do some shopping. Would you like to come?'

'No, I'll stay and read, thank you.'

He went up to his room and opened a new book. As he did so, he glanced at his desk and saw the pen there which Deet had given him as a farewell present. He picked it up and went to scribble with it on a scrap of paper, but it didn't seem to be working very well. The ink came out in blotches at first and then it stopped altogether. Tarrin saw there was ink on his fingers. He put the cap back on to the pen and tossed it into the bin. Then he went to the bathroom to wash his hands. Even Deet's presents seemed to leave you dirty.

11

Baby

One morning as Tarrin and Mrs Hartinger were walking the short distance from the house to the delicatessen, followed as ever by Bradley, they noticed a large crowd of people surrounding something in the street.

Mrs Hartinger was afraid that it was an accident of some kind, which she wouldn't want anything to do with. 'Run and see, dear. But don't stay too long. Just find out what it is.'

Tarrin squirmed into the throng, with Bradley worming in after him, afraid to let him out of his sight. He felt excited, and a little ashamed of his own excitement, as he fought his way to the centre of the crowd so as to get a better look at the body on the street, lying broken and bloody, in some unnatural position, its glassy eyes staring at nothing except death. But it proved to be just the opposite. It wasn't death that was the attraction. It was birth. It was life.

A young man and a young woman stood next to a pram. The young woman was gripping the handle of the pram. The young man was standing in front of it, his face tense and anxious. He stood as if ready to protect the child in the pram from anyone's attempt to get too close to her or to pick her up.

'Please, let us by. Let us by, please. We just need to get past. You're crowding the baby.'

'How old is it?'

'How many days?'

'Is it a boy?'

'No, it's a girl. Now, please, can we just get by?'

'A girl, a girl, you hear that, she's a girl.'

'Can we see the little girl?'

'Hold her up.'

'Is it a real baby?'

'Is she for sale?'

'How much for her? How much do you want? How much?'

'Whatever he offers, I'll double it.'

'Double that and the same again!'

'Plus a hundred thousand!'

'For God's sake! It's not an auction.'

'Can I hold the baby? Please. Can I hold the baby?'

'Let her hold the baby, you'll never see it again. Just let me hold it. Give it to me!'

The child's mother looked petrified. She had maybe expected some curiosity and attention when she took the newborn child out in its pram to take the air. But not this.

'Will you let us by? Please just let us by.'

But the crowd surged forwards and pressed even tighter around the couple and their child.

'See the baby. We just want to see the baby. Never seen a baby before.'

'What's that about a baby? Somebody got a baby? Where?'

'Over there. Middle of the crowd.'

199

The pool of people became a lake. The sleeping child woke and opened her eyes.

'Waking. She's waking.'

'What's her name?'

'How much do you want for her? I'll write you a cheque now.'

'I can give you cash!'

'How come you're fertile? What's the secret?'

The family could not move. The crowd pressed in. The pram had bodies all around it, there were faces peering, hands reaching out.

'Can I touch her – touch the baby?'

'Don't touch her!' the mother screamed, gulping in panic. 'Don't touch my baby! David!'

'It's all right.' The young man was fumbling with his mobe. He dialled the emergency number and asked for the police and told them what was happening. Then he put his mobe back in his pocket and he tried to fend the hands off and to stop them from touching his daughter.

'How old is she? Just tell me how old.'

'Is she weeks?'

'Months or years?'

'She's years. Two or three years.'

'Can she walk?'

'Talk?'

'She got teeth yet?'

'She's only two days old. Just two days. Now, please, let us through. Leave us alone.'

'Two days? How many teeth does she have?'

'None. Now . . .'

The baby began to cry.

'What's she doing?'

'What's the noise?'

'What are they doing to her?'

'What's wrong?'

'Why don't they stop it?'

'What's the noise?'

Reluctantly, not wishing to take her from the pram just then, lest she was snatched from her, but unable to let her cry any longer, the young mother reached forwards and took the baby into her arms.

'She's picking her up. Look. Picking her up.'

The crowd stopped pushing and shoving. They became hushed. Almost reverent. Like a congregation.

'What's she doing?'

'I don't know.'

'What is she doing?'

'What's she doing that for?'

Then Tarrin heard his own voice speak, and he heard his own amazement, his own awe and his own wonder.

'She's feeding her,' he said, more to himself than to anyone, in a soft whisper. 'She's feeding the baby.'

The people around him heard his words and repeated them and passed them on.

'She's feeding the baby.'

'Feeding the baby – no!'

People stood on tiptoe, craned their necks. Most of them had never even seen a baby, not a real one, but to be in the actual presence of one, when it was being fed . . .

The crowd parted without protest when two policemen came to keep order. The baby stopped feeding for a moment and let out a small belch.

'What was that?'

'What did she do?'

'She belched! The baby belched.'

'She belched!'

People were smiling, laughing, nodding to each other, touching each other's shoulders and arms.

'The baby belched. Did you hear that?'

'No! Will she do it again?'

She obliged, almost as if on cue, and did it again. Now even the policemen were charmed. They were laughing and smiling and tilting their helmets back on their heads and scratching their foreheads and looking around at everyone, almost as if it were a carnival.

'Well, that was something.'

'OK, everyone!' one of the policemen said in a loud, authoritative voice. 'Break it up. Let's move it along now. You're blocking the road and holding up the traffic. There's nothing to see here.'

Which of course was not true.

There was everything to see there, and he knew it, and he could barely take his own eyes off it, let alone expect others to transfer their gaze elsewhere and to get on with their own affairs.

Wait till he told the wife. Wait till he told her. That he'd seen a baby today. And not just that. He'd seen the kid's mother feed it too. And not just that. The baby had belched. And not just once, but twice. And then she'd kind of gurgled a little, and maybe even sneezed.

She'd be jealous green. Tickled pink to hear it, but jealous green that she hadn't been there to see it too.

'OK, everyone, now. Let's move it. Let the young people alone now.'

The crowd's mood had changed. They were willing to depart now. They'd seen something, something good, something marvellous. People took pictures with their mobes and mailed them off to family and friends.

The baby's parents were just glad to be allowed to move on.

'Got far to go?' one of the policemen asked.

'Just a few streets.'

'We'll walk you. Make sure there's no more trouble.'

On they walked. The mother pushing the pram, the father clearing a way before it, the two burly policemen walking along on either side.

'You're lucky people,' the taller and heavier of the two policemen said to the young couple.

'We know. We know.'

'How come you're fertile?'

'We don't know. Just luck, I suppose.'

'Word of advice,' the policeman said. But before he could give it he was briefly distracted by the baby smiling and gurgling at him and reaching for one of his plump, substantial fingers.

'May I?'

The mother smiled. She was grateful. The two policemen had rescued them.

'Go ahead.'

The policeman let the child take his little finger. Its touch shot through him like a current of electricity.

'You're lucky people,' he said. 'Such lucky people.' His voice was just a whisper now.

The baby's eyes closed. Her grip relaxed. Her hand fell back by her side. She slept.

'She's a cute one,' the policeman said. 'She's a cute one, right enough. Only, as I say – word of advice . . .'

'Yes, officer?'

'Get out of here, ma'am. Get out of this city. Find a spot of countryside somewhere, far from anyone, a little piece that nobody knows. And you go there and hide there, and bring up your baby, and don't let her out of your sight until she's good and grown.'

'We live in the country. We're just visiting. Just came to show her to some family.'

'Good. Well, you go back there and live safely. The city's no place for a child. You know what that little girl would be worth to any Kiddernapper here? Six, seven, maybe eight million. So you hang on to her. You hold on tight.'

'Don't worry, officer, we will.'

They were at their door now.

'And thank you. Thanks again.'

'No problem.'

'And you too, officer.'

'My pleasure. We'll watch till you're inside. And then maybe wait around a while, in case anyone's got any ideas.'

'Thank you.'

'Help you up the steps with the pram.'

'You're very kind.'

'Fine pram.'

'We found it in a shop . . . antique shop . . . bric-a-brac – needing doing up a little.'

'Did a good job.'

'Well, thanks again.'

'Take care now.'

'Bye then.'

'Bye.'

The door closed, upon baby, cradle and all.

The two policemen retraced their steps. They lingered a while, as they had promised, and then returned to where they had parked their car.

'Wait'll we tell them at the station!' the taller policeman said.

'Yeah,' his colleague agreed. 'Wait'll we do!'

As the people dispersed, Tarrin returned to Mrs Hartinger, his face blushing crimson. He had kept her waiting and should have gone back sooner.

'Sorry,' he said, 'it was a baby.'

'It's all right, Tarrin. I saw it too. Bradley came and told me. We were standing right behind you.'

'Have you seen one before?' he asked.

She nodded. 'A long time ago.'

'Surprisingly small, aren't they?'

She gave him a strange smile. 'Yes. Surprisingly.'

'I mean, to start off so small and to get so . . . well . . . big. To think that we all started off like that.'

'Yes. Well, shall we go?'

And together they walked on towards the delicatessen.

To say the Hartingers had tired of Tarrin would not be strictly true. But they had got used to him, certainly, and he to them. His novelty had worn off, just as the novelty of the Persian cat had worn off and the novelty of owning the priceless Picasso painting which hung in the hallway had worn off. That wasn't to say that Tarrin, along with the cat, the painting, and all the many other precious objects in the house, was no longer treasured, for he was. He just no longer held the same immediate curiosity and fascination for them.

Why, there were days when Mr Hartinger didn't even bother to glance at the Picasso painting at all or, if he did, it was to pay no more heed to it than he did to the hall table, the lampshade or the umbrella stand. He paid more attention to the daily newspaper.

Similarly, there were days too when Mrs Hartinger's diamonds no longer seemed to sparkle for her with their usual vitality, when even the emeralds and the pearls in her jewellery box had lost their lustre. And there were mornings when the seemingly eternal handsomeness of her unageing, time-frozen face no longer pleased her eye. She felt jaded in body and soul, as if – even in the midst of yearning to live, and in fearing and not wanting to die – she felt that she had already lived far too long.

Though she was barely a day over a hundred and twenty. Whereas Mr Hartinger was a hundred and sixty if he was a year.

Which made him a cradle-snatcher, Mrs Hartinger said.

Which was their ancient and familiar joke.

The boy, the cat, the painting on the wall – in the currency of the Hartingers' lives these familiar things were the watermarks. They were background, decor, essential, appreciated, but in the endless quest for novelty, which was a concomitant part of this long,

long life, they were not enough. There was always the lure of something new.

If you could afford it.

But, even then, what did you give to the man or to the woman who had everything? Where did those who had been everywhere now go? What did those who had tried everything try? What did those who had done everything do?

Boredom, lassitude, tedium – these had taken the place of infirmity, illness and frailty. These were the things to fear, these were the enemies now.

If you had money.

If you were poor, they were less of a problem. Your worries were more immediate, like how to earn your day's living, and how to save enough to put a little aside so that you could enjoy your retirement. All forty, fifty, sixty, eighty, a hundred or more years of it.

That evening, after dinner, the Hartingers announced that they were going to the opera and then on afterwards to eat a light supper with some friends. Tarrin was afraid that they would want him to go with them, but tonight they left him to amuse himself.

'Anything you want, Tarrin . . . just ask Bradley if you need anything.'

More than anything he wanted a friend, a friend of his own age. Not a PP. Not a pretend boy or a pretend girl, with sixty years of living hiding behind a mask of childhood, but a real live companion of his own age, with his own uncertainties, fears and feelings. Someone who would understand.

But he didn't ask and he didn't mention it. It would

have made the Hartingers feel uncomfortable, as if they were responsible for his isolation and his loneliness and for his being one of the few.

'I'll read and maybe go on the computer for a while and watch a film.'

'OK, Tarrin. And tomorrow we'll go to the stable. Maybe you can start to take riding lessons, and soon go out on one of the horses.'

'Yes, that'd be great . . . Mum.'

'We'll look in before we go.'

They did, both looking distinguished in their evening clothes.

'Bye, Tarrin.'

'Night, Mum.'

Her lips brushed his cheek.

'Night, Dad.'

A squeeze on the shoulder – in a fatherly way.

And then she was gone, in a cloud of perfume and a swirl of silk, and he was gone with her, holding the door for her, always impeccable, always so well dressed and groomed, always the gentleman.

They left the house and got into the waiting taxi. Bradley watched from the hallway until the cab had turned the corner of the street before he closed the front door. He didn't see the man in the parked car, watching the house. But the watcher noted that the Hartingers had gone, and that the boy had not, and that there had not been such an opportunity in a long time. Nor might there be another for a good long while. And tonight was the night to act.

12

Kiddernap

Maybe Tarrin heard the bell ring, maybe he didn't. Maybe the bell he heard was the one which came with the dreams – of the fields of wheat and the fields of corn, with a light breeze ruffling the stalks and stems. The fields moved like water, undulating in waves of pale, yellow surf. In the distance was the bell ringing the hour, ever so slightly cracked-sounding and out of tune. It was an old church bell in a crumbling belfry. So maybe that was what he heard as he drifted into sleep, or maybe it wasn't, maybe it was a real bell after all, and the murmuring voices were real voices, but the sounds didn't linger or bother him for long, and soon everything – real or imaginary – was silent again.

The darkly dressed man swiftly closed the front door and then dragged Bradley's unconscious body along the hall and left it to lie on the drawing-room floor. Then that door was half closed and the footsteps moved softly on up the stairs. First one bedroom, then another, opening doors to rooms containing nothing but silence and shadow, the darkness of drawn curtains, or the shimmering of stars.

Doors opened, doors were left ajar, the footsteps

moving on, up another flight of stairs again, opening another door, another, a third, and then . . .

There he was. Asleep. A book lying open on the floor, within reach of the hand that dangled down from where he slept on the bed.

Just a step or two more, a hand across his mouth so that he would not shout or scream, or make any sound of being afraid or startled when he woke, and then . . .

The boy's eyes were open, afraid, staring wildly with terror. And then the fear gave way to perplexity, to curiosity, to bafflement.

The man in black, standing in front of him, put a finger to his lips. He relaxed the grip of his other hand, the one that covered the boy's mouth.

'Hiya, kid. How're you doing?'

'Deet!'

'Thought I'd forgotten you, huh?'

'Whatever are . . . what are you doing here?'

'No time for the niceties, kid.' He went to the chair and threw Tarrin's clothes upon the bed. 'Here – get yourself dressed. Where they keep the clean underwear?'

Tarrin nodded towards the chest. 'In the drawer.'

'I see it.'

Some items sailed across the room and joined the other clothes on the bed.

'Come on, kid, let's get moving. Let's get the show on the road. No need to be shy about it. Here – I won't look. Just get yourself dressed and let's get moving.'

'But, Deet . . .'

'No buts about it, kid. Thought I'd forgot you, did

you? Didn't I say I was looking out for you? Didn't I say your uncle Deet would never let you down. Come on, kid, move it!'

Tarrin sat up and rubbed his eyes. He swung his legs over the edge of the bed so that his feet dangled over his slippers. He was still half asleep and disorientated and confused.

'Deet . . .'

'Come on, kid. Come on. Time's the essence, like I always say, and no more so than now.'

Deet went to the window and peered down into the street.

'Deet, I don't understand. What . . . why are you here? Where's Bradley? Did he let you in?'

Deet chuckled. 'Sure, kid. He let me in all right. But right now he's sleeping some chloro off down in the drawing room. He's lying there under the piano, but he ain't playing it much. He won't be waking for a while and, even when he does, he won't be talking to anyone, as he's all trussed and gagged up like a chicken for the oven. Come on.'

'Deet . . .'

'Thought I'd let you down, did you, kid? No way. Old Deet, he's one bad, bad penny. He's always turning up. Get dressed, kid, speed it up, come on.'

Mechanically, habitually, so used to always doing what Deet said, Tarrin began to dress himself while Deet paced nervously and quickly around the room, constantly returning to the window to look down into the street.

'Deet . . .'

'Come on, kid. Come on, come on, come on.'

211

Tarrin pulled his trousers on and zipped up the fly. He put on socks, a T-shirt and a fleece.

'Where's your shoes, kid?'

'Downstairs.'

'We'll get 'em on the way. Anything you need to take?'

'But, Deet . . . where are we going? Why? What's going on? I thought you sold me. Why are you here?'

'Call it a social call, kid.' Deet tittered nervously. 'Call it social.'

'What about Mum and— Mrs Hartinger and Mr Hartinger . . .'

'Mum and Dad? Is that what they got you to call them? Cheez!'

'Deet . . . do they . . . I mean . . . will they know where I've gone?'

'The hell they will, kid. Come on. Move it. Any stuff here you need to grab? You may as well take it. It's no use to them. Did they give you any cash, kid? Did they give you any spending? Take it with you, may as well. What have you got?'

'Nothing really.'

'Don't they give you spending money? What a couple of tight wads.'

'Pocket money's tomorrow, Deet.'

'Well, we don't have time to stay for it, kid. Come on. This your suitcase?'

He pulled the case down from the top of the wardrobe. 'Throw what you want in it and let's go. Hey, and don't forget that nice pen I gave you.'

'Er . . . I left it downstairs somewhere.'

'Too bad. No time. Better forget it.'

'But, Deet . . .'

'You want this book, do you? They been buying you books?'

'Yes, I—'

'Move it, kid! Move it! There's someone out there!'

But it wasn't the Hartingers back early. It was some of their neighbours. They walked up the driveway of a house across the street. The sound of the closing door echoed through the night.

'OK. Let's go now.'

Deet snapped the suitcase shut and ushered Tarrin out of the room. He stumbled slightly on the stairs.

'Careful, kid.'

'Where are we going, Deet . . . I mean, why . . . why are we going? I thought . . .'

'Tell you in the car, kid. Let's get out of here.'

As they walked along the corridor to the front door, Deet saw that the drawing-room door had swung back open and, before he had time to shut it again, Tarrin had looked in and seen Bradley lying there, his eyes blindfolded, his mouth gagged, his hands and feet bound.

'Deet . . . what did you do?'

'Never mind that. Needs must, kid. He'll be OK. They'll untie him when they get back.'

'Yes, but . . .'

'Grab your shoes. These them?'

'Yes, but . . .'

'This your coat?'

'Yes, only . . .'

'Let's go then.'

'Should I leave a note?'

'You kidding me, kid? Come on. Move. Let's go.'

Tarrin wriggled his feet into his trainers, managing

213

to get them both on without undoing the laces. Then he felt the cool night air on his face as Deet pulled the door open.

'Zip it up, kid,' Deet said, handing him his jacket. 'You don't want a chill.'

'Deet . . .' The night air woke and refreshed him, but he still had the stale taste in his mouth and that groggy feeling of interrupted sleep.

'Car's down there, kid.'

'You've got a car?'

Deet had never had a car before. He had always used taxis or trains. Tarrin hadn't even known that he could drive.

'It's a loaner. Come on.'

They crossed the road and as they approached the car Deet fired the key at it and all four of its yellow indicator lights flashed briefly as the locks clunked open.

'Get in, get your belt on and keep low, kid. And here – put that on your head.'

Deet pulled a folded baseball cap from his pocket, opened it up and put it on to Tarrin's head, yanking the peak down low. It was too low, and Tarrin reached to adjust it, but Deet knocked his hand away.

'Leave it. Just for now. Just till we're outta here.'

He bundled him into the back of the car, closed the door, got into the driver's seat and started the engine up.

Just as they came to the end of the street, a taxi turned in. Tarrin peered out and saw, from under the peak of the baseball cap, the Hartingers sitting in the back. They seemed not to notice him, nor Deet, nor the car. They were neither looking at, nor

214

speaking to, each other. Each was just looking blankly out of the window.

He caught a glimpse of Mr Hartinger's face. He looked terminally bored. It was as if he had fallen into a vacuum, into some immense empty space, and it had sucked out his soul. He looked like someone in perfect health, who had known, possessed and experienced everything that life had to offer, over and over again. Yes, he had tasted every dish on the menu, except for one rare delicacy – death.

Tarrin swivelled in his seat and looked back to see the cab stop by the house. That was the last he saw of the Hartingers. Deet turned left and left again, then took a right. Soon they were driving through an unfamiliar part of the city and Tarrin had no idea where he was.

He took off the baseball cap. Deet saw him do so in the rear-view mirror, but he didn't object.

'Deet . . .'

'When we get there, kid. I'll tell you when we get there.'

He concentrated on his driving for now, keeping an eye on the mirror, making sure that they weren't being followed.

'It's late, kid. Get some sleep for now.'

Despite his apprehensions, Tarrin slept. When he woke, Deet was shaking him, telling him to get out of the car.

It wasn't a motel this time, but a private house, which Deet must have rented. He showed Tarrin where his room was and told him he had his own bathroom and then left him to sleep. Tarrin heard Deet lock his door from the outside.

The last thing he heard before he fell asleep again was Deet calling to him through the door. 'Hey, I scammed them good, didn't I, kid? I scammed them good!'

Then he went on down the stairs, laughing to himself.

'Cereal, kid?'

'Thanks.'

Deet saw him looking around.

'Not the luxury you'd been getting comfortable with, I dare say, kid? Not the style you were getting accustomed to? Still, don't you worry, you'll soon forget all that. It's you and me, kid, back in business.'

'But what happened, Deet? I thought they . . . they'd paid you. I thought you'd sold me – to the Hartingers.'

Deet put the cereal packet down on the table so that Tarrin could help himself and he shoved the milk carton across.

'Sure they paid me, kid. And I didn't do anything till the cheque had cleared and the money was in the bank. Then I gave them a couple of weeks to get used to everything and to start taking things for granted, then I just snuck right in there and kiddernapped you away! Wasn't it the neatest bit of kiddernapping you ever saw, kid? Wasn't it?'

'But why, Deet?'

Deet's face clouded. 'I thought you were supposed to be smart, kid, and quick on the uppertake.'

'I just don't see why . . . if they paid . . . and you had what you wanted . . .'

'Because I've got the money, kid! I've got the money now! To pay for it!'

'Pay for what, Deet?'

'The PP. I've got the money now, kid, to pay for the PP implant. See, first I had you, but I didn't have the money. Then I had the money, but I didn't have you. But now, I've got you both! Smart, eh, kid? I couldn't tell you the plan in advance in case you blew it, accidental. But wasn't it a neat one? Didn't I scam them good?'

Tarrin felt his body grow cold, cold and clammy, and fear filled his heart.

'But, Deet—'

'You can be a kid for always now, see, kid. And you and me can be partners. You can do the kid act and make good money now for all your days. OK, the PP implant is big money up front, but when you think that it buys you a living for a hundred and fifty, maybe two hundred years . . .'

'But, Deet . . .'

'Why, it's not spending, it's investing, kid. You and me – partners! You'll never have to grow up now, kid. Soon as you have the implant, you can be a kid for always. You won't have to grow up ever! Isn't that great?'

'But, Deet . . .'

'Pass the coffee pot, kid.'

'I want to grow up.'

Deet stared at him. 'You what?'

'I don't want to be a boy forever, Deet . . . I want to grow up.'

'You want to grow up? What for?'

'I just do.'

'And do what?'

'I don't know.'

Deet sighed. 'Grown up, you're worth nothing, kid. But with the PP, you'll always be worth something, always wanted . . .'

'They aren't real, Deet.'

'Who aren't?'

'The PPs.'

'They're real enough.'

'They're spooky.'

'No one else thinks they're spooky.'

'Deet . . . I don't want to be a child for the rest of my life . . . I don't want to be a boy forever and ever. Always having to climb trees and drink lemonade and do what people expect boys to do because they read it once in a book somewhere . . . always to have to act like that, every afternoon, always and always, always moving on from town to town, always looking like a boy on the outside, while inside I get older and older—'

'You'll do as you're told, kid.'

'But, Deet, please.'

'You're making me angry, kid, very angry. When I think what I've done for you, the planning, the figuring out, the risks I took, and who for – all for you!'

'But, Deet—'

'Don't you "but" me. Don't you "but" your uncle Deet, after all he's done for you.'

'But you're not really my uncle, Deet . . .'

'I said not to "but" me, didn't I!'

They sat in silence. Tarrin tried to eat but couldn't. He let the spoon rest in the bowl.

Then suddenly he ran.

Deet was on to him immediately. Tarrin didn't even make it to the kitchen door.

'You're hurting me, Deet . . .'

'Don't make me!'

'You're twisting my arm!'

'I never took my hand to you, kid, not once, not ever – but there's a first time for everything – and you'd better believe it.'

He threw Tarrin back into his seat.

'Now eat.'

'I can't.'

'Got to stay healthy.'

'But, Deet . . .' Tarrin lifted the spoon to his mouth, the cereal fell from it, back into the bowl, the milk dripped. He began to sob and to cry.

'That's enough of that.'

'I can't help it.'

'Stop that.'

'I'm trying to.'

'Whadda you blubbering for?'

'I don't want to be a boy forever . . . I want to grow up, Deet. I want to grow up.'

'That's not an option any more. It can't even be considered.'

'I wanted to grow up.'

'Well, you're not going to, kid, so stop snivelling. The doc's going to be here soon and he's going to do it. He's a struck-off doc, but don't let that bother you. He's good and he's careful and it ain't going to hurt.'

'Deet . . .' The tears went on falling, the sobs shook his body.

'He'll give you an anaesthetic so you don't feel

nothing. Then after you'll maybe feel low for a couple of days. But it's nothing you won't soon get over.'

Tarrin's voice became a whine. He couldn't help himself. 'I wanted to grow up, I always wanted to grow up . . .'

Deet's voice grew hard and bitter. 'Maybe you did, kid, but it's no great shakes, growing up isn't what it's made out to be, and I know, so I can tell you. Millions would changes places with you, millions, just to have your chances, but for them it's too late. Why, if I could have had the PP when I was your age, I'd have taken it like a shot.'

'I'll kill myself. If you make me do this I'll kill myself and then I won't be worth anything to anyone!'

'No one's going to kill themselfs, kid. There's no reason or need for that. It's just a small time of adjustment is needed and then you'll see how well off you are and how you always wanted to be a kid forever after all.'

'But I don't, I don't . . .'

'I'm not arguing about it any more, kid.'

'Deet, please, I beg you, please, please . . .'

'I'm not discussing it, kid. You're making me angry now. And if we're going to be long-term partners, that's not a good idea, making your partner angry.'

Tarrin had a vision of the years and years ahead. Of the motels, the moving on; of being rented out for the afternoon to entertain those who had no children; of Deet spending every penny he made; of another train, another town, another customer, for years and years . . . of himself forever trapped in his own child's body, never able to grow, to escape from it, while inside, in his head, in his mind . . .

He went slowly but inexorably . . .

Mad.

Tarrin blacked out. He fell to the floor, taking the cereal bowl and the coffee pot with him. Luckily the coffee fell to the side and didn't scald him. Deet jumped to his feet and cursed, but when he realized that the boy wasn't faking he squatted down and gently picked Tarrin up in his arms and carried him to his room. He laid him on the bed and, as soon as he saw that he was coming round and that no damage was done, he left him there. Deet returned to the kitchen to clear up the mess, after first making sure that the bedroom door was securely locked behind him.

Tarrin's eyes finally focused and he looked around the room. How long had he lain there? Minutes or hours? Just moments, surely, and yet the room was dark. As his eyes adjusted to the gloom, he realized the curtains were still drawn. He got unsteadily to his feet and went to open them. But when he did, it was to find that there were locked and bolted heavy wooden shutters behind them.

He was trapped.

Light came in through the folds of the shutters. Tarrin lay on the bed, curled up, facing the shuttered window, watching a sliver of light inch its way towards him across the floor – towards him, towards noon, towards whenever the doctor would come.

Deet occasionally moved around downstairs. Tarrin could hear him opening and closing doors, putting the television on, then silence again when he turned it off.

Then the bell rang.

Tarrin curled up even more upon the bed, into a tighter ball, and he covered his face with his hands.

'I don't want to, Deet, I don't want to . . .'

Be a child.

Forever.

He waited to hear the footsteps on the stairs, but they didn't come. It didn't seem to be what he feared. There was joking and laughter and a woman's voice, complaining that Deet was teasing her and that, 'You always say the funniest things, Deet. You just make me giggle!'

Then, as if to prove the point, she let out a loud, affected guffaw. Whoever she was, she didn't sound like a doctor. They seemed to move into another room and there was more muffled laughter, as Deet kept her amused and she told him how funny he was.

Tarrin uncurled, but remained on the bed, watching the finger of sunlight come towards him. Maybe when it touched him, the doctor would come. That would be it, his time would be over.

How would he go?

He'd fight them. He'd kick and he'd bite and he'd scream and he'd kick and bite and spit and . . .

It wouldn't be any good. But he'd do it. He wouldn't go like a lamb to slaughter, walking meekly to his own execution.

I'll never grow up. I'll never grow up now. I'll always be a child. For all my life. Never know what it is to be grown up. Never know. Never, never know.

He sniffed, then wiped his tears from his face with

the fleshy part of his hand. The finger of light was still reaching for him. It was by the side of the bed now. In a short while it would be upon the cover, then it would touch him.

He reached out, to meet it halfway. He saw how it illuminated his hand, he saw the fine hairs, the delicate veins, the unblemished skin. Deet's wrists were hairy, his fingers strong and stubby, his arms thick and muscular, and the beard upon his face grew quickly. A few hours after he shaved, his chin had stubble on it again.

I'll never grow. Never grow to be a man. I'll always be a boy, always. Always and forever.

It had to be noon now. Maybe a little later. The sliver of light crept towards him.

'Hey, kid! Y'all right in there?'

Tarrin got to his feet, startled, and backed into a corner. Had the doctor come already after all? Had he not heard him? Was this it? Was it now?

Deet was outside, turning the key in the lock. Tarrin clenched his hands, feeling the sharpness of his fingernails against his own flesh.

He'd go for his eyes. When Deet came for him, he'd go for his eyes.

The door opened slowly.

'Y'all right in there, kid? You got the blues? You've not done nothing stupid, have you? Here – I brought someone to cheer you up.'

He stood aside to let a woman enter. She was blonde and pretty and wore a lot of perfume and lipstick. She was carrying a tray with plate of oven chips, fish fingers and peas upon it.

'Here you are, honey,' she said. 'Brought you a

little something to eat. Good, proper home cooking. I warmed it all up myself.'

Then, as she put the tray down, she turned to Deet and said, 'Isn't he the cutest thing, Deet?'

'Just like I said.'

'Why, he's a darling!' she said. And she would have ruffled Tarrin's hair, only he saw it coming and backed away.

'Ah – he's a shy one too. That's just so cute!'

Deet beamed with approval. He looked like somebody showing off his car, his pride and joy, in an effort to impress a new girlfriend. 'This here is Miss Lindy Rae, kid,' he said. 'She's a friend of mine. Well – say hello.'

'Hello,' Tarrin mumbled.

Miss Lindy Rae wriggled the fingers of her right hand at him by way of reply.

'After the op, kid, she'll be coming along with us. She'll be your new ma. We'll be like one big happy family! What do you say to that?'

Tarrin said nothing, so Deet turned to Miss Lindy Rae and said, 'He's a little nervy, about the forthcoming . . . but once that's over, we'll all be getting on like a barn on fire.'

'I'm sure we will,' Miss Lindy Rae beamed. 'Well, you enjoy your meal, honey, and we'll see each other later.'

She turned to leave. Deet looked at Tarrin and said, 'Eat up, kid. Be a while before you get another plateful. No more food after this till the PP's all done.'

Deet glanced around the room, as if to check that Tarrin hadn't been up to anything, then he nodded and followed Miss Lindy out. Tarrin looked at the food but he left it untouched. He went to examine the shutters, to see if there was some way he could unlock them or break them apart. But they were firmly secured and they were solid, built to pivot on steel bars secured to the stonework.

He went back to lie on the bed. He listened to the sounds of the afternoon and he watched the finger of light move over the bed, then over the carpet and towards the other side of the room. It touched the skirting board, it began to ascend, it crept on, up and up along the wall.

He felt hungry now. He went and ate some of the cold chips and one of the cold fish fingers and he drank from the glass of water he had also been brought.

Sometimes Deet and the lady were silent, sometimes he heard their voices. Sometimes they laughed, sometimes they seemed to be talking confidentially – maybe about him.

Then the sliver of light was going, fading, and the whole room was turning dark.

Tarrin wondered if the Hartingers would be looking for him. Of course they would. They'd have called for the police the moment they had discovered Bradley tied up on the floor. They'd have run up the stairs to see if Tarrin was all right, and they'd have found his room empty and his suitcase gone.

Had Bradley seen that it was Deet? Maybe. Maybe not.

Another sliver of light entered the room now. It was silver, the light from the moon. It began the same journey, inching its way across the floor.

Then Tarrin heard something. A soft, quiet sound. The sound of somebody stealing away and not wanting anyone to know it. It was the front door, being quietly opened and as quietly shut. Then there were footsteps out in the street and then Miss Lindy Rae's voice laughing and her saying, 'But you just crack me up, Deet!'

And Deet saying, 'Keep it down, will ya? We don't want the kid to hear.'

Then the sounds of car doors being opened and a car being driven away.

He was alone in the house. They'd left him alone. How long for, he had no means of knowing. Maybe for a few minutes, maybe for long hours. But if he wanted to get out, it had to be now.

13

Escape

Kinane hadn't given up. Not even now that some-body else had beaten him to it. He'd ask around, look around, he'd find him again. He'd find him.

He walked casually along the street, past the squad cars, and engaged one of the officers there in conver-sation.

'Something happening here, officer?'

The man was bored and tired. He'd been left outside to stand guard while his superiors sat in the comfort of the Hartingers' drawing room taking statements from both them and their unfortunate employee.

'Yeah. Kid gone.'

'You don't say?'

'Yesterday night.'

'How'd a thing like that happen?'

'Reckon someone was watching the place, waited till they'd gone out, just the kid and the one guy in there, banged on the door and jumped him.'

'Well, well . . .'

'It's how it goes. With kids like gold dust, what can you expect? If you've got food in a world full of starving people . . .'

'Someone's going to try and steal it.'

'Guess they are.'

Kinane knew instinctively who had taken him, the man who had sold him. It wasn't a new trick. Sell what you had for as much as you could get and then steal it back again.

'Think you'll get the kid back?' he asked the policeman.

'Who knows,' the officer shrugged. 'It's a big world and a big city and there's a lot of hiding places in it, and there's so many people around willing to buy a kid, no questions asked . . .'

'It's a sorry state of affairs.' Kinane looked up at the house.

'You got any kids yourself?' he asked the policeman.

'Me? I wish. You?'

But before Kinane could answer him, the policeman broke into a smile. 'Hey, tell you what – I saw a baby though,' he said, mightily pleased with himself.

'No way!' Kinane said.

'Sure did!'

'When?'

'Just a day or two ago.'

'Never!'

'Oh yeah.' The incident had turned into the policeman's favourite topic of conversation.

'So where was that?'

'Couple of streets away.'

'Never!'

'Yeah. Tell you what else . . .'

'Yeah?'

'She gave me a smile . . .'

'Gave you a smile?'

'And I got to hold her. Her mother let me hold her. And as we were going along, she reached out from the pram, and put her little hand around my finger and held on to it for a little while, just like that.'

'Well!'

'Now that was something. That doesn't happen every day.'

'And that was right round here?'

'Just around the corner there.'

'Well, I'd have liked to have seen that.'

'You ever seen a baby?'

'You mean for real?'

'Yeah. I don't mean TV. Everyone's seen one on TV. I mean for real.'

Kinane took his time to answer, then he nodded and said, 'Yes, I've seen a baby. Yes.'

'Held one?' the policeman said, feeling that he was still in the lead.

Kinane nodded. 'Yes,' he said, 'held one too . . . but that was a long time ago now . . . a long, long time ago. Well, I guess I'll be going.'

'OK. Nice to talk to you.'

'Hope you find him, officer – the kid that was taken.'

'Well, he's got to be somewhere. You take care now.'

The policeman looked after Kinane as he walked away. Had he mentioned to the guy that the missing kid was a boy? He didn't think so, but maybe he had. Yeah, he must have done. Or how else would the man have known?

*

229

Tarrin tried the door handle, quietly at first, in case Deet was still in the house after all. He listened and waited, then, no longer caring how much noise he made, he tried with all his strength to break the lock, but it was useless. In a fit of pique and anger he kicked at the door with his foot, but it made little impact, other than to cause him to lose balance and stumble to the floor.

He stayed there, lying on his back, kicking at one of the door panels with the heel of his shoe, trying to break it. But it wouldn't give. He kicked at it again, over and over, but it was solid and just wouldn't crack.

Then, as he kicked it one final time, he heard a sound. Not the sound of breaking or splintering, but a sound of metal on wood, a tinkle, a clatter.

He crawled to the door and lay face down, trying to see out through the gap between the base of the door and the floorboards.

It was the key. Deet had left it in the door and Tarrin must have kicked it out of the lock. There it lay, on the other side of the door, glinting in the light of the bulb above the landing.

Tarrin tried to wriggle his fingers under the door to retrieve it, but it had fallen too far away. He stood and looked around the bedroom, then went into the bathroom, took the toilet roll from its holder, unwound all the paper and carefully unravelled the cardboard inside, then he flattened it as best as he could and went back to the door.

He fed the cardboard out under the door, slightly to the right of the key, and then tried to scoop the key in towards him, but he misjudged and only succeeded in pushing it a little further away.

No!

He tried to reach it again, but the cardboard was now an inch or two short. He pulled the cardboard back in, tore and folded it lengthways to make it longer, then pushed it out again – gradually, carefully, no mistakes this time.

There. He hooked the peeled cardboard round the key and pulled it towards him. It moved closer, then the cardboard slid off, so he had to bring it back in, smooth it out, feed it out again and try once more.

Little by little he reeled the key in nearer to the door. Finally there it was, he could almost touch it with his fingers. But not quite.

The gap wasn't wide enough for him to get it in under the door.

Only it must be, it had to be. He tried to reach it, endeavouring to thrust his fingers under the door, but he only succeeded in skinning his knuckles.

He got up and went to the bathroom, washed the blood off his hand and opened the cabinet to find a sticking plaster. There weren't any. But there was a nail file. He wrapped his hand in some of the clean paper from the toilet roll, took the nail file and returned to the bedroom.

He lay down on the floor and started to file at the base of the door.

A few grains of sawdust at a time fell away from the wood. The blood went on flowing from his skinned fingers, turning the paper bandage red. Perspiration formed on his forehead; he felt it trickle under his arms and down his back. He went on filing. It was like grating rock-hard cheese.

After half an hour, a small indentation could be seen in the base of the door, like the top arch of a mouse hole. He could get his little finger through it. He could touch the key now, but the hole wasn't big enough for him to pull the key inside. He went on filing. His arm, hand and fingers ached, but at least the bleeding had stopped. He went on filing. Another fifteen, twenty minutes. Then he tried again.

He had it. He had it with his little finger, and he carefully and deliberately drew it in towards him, through the little mouse hole he had made. Here it was. He had the key.

Tarrin stood up, stiff and sore, his hands trembling slightly. He steadied them and then reached to put the key into the lock.

It wouldn't turn.

He felt that flush again, of coldness and fear. It had to turn, had to, had to turn, had to – why wouldn't it turn? He tried it again, again, again, with all his force, harder and harder, and then he realized.

He was turning it the wrong way. Fear, urgency and panic had made him blind to the obvious. He tried the other way. The bolt inside the lock slid away from the frame. Then he turned the handle and opened the door and stepped out, on to the landing.

He stood listening, afraid that he had heard Deet's car pulling up outside. But it was someone else. He hurried down the stairs, ran to the kitchen, then to the other rooms, looking to see if Deet had left any money. He found some change lying on the sofa, which had maybe fallen from Deet's pocket.

He ran to the front door, but there was a double lock on it, which meant that even to open it from the inside you needed a key. He went back to the kitchen and tried the side door – same thing again. He tried to open a window, but the windows were screwlocked into their frames, and again a key was needed.

He stood there in the kitchen, looking around, like a trapped animal. He made himself breathe deeply, forced himself to think. OK. He needed something heavy . . . heavy, heavy, heavy . . . he saw a solid castiron pot hanging above the cooker. He took it down and carried it over to the window by the sink. He swung the pot with both hands.

The smash seemed terrifically loud to him. Had anyone heard? If so, they didn't come running. He found some oven gloves and used them to pick the shards of glass from the window frame so that he would not be cut as he climbed through.

Just as he was about to go, he noticed the baseball cap which Deet had made him wear the night before. He stuffed it into his coat pocket. Then he was carefully climbing out through the window and then he had dropped down to the path. Then he was gone.

He'd been gone exactly four and a quarter minutes when a car turned the corner and stopped outside the house. There were three people in it – Deet, Miss Lindy Rae and a man who sat in the back seat, with a doctor's medical case upon his knee, while beside him was a leather bag, containing a selection of drugs and surgical instruments.

'Here it is, Doc,' Deet said. 'You get your money when it's done.'

The man in the back nodded and reached for the door handle. The three of them got out of the car and walked up to the house.

14

Dainty Town

If nobody knew where the boy was, then maybe somebody would know where Deet was, and when he found where Deet was, he would find the boy too. That was Kinane's way of thinking. He was in no mood to give up yet, not by a long way.

You couldn't hide a child indefinitely. Not if you wanted to make money out of him, which Deet undoubtedly did. So Kinane put the word around that good information was something he'd be willing to pay for, then he sat in a bar, with his mobe beside him, waiting for it to ring.

Someone would spot him, sooner or later. You couldn't hide a child in this city, not for long. People would come to him. Like bees to the flower. Like jackals to a carcass.

Tarrin pulled the baseball cap down and hurried on through the night. He neither knew where he was, nor where he was going, but he moved swiftly and with the appearance of certainty just the same. If he acted self-assured and confident, people might leave him alone.

As he walked, some lines from the Gideon Bible –

those bibles left in every motel room – came into his head.

The foxes have holes and the birds of the air have nests;
But the son of man hath not where to lay his head.

That was him all right – a son of man, with no one to turn to.

Where to go? Where to hide? Where to shelter? He was the most conspicuous thing in the world – a child, alone in the night.

It was like money walking the streets, like a gold bar left out for the taking.

Tarrin squared his shoulders, increased the length of his stride, plunged his hands deep into his coat pockets, even swaggered a little, the way he had seen Deet do.

Maybe people would think he was grown up, an adult, as long as they didn't see his face – yes, a young man, a small one, on the slim and the slender side, but an adult just the same, and they would leave him alone.

'Was that a kid?'

'No. I don't know. Was it?'

A man and a woman stopped to look back at him. He felt their eyes staring and he hurried on around the corner. They'd only sounded curious, they hadn't sounded as if they'd meant him any harm, but you never knew, never knew at all.

Where to go? There had to be somewhere. The Hartingers? Back to the Hartingers? They'd be looking for him, wanting him back, if only because he had cost them so much money. And the police had to be looking for him too, and possibly for Deet. He'd surely be on the list of suspects.

Only where did the Hartingers live, in relation to where he was now? The city was immense, it was a panorama of streets and houses, high-rises and office blocks; it went on to every horizon.

> *There's a green land far away,*
> *Going to get there one fine day.*

Only where was it, that green land, and why did he feel he belonged there?

No, Tarrin didn't want to go back to the Hartingers. He didn't want to be a possession any more, a trophy, a pet. He didn't want to belong to anyone, not to Deet, not to the Hartingers, not to some stranger who had hired him by the hour. He wanted somebody who belonged to *him*.

'Was that a boy?'

It was a woman's voice, a good, kind, nice voice, a voice of concern.

'No. It couldn't be. Not out on his own. Not in the night.'

Tarrin ducked down an alleyway. It was long and dark and dangerous-looking, but then the open streets were hardly safe. He wondered if Deet would be back yet, and his absence discovered. He'd come after him, he knew it.

He had to go to the police then. If it was Deet or the Hartingers, it had to be the Hartingers, the lesser of the evils.

And yet.

Yet what?

237

Still he walked on. He saw a police car cruising along past the end of the alley. He could have run after it, waved, shouted, 'Stop! Stop! I'm the boy! The one who was kiddernapped! From the rich people's house!'

But he didn't.

He walked on, telling himself, repeating over and over, that, yes . . .

> *There's a green land far away.*
> *Going to get there . . .*

He left the alley and walked on along a wide, empty street. Behind the curtains of a hundred houses there was the flickering of television screens.

They'll have my picture up, he thought. The Hartingers will have my picture, up on a lamp post. Just like I was a cat gone missing. It'll be my picture and underneath it will say: 'Reward. Have you seen this boy? Reward for any information leading to his recovery. Contact . . .'

Just like a little lost cat.

I want to go home. Mum, Dad, somebody. Come and take me home. I must have had a home once. I want to go home.

'Cheez! Did you see that?'

'What? What you talking about?'

Tarrin looked up and saw trouble. Two men standing under a street lamp. Two chancers in search of an opportunity. And one had just walked by.

He put his head down and kept going. One of the men turned to the other.

'Didn't you see that?'

'What? What?'

'Kid, wasn't it?'

'Who was?'

'Him there, that there.'

'Nah!'

'It was, I'm telling ya.'

'Kid on his own?'

'I'm telling ya!'

'Let's go get him then!'

'Let's go!'

'Money walking the streets!'

The two men took to their heels and came after him, but Tarrin was already running. He fled down another alleyway and cut across some back gardens and then he hid, as quiet as a sleeping bird, hunched by the side of a conservatory, where the shadows were long and deep.

The men looked for him a long time, but gave up in the end. They walked away, cursing their luck, but somehow finding it amusing too.

'Could have sold him for a bundle.'

'Easy street!'

'Or kept him and set him working.'

'People'll pay anything for a kid.'

'Come on. Let's get a beer.'

Tarrin waited another ten minutes, just in case they were shamming and hadn't really gone, then he crept out from his hiding place and climbed over the wall to drop down into the alleyway at the back.

He took out the money he had found on the sofa and counted it. It wasn't much. Enough for a drink and something to eat, but that was all.

What'm I going to do?

The bleak reality hit him. He had to return to the Hartingers. There was nowhere else for him to go that wasn't somewhere worse. It was his only choice – to find a police station, to explain who he was, to turn himself in.

I was free. I was free. For a few brief hours I was free, Tarrin thought, both proud and sad. I was me, and I didn't belong to anyone. And I didn't have to pretend to be a child – because I *was* a child. I didn't have to be a child for an hour or a morning or an afternoon – I was me. Just me. For a little while, I was me. To be who you really were, it was the best thing in the world. Even when it meant being alone.

Tarrin moved on into the night. Attracted by a haze of light, he hurried towards it. He found himself in a warren of cobbled streets and small, picturesque squares, lit up with the neon glare of clubs, bars and restaurants. There was bustle and movement and people of all colours and nationalities mingling together. And for once nobody seemed interested in the small, childish figure. They were preoccupied with themselves and their companions.

He stopped, looked around, tilted the baseball cap back on his head, then took it off. Nobody remarked on anything. Nobody cared. They barely gave him a second glance. They weren't interested in him. He was nothing unusual to them.

He didn't understand it. Why weren't they staring at him, hassling him, whispering to each other about him, saying, 'Look – it's a child, it's a boy!'

They let him be.

'Excuse me . . .'

The man looked at him. 'Yes?'

'Is there a police station around here?'

The man pointed. 'Down there, left, left again, keep going. Ten minutes' walk. You can't miss it.'

'Thank you.'

'No problem.'

The man smiled, nodded, walked on.

Tarrin had been braced for all the expected questions as to what a child like him was doing out on his own. But they hadn't come. He felt surprised and puzzled, even strangely disappointed.

Tarrin followed the man's directions and went along the street he had pointed to. This street was also cobbled, with narrow pavements, and it was lined with bars and cafes. He came to the end of it and turned left. This street was darker. No bars or cafes here, save for one, halfway along, a small beacon of light in the darkness. As Tarrin passed it, he looked in, down through a street-level metal grille and into a basement room.

He saw the most amazing, the most wonderful sight. He stopped and he stared, his heart pounding with excitement, with disbelief.

The room was full of children. There must have been forty or maybe even fifty of them. They were sitting at tables playing card games, or sipping from drinks and talking, or they were playing table football or computer games.

But they were children, all of them, even the people working there, the waiter and the waitress and the boy behind the bar.

Children. They were all children.

Children . . . I've found children.

Tarrin moved closer to the grille. He had to be mistaken. But no, they were children, right enough. Only what were they all doing there? What was going on? A celebration? A party? A birthday, perhaps?

He went to the steps and walked down them to the entry door. A sign above it read Dainty Town.

A security man stood there in the shadows. He was no child. He was big and mean and meant business.

But when he saw Tarrin he just nodded and smiled and said, 'Evening, sir.'

And he held the door open.

Tarrin looked at him, shocked, surprised, but trying not to show it.

'Evening.'

'Please, go right in, sir.'

'Thank you.'

Tarrin entered and the door closed behind him. He looked around him with a sense of delight mingled with disbelief. This wasn't possible, was it? But it was. The adult world had gone and was forgotten. They were all children here, every one.

As he stood, looking around him, a hand touched his shoulder and he turned to find himself looking at the prettiest girl in the world. Or if she wasn't the prettiest in the whole world, she was the prettiest girl he had ever seen. Her hair was brown and her teeth were white and straight and her smile could have melted chocolate, and although she was a stranger to him he had the feeling that he knew her from somewhere. She wore small heart-shaped glasses with rose-tinted lenses, perched on the tip of her nose.

'Hello, stranger,' she said. 'I've not seen you here before.'

'N-no,' Tarrin stuttered. 'N-never . . . I've never been . . . that is . . . I never knew . . .'

To help him out of his difficulties, she held up the glass she had been drinking from and let him see that it was empty.

'What say you buy a girl a drink?' she said.

'Y-yes,' Tarrin said. 'Of course.'

She beckoned to the bartender.

'What can I get you, folks?' the barman said.

Well, he was the bar-child really. He looked about ten, with stick-em-up hair and a freckled face. 'Name your poison,' he said, in a squeaky voice.

'A juice, please,' Tarrin said. 'Orange.'

'And the lady?' the barman asked.

'The usual, Jim,' the girl said.

'Coming up.'

Tarrin watched with some astonishment as the barman picked a glass up, took it to a bottle labelled Finest Malt Whisky and pressed it against the optic. He put it down in front of the girl and got Tarrin an orange juice. Tarrin handed money over and waited for change – but it didn't come. He realized with dismay that he'd just spent all his money on two small drinks. He looked warily around the room and saw, to his amazement, that everything in the bar was child-sized. The tables, the chairs, the lot. The signs for the toilets read 'Little Girls' Room' and 'Little Boys'.

'Well, cheers,' the girl said. 'Good luck. Here's mud in your eye.'

She put the glass to her lips and took a sip from it. 'My, my!' she said. 'That hits the spot every time.'

Then she made herself comfortable on a bar stool, invited Tarrin to do the same on the stool next to her, curled one leg around the other and said, 'So tell me about yourself. What do you do?'

Tarrin looked perplexed. 'Do?'

'Yes. Do. You sing? Dance? Tell fortunes? Play an instrument? What do you do?'

He stared at the little girl. She really was so, so pretty. In a way, quite unbelievably pretty. In fact, the more he looked at her, the more he had the feeling that he had seen her before.

'I . . . I . . . don't really do anything.'

The girl laughed. 'You have to do something, mister. And how come I've not seen you here before? You new here? You on tour?'

'Tour?'

'Yes, tour. Are you touring a show?'

'A show?'

'Aren't you in show business? You're either in show business or you're in the wrong bar.'

'I'm sorry?'

'You're sorry? What're you sorry for?' And she giggled, though he couldn't see what was funny. His eyes drifted over the other people in the dimly lit room. He had never seen so many children, never.

'What's your name, mister?'

The word sounded strange, in the mouth of a child. 'Mister!' It seemed harsh, world-weary, a little cynical. He was more and more convinced that he had seen her before, but where?

'Tarrin,' he said. 'My name's Tarrin.'

'That's nice. Unusual, but nice.'

The little girl sipped her whisky. Was it *real* whisky? Surely not. Yet it smelt like whisky, and Tarrin knew what that smelt like. Sometimes Deet used to drink it. He kept a bottle in his suitcase 'for emergencies.' And the other children in the bar, they were drinking spirits too, and beer, and some had bottles of wine at their tables.

'What's your name?' Tarrin asked.

'Davina,' she said. 'Miss Davina.'

Then he knew who she was and where he had seen her. The poster, outside the club.

Miss Davina 'Bo-Bo' Peep. The cutest thing on two legs. And there had been a photograph of the prettiest girl you had ever seen (even prettier than Miss Virginia Two Shoes), dressed up in ribbons and bows.

He remembered what Deet had said about her.

'Forty if she's a day, kid. Forty at least and then some.'

'She's had the PP, Deet?'

'You betcha,' he'd said. 'And you think of the money she's making. There's one rich little girl.'

Miss Davina had taken her tinted glasses off now and set them beside her drink, on the bar. Tarrin stared at her, looking right into her eyes.

'Why do you stare so, honey?'

He looked around again, at all the children there.

None of them were children at all. They were all PPs, their growth stopped forever.

Forty if she's a day, kid.

Forty years old and then some.

He couldn't stop himself from staring at her. She looked so pretty, so sweet, so nice.

Forty if she's a day . . .

She sipped at her drink and then put it back on the bar. Whatever he had found absent in her eyes, she had seen in his.

'Good lordy,' she said. 'You're real. You're real, aren't you? You're real?'

The room fell quiet. An uncomfortable silence ensued as the customers turned or swivelled in their chairs and looked at the boy at the bar, sitting next to Miss D.

'Is he real?'

'She say he was real?'

'He real, is he? Isn't he a PP?'

Tarrin looked back at them, a knot tightening in his stomach, feeling inexplicably afraid, not knowing if he was afraid more of them or of what they had become.

They were men and women; old men and old women in some cases. They were professional children, entertainers, people who sold an image of childhood to those who could have no families of their own. They were adults in children's bodies.

For an awful moment Tarrin felt that they would rise from their chairs, rise as one person, advance on him, take him, lynch him, destroy him for being the reality of what they were only the appearance – avenge themselves on him for still having the opportunity which had been taken from them . . .

The opportunity to grow up.

But they didn't seem resentful, they just seemed curious, and wistful, and maybe a little sad to see this reminder of who and what they had once been. Then, one by one, they turned away and resumed their games, their conversations and their drinks.

Miss Davina sipped at her whisky and ordered another.

'Want one, honey?'

'I'm OK – thanks.'

His juice was barely touched. He watched her drink. She was old enough to be his mother, maybe even his grandmother, yet she looked . . . she was . . . just a girl.

'So what brings you here, honey?'

'I just . . . found it.'

'No one told you?'

'No.'

'You're on the run, aren't you? There's someone after you.'

He nodded.

'Someone own you?'

Tarrin hesitated. He wondered how much it was safe to tell her. But before he could answer, a voice rang out from a dark corner of the bar.

'You *cheated*!'

'I didn't cheat!'

'You cheated! I saw you! You did!'

An argument had broken out between two of the card players. They were sitting at their table, squabbling like any two children over a game of snap. Yet the game was poker, and there was money on the table, and the two boys playing the game were not boys at all, but men, maybe thirty or forty or fifty years old, and there were two or three thousand units at stake.

'I'm telling you, that wasn't your card!'

'And I'm telling you it was!'

One of the two boys lurched to his feet, knocking against the table as he did so and overturning a bottle of beer. It rolled off and fell to the floor, clattering but not breaking, spilling brown liquid and foam.

'Hey! You two! That's enough!'

The barman hurried out from behind the bar to fetch the doorman to stop the trouble. Both of the card players were on their feet now, squaring up to each other. One pushed the other on the shoulder with the heel of his hand, the other retaliated in kind. Tarrin watched, fascinated and a little horrified. They stood fighting like two little boys, like Tweedledum and Tweedledee quarrelling over a rattle.

'You do that again, I'll kill you!'

They were both drunk and bleary and by the look of them had been drinking for most of the night.

It's way past your bedtime, Tarrin couldn't help but think. You ought to be tucked up and fast asleep by now.

The doorman hurried over to break up the trouble. His adult stature allowed him to tower over everybody in the room. He had to stoop slightly or his head would have touched the ceiling.

'OK, gentlemen, OK. What seems to be the problem here?'

'He started it.'

'Did not!'

'He was cheating.'

'I was not! He was the one who was cheating. He was!'

'OK, OK . . . I think you've both had enough, gents, let's call it a night now, huh?'

Reluctantly, sulkily, the two boys gathered up their things, their money, their coats, and first one and then, after an interval, the other staggered out into the night.

As he left, the second boy swore at the doorman, letting fly with a great long stream of threats and expletives, telling him what he would do to him if he ever caught him in the dark.

The doorman ignored him.

'Goodnight now, sir,' he said.

The boy went out in the street, almost walked into a dustbin, then lurched on his way, looking like a drunken, bad-tempered child, who should never have been let near a glass of alcohol, but who had opened up the drinks cabinet while his parents had been out.

Miss Davina smiled. 'They're always quarrelling,' she said. 'They start off all right, but it always ends in a fight.'

'Who are they?'

'You don't know?'

'No.'

'It's Baby-Face Chester and Little Joe.'

'What do they do though?'

'*Everybody's favourite ragamuffins – the naughtiest boys on earth. The two little rascals you wish you'd had.* They do a comedy act and work the clubs. Or people hire them for parties and they fall in the trifle and have food fights and things like that.'

'Are they brothers?' Tarrin asked.

'I don't think so.'

Tarrin sipped at his orange juice. He watched with fascination as a boy drinking alone at a table extracted an expensive-looking cigar from his pocket. It was in a small tin tube. He unscrewed the top, took the cigar out, smelt its aroma, clipped the end, put it into his mouth, then lit it with his lighter. The cigar seemed huge in his hand. Yet he seemed unaware of any incongruity, and he went on smoking, quite unselfconsciously, as he sipped his brandy and read his newspaper.

Further down along the bar two girls, who looked no more than ten or eleven years old, were perched on bar stools, drinking cocktails with cherries and little paper umbrellas in them. One seemed to be commiserating with the other, whose heavily made-up face was streaked with dried tears.

'He said he loved me,' she told her friend. 'He told me he loved me and we could have a life together. And then he left me for her!'

She glared towards the far corner of the bar, where a boy and a girl sat together in the shadows, staring into each other's eyes, holding each other's hands.

'Men!' the girl at the bar complained to her friend. 'You can't trust them!'

A boy sitting along from them looked up from his glass of wine, turned his head in their direction and said, 'Oh yeah? And you think women are any better? Because if you do, I could tell you stories . . .'

'Leave us alone,' the girl's friend said. 'We're not talking to you. We don't want to hear your stories. And mind your own business.'

Then she beckoned the bar-boy over.

'Same again, Jim,' she said. 'Large ones.'

Tarrin couldn't help but feel that the whole scene before his eyes was contrived, unreal, that at any moment the director would step from behind the scenery and shout, 'Cut! OK! Stop the camera! Not bad, but let's go again on that one, and little more pizzazz in it this time, boys and girls.'

But it was real.

'A penny for them—'

Miss Davina had been watching his face all the while. She was smiling now. 'What were you thinking?'

'Oh, I don't know . . . just how . . .'

'You don't want to be like us?'

'It's not that.'

'You don't like us?'

'No, no, it's just . . .'

'You feel sorry for us. You pity us. And, in another way, you're very afraid of us too?'

Tarrin didn't answer her. He looked down and he toyed with his glass, moving it around the bar, watching the damp circles it made.

'And you wouldn't like to be like us . . .'

'Nobody wants to die, I suppose,' Tarrin said. 'And nobody wants to grow old either. But maybe nobody really wants to be a child forever, either, though they maybe thought so once . . .'

'So what does everyone want, honey?'

'I don't know . . . I don't know if they know either. Why . . . that is . . . when . . . did you . . .?'

'Have the PP? Long time ago, honey, when you were just a gleam in your daddy's eye. My parents wanted me to have it. They didn't want their little girl

251

to grow up. I was always going to be my daddy's little girl. They intended it for the best, I guess.'

'Are they . . .?'

'No. They're dead now. You can only postpone it – maybe for a long time, but it still happens to everyone in the end. Come on.'

She finished her drink and got to her feet. Tarrin hesitated.

'Where are you . . .?'

'I'm going home. You want to come home with me?'

'Well, I . . .'

'Come on, honey. I'll hide you. You'll be safe there. Look, I'm old enough to be your mother,' the little girl said, and her little girl's eyes looked at him with compassion and some sadness.

'Well, you see . . .'

'Where else have you got to go, kid?' she said.

Tarrin hesitated still, not knowing if he could trust her.

'Come on, honey. Like I say, I'm old enough to be your mother. Come home with me. I get lonely sometimes. I always wanted a kid of my own. I'll take care of you. You can be my boy. You can hide away there. You can grow up. That's what you want, isn't it? Then when you're big and tall and starting shaving, you'll be safe. You'll be grown up. They'll all leave you alone. And you can look after your poor, old ma. And that'll be me!'

She giggled and Tarrin smiled too at the absurdity of this pretty little girl being the mother to some hulking and possibly moody adolescent.

'What do you say, honey? Because I'm going now. I need my beauty sleep.'

Miss Davina gathered her coat about her. It was soft and expensive, with a fake fur collar, which perfectly framed her gorgeous curls and her pretty little face. She picked her tinted glasses up from the bar.

'Well, honey?'

Still he hesitated. He wondered whether he could trust her promise of safety. Yet where else did he have to go. His only other choices were the hunters on the streets or a cat basket back at the Hartingers' – prey or pet. He wanted to be neither.

Tarrin nodded and got to his feet. He was a little taller than her. Not by much, just a few centimetres.

'Thank you. If I could stay for a while . . .'

'Let's go then, honey,' Miss Davina said, and she called goodnight to the bar-boy.

'Goodnight, Jimmy.'

'Goodnight, Miss Davina.'

She led the way to the door. The doorman opened it for her and said goodnight to them both. Miss Davina took Tarrin's arm as they walked on along the street.

It felt a little strange to have her arm linked in his and to feel the fur collar of her coat brush against him from time to time as they walked.

'You can call me Davina, honey,' she said. 'Or, if you want to, you can call me Ma.'

How could he ever call her Ma?

She was only eleven years old.

He looked back once towards the bar they had come from. He saw the neon sign-board flash on and off – Dainty Town – then darkness – then Dainty Town again.

He couldn't see inside it any more. And there was no way he could have seen Jimmy the bar-boy go to a quiet corner and pick up his mobe and make a call to the number he had been given and say, 'That merchandise you were looking for? I may be able to give you a location on that. Of course, I'll be needing the rest of the money first. That's right. No dough, no info. OK. I'll expect to see you then. OK. Gotta go. Got people wanting drinks here. OK.'

He killed the call and went to serve the children at the bar.

A small eight-year-old-boy had come in. He wanted a vodka and tomato juice for his companion, with a Scotch on the rocks for himself.

'I don't think I've seen you before,' Jimmy said. 'You've got to be over eighteen to buy alcohol in here. Let me see your ID.'

The two children took their ID cards out and placed them on the bar.

'OK,' Jimmy said. 'That'll do.'

He got them their drinks.

At first Tarrin wondered why a Kiddernapper didn't come after them, or why Miss Davina had never been snatched from the street and bundled into a car, taken off to be sold to some rich, childless couple like the Hartingers, with a big, empty home. But he didn't wonder for long. There was something about her, the look in her eyes, the way she walked and held herself. Anyone could see – who cared to look long enough – that she wasn't a girl at all. She had none of the mannerisms. Sure, she could probably imitate them, as she must do in her stage act, but now she walked ahead, determined, confident, grown up.

A Kiddernapper would know from looking at her, though more amateur eyes might have been fooled. Tarrin felt that if she was safe, then he would be too. People would assume that he was a PP as well.

Just as long as he didn't run into Deet.

When they got to a road junction she let go of his arm, positioned herself conspicuously on the kerb, put two fingers into her mouth and let out a shrill, piercing whistle to attract a passing cab.

The taxi did a U-turn in the street, but the night was busy, with bars and theatres closing, and there were plenty of other people looking for a ride home. A man jumped in front of them and put his hand on the taxi door.

'Take me to—'

'Get the hell away from my taxi!' Miss Davina screamed.

The man turned and looked down at her, half shocked, half amused.

'Yeah. It's you I'm talking to!' she said in her little girl's voice. 'That's my cab. I whistled for it. Now get your hand off the door!'

The man glared at her. 'Now look here, little girl, I don't know what you're doing out at this time of night—'

'Don't you little girl me, you great bozo!' Miss Davina said. 'I'm old enough to be your mother and if I was I'd drum some manners into you for taking other people's taxis! So out of my way!'

The taxi driver watched, amused but otherwise

indifferent to what was going on. The big man stood his ground, so Miss Davina ducked between his legs and pulled Tarrin through after her and, before they could be stopped, they were in the cab.

'Where to, lady?'

'I'll tell you when we get there. It's straight on for now.'

The taxi pulled away. Miss Davina glared out of the window at the man who had tried to take her taxi.

'I hate that,' she said. 'They way they patronize you. They way they think you've got no rights and they always come first because they've got grown-up bodies. Well, I tell you, honey, a lot of adults may have grown-up bodies, but they've only got pea-sized minds. I just hate being small sometimes and never getting taken seriously. OK, left here, driver.'

The cab turned off the main road and stopped outside an apartment block. Miss Davina paid the driver and gave him a tip. She had to stand on tiptoe to hand the money in through the window.

'Thank you, miss.'

'Thank you.'

The taxi drove off to find another fare.

Her apartment was not large, but spacious enough. It was furnished the way she was dressed, in designer fabrics and fake furs. The carpets on the floor were deep and soft. Tarrin took his shoes off, afraid of making marks.

'Nightcap?' Miss Davina asked, heading straight for the collection of bottles on the shelf. But then she stopped and smiled.

'I'm forgetting myself. Can I make you something to eat maybe?'

'Well, I am a little hungry . . .'

'Come in here. I'll fix you something.'

She led the way to the kitchen and made him sit down while she cooked some pasta. He watched, impressed, as she diced vegetables and sliced tomatoes to make a sauce. This was better than a burger. The only cooking Deet had ever done was opening a sachet of ketchup.

Davina poured herself a glass of white wine from the bottle in the fridge and sipped as she cooked.

It just looked so strange, to see the pretty little girl in front of him cooking and drinking wine and occasionally humming a snatch of a song from a musical of long ago.

'Here.'

She had poured him some milk.

'To us.'

She clinked her wine glass against his milk-filled one.

'Here's looking at you, kid,' she said and then giggled, as if at some private joke.

She ruffled his hair with her hand, just the way adults had, when Deet had rented him out for the afternoon to be the child they had never had. It seemed wrong somehow that she should be doing this, that she – a child too – should be treating him as if, well . . .

It gave him the creeps.

The pasta and the sauce were soon ready. She set a place for him at the table.

'Here's your supper, honey. Eat and enjoy.'

She herself didn't eat, but watched him for a while, then said, 'I'll go and make your bed up.'

He watched her go to and fro, taking pillows and sheets and covers, and going to make up the bed in the spare room.

'Come and see,' she said.

He put his plate in the sink and went to see his room. It was all decorated in blue.

'Do you like it, honey?'

'It's nice. Very . . . nice.'

'Is it a boy's room, would you say?'

'Yes. It's a boy's room.'

'Good. Come on. Do you want some ice cream?'

She took him back to the kitchen and fetched two bowls. Then she took a tub from the freezer and scooped ice cream out. They sat and ate, and as she ate hers, she went on sipping at her wine.

It should have felt secure and comfortable, there in her apartment. And it was safe – safer than the streets, anyway – but somehow all the old feelings began to resurface. Tarrin felt the same as before, just as he always had, during those afternoons when he had had to please the paying customer, to keep them satisfied, to be who they wanted him to be.

I don't want to be this any more. I want to be me. What about me? Who'll be for me? Who'll be for me what I want them to be? Be the mother I must have once had, the father I once had? What about me? What about my home? What about how I feel?

What about me?

Miss Davina was getting a little drunk now.

'You're so sweet, honey,' she said. 'You're a poor, poor boy who's all alone. But you mustn't worry, because Mummy's here now, and she's going to take good care of you and won't let those bad people come and take you away. You'll be nice and safe here all the day. You can hide in here while Mummy's working, and when she comes home, she'll cook dinner and read you stories and everything will just be so lovely, so, so lovely. We'll be one big happy family – my little boy and me. Isn't that so, honey? Isn't that so?'

She placed her hand over his, as it rested on the table. But whether this was to give comfort or to receive it, who could tell.

Tarrin looked at her little girl's face. She gave him the chills, the way she was acting. But he felt sorry for her too.

'Isn't that so, honey? Isn't that so?'

'Yes, yes, that's so.'

'Say it properly, honey . . .'

'Yes, Mummy, yes, that's so.'

The little girl's face beamed with pleasure. Her eyes brimmed with tears. She squeezed his hand. 'My little boy,' she said. 'My little boy . . .'

Then she noticed the clock.

'And my! What am I thinking! Look at the clock! It's way past bedtime! I'll find you a toothbrush and show you where the bathroom is.'

She left the things in the bathroom for him, then, as he was using the toilet, she called through the door, 'Mummy's got no pyjamas for you, but she'll buy some in the morning.'

'I'll be OK. Thanks.'

She heard the toilet flush.

'Remember to wash your hands,' she admonished.

'I know . . .'

She giggled. Still a little drunk.

'You know *who*?'

He almost screamed. But he was afraid that if he broke the spell she might make him go back out into the night, and where would he sleep then?

'I know . . . Mum.'

'There's a good boy. Be in to say night-night.'

He heard her go to the kitchen. He hurried to his room and got into bed. She came in, holding a glass.

'Brought you some water.'

'Thank you.'

He noticed that she was also holding a book in her other hand.

'Would you like me to read you a story?'

'I'm sort of tired . . .'

'I'll read you to sleep then.'

He was too tired to protest any further, too exhausted to care.

'Once upon a time,' she began, 'in a land far away . . .'

But Tarrin heard no more than that, for he fell asleep immediately. Miss Davina saw his eyes close and heard his deep, regular breathing. But she still went on reading the story. Just to hear for herself about the far-away land and what had happened a long time ago.

15

All the Years and Days

Kinane knew he had him now. He sat in the car across the street and waited. Eight, nine, ten o'clock, ten thirty. Time drifted by like a slow-moving river.

Finally the curtains were opened and the face of a little girl looked out from the upper apartment window. She peeked down to the street, as if standing on her tiptoes in order to get herself up above the high window sill. She looked out at the grey sky and the light drizzle, then, seeming to not much like what she saw, she turned away and disappeared from view.

'You want some breakfast, honey?'

Tarrin opened his eyes and saw her standing in the partially open doorway.

'Want some breakfast or would you like to sleep longer? We were up late, weren't we?'

'What time is it?'

'It's just after ten.'

'I'll get up. Yes. Some breakfast please. Thanks.'

He dressed and went to the bathroom, then joined her in the kitchen.

'I have to go out,' she said. 'I have to work. First there's a rehearsal and then a matinee, then another evening show. I'll get back in between if I can; if not

I'll try to pop out and buy some things for you and see you here when I get back later.'

'Is there anything I can do?'

'Do?'

'Tidy up?'

'If you want to, honey. Here – there's the cereal. Help yourself. Mummy's got to go now.'

He shuddered. She noticed.

'You cold?'

'N-no. Just . . . you know . . . stretching . . . waking up.'

He watched her get her things ready, check that she had her stage clothes, her dancing shoes.

'What do you do?'

'Sing, dance . . . be a little girl. Be what people want. You know.'

'I know.'

'Come and watch one day. One day soon. But not today.'

'Yes. That'd be nice.'

'OK. I'll see you later, honey. Be good. Maybe better stay in today, huh?'

'Yes. OK.'

'Bye, honey.'

'Bye . . .'

She waited expectantly.

'. . . Mum.'

She smiled, then, satisfied and content, she left the apartment, and her steps echoed and seemed to fall like coins down the well of the stairs.

Tarrin went to the window and watched as she hailed a cab and got in, and as the cab drove away. Then he returned to his breakfast. The doorbell rang, but he didn't answer it. It was probably the postman, but he wasn't going down. It rang a while longer, then the postman must have given up and left the parcel or whatever it was with a neighbour.

When Tarrin had finished, he washed the plates and bowls up, then looked around for a pen and some paper, which he brought to the kitchen table. He sat and began to write.

Dear Miss Davina,

Thank you so much for all your kindness. I really do appreciate your offer to me and I hope you don't feel I am letting you down. I wish I could be the son you are looking for but I cannot. I have to be me, just me, though in many ways I don't even know who that is - and that is what I have to try to find. I'm looking for someone too, you see. Maybe a memory, maybe a dream, I don't know. But I can't stay and give up on all I've been searching for, not now. I'm so very sorry and I hope you won't think bad of me or that I took advantage of your kindness.

Thank you again and good luck to you always and I hope that you can be happy.

Your friend,

Tarrin.

PS - I think you are very pretty. Maybe the prettiest person I have ever seen. I would love to hear you sing and see you dance one day. Bye.

He folded the letter and left it in the middle of the

kitchen table where it could not be missed. Then he gathered his things and found his coat in the wardrobe where she had hung it up for him and he got ready to leave.

Where he was going he did not know. All he knew was that he couldn't stay. All he had was himself and the clothes he stood up in and a handful of memories, which he wasn't even sure were memories at all.

That was all he had. The light coming through the trees and the warmth of the sun and the smell of the freshly cut wheat, or was it corn, and the perfume of the woman and the sound of her singing and how she picked him up and held him in her arms, and he was just a baby, only a baby, a long, long time ago.

In a green land.

Far away.

His hand reached for the door. The streets waited for him. With the fear and the freaks and the failure of mankind's great hopes for life eternal.

And in that moment Tarrin realized the truth at last – which was that he would never find her. He would never find the woman in the memory and the dream. He would never find her, nor the sunlit avenue of trees, nor the man who stood by her and took him from her and held him up high so that he was tall as a mountain and the ground was far below. And then the man laughed and spun him around and he smelt nice too, warm and of animals and the scent of leather.

In the green land.

Forever lost now.

Forever.

Tarrin looked around the apartment one last time.

He knew where he was going now: how to find them, how to be reunited. There was a way, after all.

He opened the door, closed it softly behind him and walked down to the street. He still didn't know where he was, but he knew that if he walked then sooner or later he would find it. You always did. It was always there in the end. So he could have chosen left, but he chose right, but what did it matter if all roads took you to the same place in the end? It was just a matter of how long the journey was, that was all. But all the roads went there, eventually.

He walked on, lost in thought, absorbed in all the sadness of his own short and unhappy life. Neither feeling bitter, nor sorry for himself, just wishing that it could have all been otherwise.

Kinane watched him, then gave him a moment before getting out of the car and following on, at a discreet distance, so the boy wouldn't even know that he was there at all. He didn't want to startle him. He didn't want him running. He didn't want him yelling and screaming to some passer-by, 'Help, help! I'm being taken. There's a Kiddernapper after me!'

Broad daylight wasn't a good time, but it was the only time there was, as it had turned out. He'd waited a long time, he'd been nice and patient – he wasn't going to ruin everything now with any sudden moves. He didn't want the kid running. Running and getting lost again, that was the last thing he wanted. So he followed on, nice and easy and casual, as though he had all the time in the world, as though he would live for two hundred years.

Tarrin walked on. He wondered about Deet – if he'd still be looking for him, where he would be looking for him, or if he'd maybe have given up and just kept the money and have moved on, looking for another card game where he could win another meal ticket and another few years on easy street.

He walked and walked, lost in his thoughts, no longer caring about the people who stared at him and the voices that whispered about him.

'Look – a boy there, all on his own.'

'Do you think we ought to . . .?'

'I'm not sure . . .'

Before they could decide he had moved on.

At last he came to it, as he knew he would. Almost all great cities are built on rivers. And there it was, glistening in the sunlight, wide and weary, like some great coiled serpent.

Tarrin followed the embankment until he came to a derelict, run-down area of empty shipyards and rusted cranes. He walked on past barges and tugs, then he climbed upwards until he came to a bridge, and there he stopped.

He leaned upon the parapet and looked down into the dark, fast-flowing water. Deet would never find him there. Nobody would. The river would put a stop to it, put an end to everything. The PP implant could make people children forever, and the Anti-Ageing pills could stop those who had grown from growing older still. But the river could undo all that. Everything that mankind could create, nature could undo.

He watched the swirling water, almost hypnotized by it, knowing what he had to do, and not afraid to do it. He just wanted a few last moments to himself, to say goodbye to . . . to what, to whom? He could think of no one.

He didn't see the man at first. He only noticed him after five minutes or so. He had stopped thirty metres away and he too was leaning on the parapet and staring down at the murky water.

Tarrin saw him out of the corner of his eye.

Kiddernapper.

His body tensed. He prepared to run. Then he remembered that he didn't have to run. Not any more. He just had to jump, to fall, all the way down.

When he moves, I'll go. Soon as he moves. That will be the trigger. When he moves.

But the man did not move. He stood, staring at the water. Tarrin looked at his features. He was tall, with large hands and a square, broad face. He looked old – a little too old, as if he hadn't taken his Anti-Ageing for a while.

Move and I'll go. When you move, I'll go.

But still the man didn't move. He stared at the water, as if looking for his soul, for his heart, for his own life. Then finally he looked up and he raised his head and he turned his face to look at the boy.

He looked so sad. So sad. And so defeated.

'Is it you, Danny?' he said.

Tarrin stared. What had he said? What did he say?

'Is it you, Danny?' the man repeated, his voice rising as he said the name, as if even after all these years there was still a little hope in him.

Tarrin stiffened. It was a trick. He was going to grab him. He'd start edging near, keeping talking all the while, and, when he was near enough, he'd grab him, before he could jump. Well, he wasn't going to let that happen.

A truck passed and the noise stole his voice. He asked again, 'Is it you, Danny? Is it? If it isn't you I have to stop now . . . I have to go home . . . give up now . . . if it isn't you.'

He made no effort to move, to draw nearer, to trick him into giving his confidence.

'W-what did you call me?'

Kinane looked at Tarrin, looked at his eyes, his face, the shape of his nose . . .

'You look so like your mother, Danny,' he said. 'You look so like her.'

And then he moved. He raised his hands to his face. And Tarrin saw that he was crying.

Trick. It was a trick. Gain your confidence. Get you to go to him. Trick.

'My name's not Danny.'

The man looked up and wiped his face on the cuff of his coat.

'It was once, Danny. A long time ago. That was the name we gave you.'

'My name's Tarrin.'

'That's your middle name. It's your mother's sur-name. We gave it to you for a middle name. It was maybe stitched on some of your clothes.'

Tarrin erupted in anger. He screamed at the man, spittle flying from his lips.

'I don't believe you, you're a liar, you're a Kiddernapper, you're trying to trick me and sell me and make money like they all did and then I'll have to go on pretending. But I won't be what other people want any more, not ever, I'll kill myself first,

I'll kill myself, if you come a step nearer I'll kill myself.'

The man didn't move.

'She took you into town. We kept you all in the country, at the farm. Most other people had no children, but we did, we did, and she took you into town and left her bag in the store and ran back in and you were there alone no more than fifteen or twenty seconds and when she came out . . .'

'What? What!'

'You were gone.'

'You're a liar!'

'I'm not a liar, Danny. If you're Danny I'm not a liar. I'm not a liar.'

'Why didn't you look for me, why didn't you find me!'

'We got the police, we looked, we all looked, and when the rest gave up we didn't. I've looked for years and for years. I've stayed in a thousand different hotel rooms and I've met people you'd never want to meet and been to places you'd never want to go. I've travelled to a hundred cities and I've searched in every one of them for every child I could find and I've searched their faces for some sign of you, of me, of your mother . . .'

'It's not true. You're a liar! You're a liar! You're a dirty kiddernapping liar!'

The man reached into his coat pocket and extracted something. He held it up.

'This is a photograph, Danny. Of all of us. When you were small. Me and you and Mum and your brother and your sister . . .'

'What . . . what did you say?'

'Come and see it. You'll see yourself in them, and them in you. Come and see.'

Trick. Don't move. Don't fall for it.

Kinane saw it in the boy – the reluctance and the curiosity. He knew the unpredictability of wild, cornered things, and he knew when to back away.

'OK. I'll leave it here. I'm leaving it on the parapet and I'm weighting it down with some coins so it can't blow away. Then I'm going to walk away, another thirty metres, and you can come and see it.'

He did as he said he would. When he had moved the extra distance, Tarrin gingerly walked forwards, grabbed the photograph and held it in his hands. The coins tumbled into the river.

He held the photograph and he looked at the picture.

It was of a family. A real, proper family. It was a picture like the ones in the Museum of Childhood.

A woman held a child; she was smiling for the camera. The man standing next to her was the man on the bridge with Tarrin now.

The photograph had been taken outside, in the open air, in the country, in early summer perhaps. In the background was a white-painted farmhouse, and behind and to the right of that a long avenue of trees. Beyond the trees were fields of maturing wheat and barley and also some fields of oilseed rape, a brilliant, shimmering yellow.

It seemed like a green land.

Far away.

Tarrin studied the photograph; it was creased and cracked and dirty, as though it had been taken out and looked at and put away and taken out to be seen again, many, many times.

Is this me? Really me?

The baby was just a baby. It could have been anyone. But when he studied the woman's features, he saw traces of his own: his own bone structure, his own eyes and hair, the same small, white, regular teeth. She was looking at the baby and smiling, as if he were the most marvellous thing in the world.

He looked away from the photograph and saw the man watching him. He was standing tense and nervous, as if afraid of making any sudden noise or movement which could frighten Tarrin away. Like a predator which had stalked its prey for a long time, and now, having it cornered at last, was getting ready to pounce.

Tarrin moved backwards a few steps. The man watched, concerned.

'Leave me the photograph,' he said. 'Leave me that . . . if it isn't you . . . at least leave me that.'

Tarrin smiled at him. He held the photograph out over the parapet of the bridge, as if to drop it into the water. He saw the worry and the pain on the man's face, the fear that he might lose the picture and this last trace of his precious son would be gone forever.

'Come nearer, I'll let it go.'

He felt powerful. Nobody telling him what to do now. He was the one in control of lives and destinies. No one could hurt him now.

He altered his grip on the photograph. He held it only between his index and his middle fingers. It quivered a little in the wind. He just needed to loosen his grip a fraction and it would fall to the water far beneath, fluttering like a leaf.

The man just watched. He said nothing, he made no attempt to run and grab it from his hand before it was too late. He just watched.

Then Tarrin climbed up on to the parapet, still holding the old photograph. The wind blew his hair, he could see down into the swirling river, with its dark brown water and clean white foam. He looked at the man – his hands were balled into fists, his nails digging into his palms.

'Danny . . .'

'I'm not Danny . . . I'm not anyone . . . I'm just . . . me . . . whoever that was . . .'

'I came to take you home, Danny. They're waiting for you, all waiting. Mum and Grandma and your sister and brother . . . they're waiting . . . all waiting . . . I said I wouldn't come back without you . . . I've been looking so many years now . . .'

'You know something . . . it's clever . . . it's good . . . almost convincing . . . yes, it's very clever, mister. I have to give you credit for that. But you're all liars, mister, you know that? You're all liars. Every one of you. You all want something and you're all liars. You think we're just things, to make money off, and you want to catch one. You're all—'

Tarrin almost lost his footing. He swayed and saw the water beneath him swirl and spiral as a barge passing under the bridge emerged directly below. He could have dived, straight on to the deck. The water eddied between the barge and the pillars.

'Danny . . . Danny . . .'

He'd go now. Count to five, then close his eyes and fall. And it would be done.

'Danny, there's a mark, on the baby's leg, look at the photograph, on the baby's leg, by his knee, on the inside, there's a birthmark there. Look for yourself.'

He opened his eyes and looked. The baby was fat-faced, well fed and happy. It had chubby arms, so fat they dimpled at the elbows. The baby was wearing a nappy and a vest top but nothing on its legs. He looked at the mark. He'd missed it at first. That part of the photograph had almost been worn away. The mark was the same shape now as it had been then, just larger. It had grown with him, so it seemed.

Tarrin got down from the parapet, more falling than climbing. He squatted on the pavement with his back to the bridge, just staring at the photograph, as if there was nothing else in the world.

After a while the man walked towards him and squatted down beside him, not too near, a good few metres away, just in case he still didn't believe him.

At length the boy looked up.

'You're my father?'

He nodded. 'I believe so, Danny.'

'And you always looked for me . . . ?'

'I always looked for you . . .'

'All the years . . . ?'

'Down all the years, Danny . . . I looked for you down all the years . . . all the years and days . . . I never stopped looking . . . never . . . I never . . . I couldn't . . . I just went on looking . . .'

Tarrin turned away. He stared down at the pavement beneath him, at the dirt upon it, the cracks in it.

The man stood and walked a little nearer; then he squatted down again, next to the boy. He slowly reached out and he touched him on the shoulder.

'Let's go home, eh, Danny,' he said. 'Let's go home now . . .'

The boy nodded. And yet he didn't make any move to stand up or to raise himself, he just went on staring down at the ground.

Eventually the man half lifted, half pulled him up to his feet. He went to take the photograph from him, but Tarrin wanted to hold on to it still, so he let him. He put his arm around his shoulders.

And, eventually, they walked on.

They drove and kept on driving, all that day and well into the night. They stopped to rest for a few hours in a Rapid Link Motel. Tarrin thought of Deet, and all the rooms they had stayed in. His own father felt like more of a stranger. Deet was predictable and familiar, but this man, who knew? What made him laugh, made him sad, made him angry? What made him the kind of man who would never give up? What made him the kind of man who would hunt you down through all the days and years, because you were his son and he loved you?

And Tarrin momentarily felt afraid of the very thing he had yearned for.

At daybreak they resumed the journey and after a few more hours the countryside began to change around them. The soil was rich and red; there were dairy cattle and sheep and verdant pasture, and then the land changed again and arable crops took over from the pasture. They passed through a small town, little more than a village. His father stopped the car and pointed to a shop across the road.

'It was there,' he said. 'Outside that store.'

Tarrin looked to where he had been taken, as he had sat in his pushchair, all those years ago.

'Who was it?'

'Who knows? Stranger in a car. Someone passing through. Saw their chance and they took it, and the chance they saw was you.'

Tarrin looked from the place back to his father. The lines in his father's face were deep, deeper than most people's, deeper than they needed to be.

'Can I ask a question?'

'Of course.'

'Do you take the Anti-Ageing?'

'No.'

'Why not?'

'Why not, Danny?'

'I'm used to Tarrin – Danny sounds like someone else.'

'Aren't you someone else now? You've come home.'

'I'm used to Tarrin. That's who I am.'

His father nodded. 'OK.'

'Your lines are deep,' Tarrin said, 'on your face.'

'We don't take any Anti-Ageing. None of us do.'

'You grow old?'

'Yes. And I've got to tell you, your mother's not like in the photograph. She's still your mother, and still a treat to look at . . . but she's aged too. And your grandmother, well . . . she's got more lines than a railway station. But you'll like her.'

'Why don't you take it? Do you want to grow old? Do you want to die?'

'Of course not.'

'Then why?'

'We think it's wrong . . . it's why there are hardly any children . . . people hang on to life . . . and won't let someone else take a turn.'

'So will you die soon?'

He felt suddenly lonely, to think that he had only just found them and now he might lose them all again. His father smiled.

'Not unless something falls on me,' he said. 'In fact, we Kinanes live a long time.'

'How long?'

'Eighty-five, ninety years.'

'That's not long.'

'It is for unassisted.'

'Dad . . .'

The man swallowed, he ran his hand around his neck, as though his collar were too tight for him.

'Yes, son . . .'

'How come there's so many . . . me and a brother and a sister . . . when most people have no one?'

'Maybe we were just lucky. Maybe it's the way we live.'

'Are there other children here?'

'Some.'

'Girls too?'

His father laughed.

'Yes. Girls too. They're around.'

'I met a girl,' Tarrin said.

'You did?'

'She was really pretty,' Tarrin said.

276

Kinane didn't say anything for a while. He didn't want to say anything that might spoil the moment – a father with his son, just being there.

'You like her?' he finally asked.

Tarrin nodded. 'Yes, only . . . she wasn't really how she seemed. She was . . . older.'

'Ah. She like you too?'

'I think so. She wanted to look after me.'

'Did you want her to?'

'No. I wanted to go home. I've wanted to go home all my life. Only I never knew where it was . . . or if it even existed.'

Kinane tried to smile, but he didn't really feel like smiling. 'You ready to meet them now?'

Tarrin nodded. 'I think so. Do they know I'm coming?'

'Of course. I phoned ahead.'

'Dad . . .'

'Yes?'

'I'm frightened.'

'I know,' he said. 'I know . . . but not half as frightened as they are of you.'

That made him laugh and, while he was distracted, Kinane slipped the car into drive and drove on out of the town.

The farm track led on down under a canopy of plane trees, their branches curling over. As the car passed, there was a strobe of light and shade, light and shade from between the branches and leaves.

'I remember that . . .'

'What do you remember?'

'The sun and the trees shielding you from it . . . and the smell of things . . . animals . . . and you . . .'

'Me?!'

'And her . . .'

'Well, here we are.'

The car bumped over some cobbles and drew up in the yard.

'Are they older or younger?'

'Older brother, younger sister. Just two years in it either way. That's them all.'

Tarrin and Kinane didn't get out of the car. Not for a while. The four people stood, waiting, watching, trying to seem welcoming, yet not really knowing how to act, wanting to be friendly, but afraid and apprehensive, fearful that he would be too much of a stranger, that it was all too late now, and that things could never be repaired.

'Shall we . . . Tarrin?'

'OK.'

His father got out, then walked around the car and opened his door. Tarrin got out and stood next to him.

'This is Tarrin,' his father said. 'That's how he likes to be called. Tarrin, this is your grandma, Nina . . .'

'Hello, Tarrin . . .'

More lines than a railway station. She had those all right. But she was nice too. Brown as a walnut, and so sear and old, as beautiful as an autumn leaf. She watched him with her pale, grey eyes.

'Your brother, Ed . . .'

'Hi.'

'Hi.'

'Your sister, Bella . . .'

'Hi.'

'Hello.'

278

'And . . . and this is . . .'

There she was. Like in the photo, but, yes, older, just as his father had said.

'How are you, Tarrin?'

'Fine thank you, ma'am.'

'It's good to have you home . . .'

She put her hand out, as if in friendship, to shake his own hand, neither expecting nor feeling entitled to any greater intimacy. He reached out and touched it, his fingers brushing her own.

'Pleased to meet you, ma'am . . .'

How many times had he said that, to how many customers, on the thresholds of how many doors? And then he had tried to be the boy they had wanted him to be, for an hour of the afternoon.

Will you love me, he wondered, watching her. Will you love me . . . for being myself? For who I am?

'I'm sorry, Tarrin . . . I'm so sorry . . . it was only for a moment, that was all, only for a moment and I lost you . . . I'm sorry, oh so sorry, it was all my fault . . .'

Then to his anguish and for some reason – though he did not know why – to his shame – she began to cry. And as she did, she put her arms out, the way a parent would do to a child, a small child, running towards them, ready to scoop that child up and swing it in the air.

Only what if the child swerved away, didn't run, didn't come, turned and fled?

'I'm so sorry, Tarrin, so sorry . . . I am, I am, I am . . .'

He stepped forwards and he put his arms around

her, and he rested his head upon her as she stroked his hair.

'It wasn't your fault,' he said. 'It's all right. It wasn't your fault.'

She didn't say anything. She just went on holding him and stroking his hair. She smelt just as he remembered. Just the same. The very same. Just like all those years ago.

It was difficult. There were long silences at meal times when nobody really knew what to say, or quite how to say it. Nobody knew how he felt. He didn't really know himself. Maybe he felt bereaved more than anything, that the years which should have been his, here in this place, with these people, had been taken from him, that his childhood had long ago died. In some ways, they all seemed innocent to him, even naive. What would they know about his life? How could they understand?

It took Tarrin a long time to settle. Sometimes he helped out around the farm, sometimes he just wandered off alone – though they were loath to let him be alone, but realized that sometimes you just have to be, whatever the risks and the chances.

One afternoon, as he was sitting in the yard, Ed appeared, kicking a football, tapping it from one foot to the other, then kicking it up, hitting it with a knee, passing it to the other knee, letting it fall to his feet again.

Tarrin watched him and his brother saw him watching.

'You want to play?' he said.

'I don't know how . . .' he said. 'I don't know how.'

And that was it. He didn't. He had no idea. He didn't know how. Not really. Except for money, except as work, except to do what was expected. And maybe it was too late to learn.

Ed went on kicking the ball. He booted it against the wall of the barn and trapped it with his foot as it rebounded.

'I'll show you,' he offered. 'If you like. I'll show you how to play.'

Tarrin remained where he was for a time, sitting on the base of an upturned feed-trough, shredding a blade of grass with his fingernails, then he stood and walked towards his brother.

'OK,' he said, 'show me.'

'Here.' His brother tapped the ball over, it dribbled to his feet. 'Kick it against the wall,' he said.

Tarrin did as instructed. The ball rebounded. He missed it and had to run after it, then he carried it back.

'What now?' he asked.

'Do it again,' his brother said. 'Only this time we both try to get it.'

'And then what?' Tarrin said.

'Just do it,' his brother said. 'Just do it, and you'll see.'

'OK,' he said.

He kicked the ball again. It once again rebounded from the barn wall and the two of them chased after it, trying to be the first one there. Their legs nearly entangled and they bumped against each other as they struggled for the ball. His brother got possession of it but Tarrin went after him and got it back, so his brother came after him now and Tarrin ran with the ball across the yard, kicking it in front of him as he ran and as his brother followed him in hot pursuit.

Then he realized.

He suddenly realized what he was doing.

He was laughing.

He was laughing out loud.

16

Miss Virginia

Tarrin lived another seventy years, and he too met a girl and they were lucky and able to have children.

He never forgot Deet though, much as he tried to. Memories kept returning to him, like recurring bad dreams: recollections of trains and motel rooms and flickering TV screens; they stayed with him like scars. Some nights too, Tarrin would wake in panic and rush to the bedside of his own sleeping children, to check that they were still there. He half expected to find Deet out on the landing, saying, 'Listen, kid, I've got a proposition . . .'

Some decades down the line, he recollected the money he had taken from Mrs Weaver and his vow to repay it. He managed to track down her address, and he sent her a transfer for the 500 units he had stolen from her, along with his apologies. By the time she received it, she looked younger than he did.

On the day of his death, in the street of a distant city, a figure in a coat with a fake fur collar stepped from a taxi outside a small establishment and she headed for the door around the back, the one with the sign above it which read 'Artistes Only'. She went inside, went to her dressing room and started to get ready.

At the front of the building, a matrix sign advertised the attraction of the day.

'For a limited season only. Miss Virginia Two Shoes', the light-board read. '125 years young and still dancing. Come see the daughter you never had. Everybody's Favourite Girl. Performances Twice Daily.'

It was two in the afternoon and a queue was already forming of those wishing to see the matinee. There was no shortage of takers for that afternoon show, and by four o'clock the tickets for the evening performance were also fully booked.

A board was put up in the foyer to inform the public.

It said simply:

All Sold Out.